# SILENCED FOR GOOD

ALEX COOMBS

Boldwood

First published in Great Britain in 2020 by Boldwood Books Ltd.

Copyright © Alex Coombs, 2020

Cover Design by Nick Castle Design

A CIP catalogue record for this book is available from the British Library.

Paperback ISBN 978-1-83889-854-0

Ebook ISBN 978-1-83889-856-4

Kindle ISBN 978-1-83889-855-7

Audio CD ISBN 978-1-83889-848-9

MP3 CD ISBN 978-1-83889-849-6

Digital audio download ISBN 978-1-83889-851-9

Boldwood Books Ltd
23 Bowerdean Street
London SW6 3TN
www.boldwoodbooks.com

# 1

'I think that you're addicted to violence. I think you like the adrenaline rush, the danger. I think you like losing control.' Dr Morgan's gaze was steady, her voice calm. 'I've seen this so many times before, usually in drugs and alcohol. Starting off as fun, then a remorseless escalation until we have total addiction, an inability to live without it.'

She glanced at Hanlon. Over to you, the look said.

'I never lose control,' Hanlon replied icily. She let her gaze wander around Dr Elspeth Morgan's consulting room while she struggled to maintain her composure. It was a large, airy first-floor room overlooking a quiet residential road. It was a reassuringly expensive area. Dr Morgan's fees were not reassuring; they were alarmingly high. They were in Hampstead, in North London, just up the road from the Freud museum. Freud had tribal art in his consulting room; Dr Morgan favoured modern, abstract paintings and sculpture.

Hanlon disliked them intensely.

'Then why are you here?' countered Dr Morgan, her voice

sceptical. 'For showing a worrying amount of kindness to a suspect avoiding arrest? I think not. You broke his nose.'

Hanlon had been temporarily suspended from duty while an assault charge was investigated. She didn't blame the criminal responsible for struggling while she arrested him, but she did blame her colleagues for not backing her up. She had been in the police for twenty years now, and her career had plateaued. She was high-ranking, a DCI, but somewhere a line had been crossed from respected elder statesman – she was forty – to dinosaur. Embarrassing dinosaur. Her opinions were old-fashioned, as was her approach to policing.

'He was resisting arrest.'

Dr Morgan raised an elegant shaped eyebrow and looked at her quizzically. She was about sixty, tall and sophisticated. She had short, skilfully cut grey hair and a shrewd face. She was wearing a grey silk trouser suit and a patterned blouse. Hanlon could imagine her in court giving evidence as an expert witness, unflappable, convincing.

Now she said, 'I would imagine a lot of people resist arrest where you're concerned, DCI Hanlon. Well above the average.'

'The suspect didn't complain at the time.' She shrugged.

'No, indeed. Not at the time, but he did later, didn't he?' Dr Morgan gave her an uncomfortably penetrating look and Hanlon moved uncomfortably in her chair. Not because it was badly designed; it was guilt. Hanlon had spent her life hiding things deep inside, and now here was this woman shining a light on things that had been in a cavernous darkness for years, decades sometimes. The present events that they were discussing would be a portal to the past, and Hanlon, although she would never have admitted it, was scared. She was beginning to regret coming here.

Dr Morgan looked at the hard-faced, dark-haired woman

sitting opposite her and continued, pressing the point, 'And your colleagues failed to back you up. I think we can draw our own conclusions from a rather deafening silence.' Dr Morgan looked at Hanlon. 'Bit unusual, isn't it? You normally close ranks. When it's the police worrying about police violence, surely alarm bells should be ringing in your head.'

'I think I am suffering from stress,' Hanlon lied, trying to shift the ground. The interview with the clinical psychologist was not going to plan. She had hoped that Dr Morgan would sympathise with her, agree that the Metropolitan Police had treated her shamefully and agree to help her fight her corner. She didn't need this. Dr Morgan seemed to be casting herself as a hostile witness.

The psychologist raised a sceptical eyebrow. 'You can't control yourself, Hanlon – worse, you don't want to.'

'That's not true.' She looked around the room again. There were three plain pale grey unadorned ceramic vases on a table against the wall. They were very simple in design. Her fingers curled and her knuckles whitened.

She was reliving the incident, the four of them following the BMW 3 series through the streets of South London. A suspected arms drop. They didn't want the driver, he was just the delivery man, they wanted the customers. Then the brief chase as the driver realised he was being followed. The car stuck in traffic, two men abandoning it, Hanlon chasing the driver on foot.

'They're Bauhaus vases,' Dr Morgan said, misinterpreting Hanlon's gaze but not the anger and frustration underlying it. 'Please don't even think of smashing them. They're rather beautiful and rare.'

Hanlon ignored her. She was still in South London. Running down the alley. Behind a Chinese restaurant. The smell of five spice from the extractor fans and rotting food from the black binbags outside the kitchen door. The man, twenties, stocky. The alley had been a dead end, a chain-link fence. Shouting at Hanlon in some unknown Eastern European language. She glanced around, no one there, no witnesses. She hit him hard in the stomach, saw the pain and surprise in his face – it felt good... *'you can't control yourself'* – spun him round, cuffed him. More perceived insults, the frustration inside her, another punch and then, quite casually, an elbow into his face... *'Worse, you don't want to...'*

She stared hard into Dr Morgan's eyes. 'He was resisting arrest. He brought it on himself. There was no excessive force – it was necessary, proportionate and reasonable.'

The doctor drummed her fingers thoughtfully on her desk.

'There's a technical term, Hanlon. In layman's terms it's called pushing the fuck-it button. That's when addicts give in to their chosen addiction big-time. They know it's going to have terrible consequences, but they've ceased to care. They almost seem to relish it.'

'Really?' She tried to sound unconcerned.

'I know you know that feeling, Hanlon.'

'No. That's not the case.' She frowned, angry with herself; her voice sounded hollow and unconvincing.

'Isn't it? Really?' She noticed how still the doctor was. And worst of all, she was right, and Hanlon knew it. She knew it only too well. The alley incident was far from isolated. In the past few days there had been a road-rage incident and a furious row with the woman in charge of line-ups at Lewisham. How many times had she said to herself, 'Bring it on!'? She looked into the shrewd face of the therapist; she had no intention of bringing any of this recent history up.

Dr Morgan continued, inexorable.

'From what you've told me, the heavily edited version, I

assume, things are escalating. You deliberately put yourself in positions of extreme danger—'

'That's not true.'

'You could have called for assistance at least three times that I know of, from what you've told me.' Hanlon considered this; it was true. Even at the planning stage, she'd been offered another car, she'd turned that down. When the chase had started, she'd been adamant they could handle it. It had been her decision to pursue the suspect alone. She hadn't wanted any help, maybe she hadn't wanted any witnesses.

'But I couldn't trust...' This wasn't fair, Hanlon thought.

'No, you don't trust people, do you? Don't you think that's part of your problem, an inability to trust? And those you do trust, you seem to treat them in a very high-handed way. This man Enver, your former colleague, the man you claim is your best friend, he's not talking to you.'

Hanlon shifted uncomfortably in her chair.

'That's because of his wife. She's a bitch.'

'Is she? Is she really?' Dr Morgan raised an eloquent eyebrow. 'Or is she just angry with you for exposing her husband to danger, not to mention morally blackmailing him into actions that would get him sacked if they had come to light?'

'You're twisting the facts,' Hanlon complained.

'When we discussed past relationships, you told me you had even managed to find a lover with a similar laissez-faire attitude to the law. Even though like calls to like, it's quite an achievement.'

'He's Russian,' Hanlon muttered. Whatever Serg got up to was no business of the Metropolitan Police in her view. There was no conflict of interest. Part of her thought, Well, I'm not sure that is true at all. She buried the thought. Another skeleton from the past.

Dr Morgan laughed. 'So what? What difference does that make? I'm half Russian if it comes to that.'

In her life outside work, in the boxing ring and in triathlons, she had inevitably come across people better than she was and when she recognised it, when she knew she was beaten, sometimes it came as a huge relief. To stop pointlessly fighting. She knew she was beaten, she knew, deep down, that Dr Morgan was right. Hanlon was suddenly tired of herself. As with so many events in her life, she had managed to alienate someone who could help; she had managed to turn an appointment with a doctor who she wanted to assist her into a fight.

Maybe it was time to stop fighting everyone and everything.

'What should I do?' she asked quietly. She suddenly felt that what she really wanted was a set of easy-to-follow rules laid down by Dr Morgan.

'Go on holiday,' she said. 'There, simple advice. Like you told me you had planned to do. Get out of London. Go on this holiday to Scotland. There is nothing you can achieve down here. Then when you feel calmer, call me and arrange for a follow-up appointment. Then we'll talk about your future.'

Hanlon stood up and went to the door.

'Oh, one more thing...' Hanlon turned. Dr Morgan said, 'You have a problem with life. You might have noticed this by now – I certainly have. Now, as you can't avoid that, just avoid crime, OK. You're going to a sparsely inhabited Scottish island. Don't get into trouble.' She looked hard at her. 'That should be an achievable goal.'

'I'll do my best,' Hanlon said and walked out of Dr Morgan's tasteful house into the expensive, manicured Hampstead street.

## 2

The woman's body was lying on the shingle and stones of the beach. She was wearing a black one-piece swimming costume. Her skin was very pale against the dark material. There were tattoos on her upper arms and shoulders. Her head was on its side, her ear had multiple piercings. She had short, badly dyed blonde hair and her micro-bladed eyebrows were very dark on her forehead. She looked very young and terribly fragile against the hard black and grey rock of the foreshore.

DI Campbell shook his head sadly as he looked down at her.

He remembered the last time he had seen her. The party. She had been working the bar. He closed his eyes for a second; the cold grey rocky beach disappeared. He was back reliving the past.

'Can I get you a drink, Mr...?'

'Murray.' He had smiled, he remembered doing that. She had smiled back. Women often did – he was good-looking and knew it. 'You can call me Murray. Aye, I'll have a Guinness.'

'Certainly, one Guinness coming up...'

Murray had been the name he had used when he had seen her. Not his real name. The dark bar, its lights low. Then she had been in full party mode – the illumination might have been dim but her smile was bright, her blouse buttoned low, the music loud, the guests flushed with excitement and alcohol. He couldn't remember her name, but he could remember her eyes, pupils dilated, she'd been high, her hands brushing his suggestively as she had handed him the pint. Some of the head from the Guinness had splashed on her forearm and she had licked it off, catlike, provocatively. She had been so full of life and now... this.

He straightened up and pulled off his latex gloves. There were no red-flag indicators of foul play, no obvious external cuts or abrasions. There was nothing to indicate anything other than an accident. No need to get a team over to the island. He was only here because he happened to be staying just up the road. The call had come in from the station on Islay, the neighbouring, larger island – could he deal with it? He most certainly could.

'What a waste,' said the elderly man standing close to him on the shoreline. He was the one who had found her an hour or so earlier and called his discovery in.

'Yes,' Campbell said, 'it's very sad.'

The sound of vehicles – he looked up to the road above the shore – an old Volvo followed by an ambulance.

DS Catriona McCleod pulled up next to the familiar Land Rover of her colleague and the ambulance stopped behind her. She got out of the car and shivered in the cold sea breeze. They were on the east side of Jura, a hundred or so miles west of Glasgow, the Kintyre peninsula a low dark smudge across the choppy grey Atlantic. The cloud was low and, although it wasn't raining yet, there was moisture in the air. Behind them the enormous shapes of the island's mountains, the Paps of Jura, were invisible in the mist. But you knew that they were there. They were always there, stone giants dwarfing human activity.

'Down here!' called DI Campbell to her from the seashore below. The tide was out and she could see her colleague and another man bending over something invisible from where she was standing.

'Wait by the ambulance,' she said to the two paramedics. She'd met the ambulance at the ferry – a drowning, no suspicious circumstances – and escorted them to where the body was. Like Campbell, she was local, she knew where to go.

'We're in nae hurry,' said the burlier of the two, grinning.

McCleod went to her car and took out a pair of latex gloves from a packet in the door compartment. 'Stay!' she ordered the border collie who was crouched in the rear hatch space of her Volvo, panting, eager to join in.

She sat down on the driver's seat, kicked off her trainers and pulled on a pair of green wellingtons. She clambered down the slope with its coarse grass and made her way over the rocks to the seashore, where Campbell was standing with an elderly man.

The wind blew her long hair around her face. She twisted it back into a ponytail and secured it with a band. The breeze was ruffling Campbell's short red hair. The old guy was bald and weather-beaten; he was wearing an old yellow oilskin. Retired fisherman, she guessed. He had that look. The sea was grey today and looked rough. Although the wind wasn't that strong, white horses danced on the waves away from the shore. She could see a fishing boat rising and falling, tossed by the Atlantic as if it were weightless, ploughing through the swell a few hundred metres away.

The three of them looked down at the drowned girl. McCleod looked questioningly at Campbell; he shrugged as if to say, nothing to get excited about. They could hardly talk freely in front of the civilian but it wasn't her place to send him away. Campbell answered her unspoken question.

'It looks like a tragic accident,' he said.

'Do we know who she is?' asked McCleod.

Campbell looked at her. He had very green eyes and McCleod noticed how they almost changed colour to a dark shade of jade as they reflected the grey from the sea and sky. She couldn't say that she liked him very much, he was arrogant, stand-offish, but competent enough.

'She's from the Mackinnon Arms,' he said. 'I saw her working there.'

'Och, of course,' said McCleod, 'Eva Balodis.'

Campbell, surprised, looked at her questioningly. 'You know her, then?'

'That woman Harriet – Harriet the manageress, I can't recall her surname now – she called in a missing persons on her yesterday. Said she was very worried about her.'

'Did she say why?' Campbell asked. 'I mean, other than the fact she hadn't turned up for work?'

'Well, she's from Latvia, as far as the manageress knows, she has nowhere else to go, all her stuff is still in the hotel, so she hadn't done a flit.'

She looked down at the girl. 'Seems she was right to have been worried.'

The old man watched them impassively, taciturn like many of the islanders. He was dressed in scuffed and work-worn clothes and an old oilskin. Campbell, in a green Barbour jacket and worn cords, looked as if he'd stepped from a Boden catalogue. Even the trousers looked artfully distressed rather than old.

'She said that Eva had talked about swimming the Corryvreckan whirlpool – in fact, Harriet made quite a point of it

– and now...' she nodded in the direction of the body '... here she is.'

'Well,' said Campbell briskly. 'Well, there we are, then. Almost certainly an accident.' Jumping the gun a bit, thought McCleod. It was as if Campbell wanted this done and dusted as quickly as possible.

'How did you know her, sir?' asked McCleod.

'Oh, I don't really know.' He was studiously vague in that way that people have when they want to avoid a question. 'I must have bumped into her at the hotel with my grandmother; you know she lives near Craighouse.'

Craighouse was the only village on the island. Not many people lived on Jura, the ones that did were mainly retired. During the summer the population swelled slightly with tourism but in general, everybody knew each other. It was odd that Campbell should have been so unaware of how he knew the girl. More than odd. And the whole way he was handling this was unusual for him. Normally he was a stickler for procedure, cautious in the extreme. Today he seemed very rushed, anxious to get everything tidied away.

'Can I go now?' said the old man, who had moved away from them and was now sitting a couple of metres away on a boulder while the two police officers talked.

'I'm sorry,' Campbell said, giving an apologetic smile. It transformed his face, making him look very boyish. 'DS McCleod, this is Ronnie Fraser. He found the body and called us. Mr Fraser, could you go with my colleague? She'll just be asking you a few questions, then you're free to go.'

'Aye, come along with me, sir. We'll just go up to my car...'

'Oh, and, Catriona, send the paramedics down. They can take her away. The tide's coming in. Don't want her floating away.'

'Yes, sir.'

She walked back up the beach with Ronnie Fraser. He walked with the unhurried trudge of the countryman. She told the waiting men to fetch the body. As they unpacked the stretcher from the back of the ambulance and scrambled down to the shore, she looked back at Campbell, who was standing with his back to her, staring out to sea.

She turned to the old man. 'Now, sir,' she said brightly, 'just a few wee questions. Firstly, your full name please...'

As the questions rolled on, where he lived, the sequence of events, the chronology of the discovery of the body, she found that she was operating almost on autopilot as she took down the answers. Her mind was more preoccupied with Campbell. It wasn't just the way he was handling things or the uncharacteristic forgetfulness about where he had met Eva.

Campbell's grandmother was ardent Free Church of Scotland. They were a strict, some would even say fanatical, Calvinist branch of Christianity. They were no fan of drink. She would no more have gone into a hotel bar where alcohol was served than McCleod would have visited a brothel.

Campbell was lying.

As if aware the DS was thinking of him, Campbell turned and looked directly at her. She recalled stories that she had heard, pub rumours, that Campbell was a bit of a ladies' man. It was very believable. Maybe she would have been tempted herself, if he weren't such a stuck-up prick.

As McCleod thanked Ronnie Fraser and watched him walk away back to where he lived, she wondered, were Campbell and Eva an item? No, they could never have been an item – she wouldn't have been presentable enough for Campbell. She would have been an embarrassment.

Was she your side-piece, sir? That was far more likely. Not good enough to be a fully accredited girlfriend, but just good enough for a quick one when need or the opportunity arose. Was that why the DI was being so economical with the truth, why he was in such a hurry to close the book on this one, an embarrassing ex-lover? Self-interest seemed to be taking precedence over justice. Whatever had happened to Eva Balodis was not going to be gone into with any great rigour.

Well, she thought, I for one will be keeping a close eye on the investigation, that's for sure.

## 3

DCI Hanlon looked out of the small window of the plane – a Twin Otter according to the information sheet from the airline – on the flight from Glasgow to Islay. The laminated leaflet also showed a stylised map of Scotland with the flight routes indicated by red dots. The one she was on went west of Glasgow, down the river Clyde, over the Argyll peninsula that hung down from the main body of Scotland, as if stretching out to Northern Ireland, towards the island of Islay in the Atlantic and its northern neighbour, Jura. It was the smallest plane that she had ever been on. The interior was basic, with seating for a dozen or so people on either side of the short, cylindrical fuselage, and the pilot and co-pilot separated from the passengers by an undrawn curtain. If she'd leaned forward, she could have tapped the female pilot on the shoulder.

Her mind was far away from the flight, from the now of things. She might have left London physically, but mentally she was still there, in that small, sparsely furnished police office with a view of the Thames.

On the one side:

'*Professional misconduct... Unacceptable use of force... Gross misjudgement...*'

Phrases from the charges she was facing and the ongoing disciplinary hearing and meetings with the IOPC.

On the other:

'*Proportional use of force... The officer felt threatened by the arrestee... Self-defence...*'

She looked out of the window to take her mind off recent history. She felt conflicted by the turn of events. Part of her was outraged that it had come to this, but part of her, she now realised thanks to Dr Morgan, acknowledged that she had overstepped the mark. But how she felt was comparatively unimportant. Her future was out of her hands. She was under few illusions as to her career path. Corrigan, her boss, mentor and protector, had retired. She wasn't exactly friendless in the Metropolitan Police, but it surely felt that way. She was like a wounded lioness in a pack; the others had smelled her weakness and were moving away from her. Hyenas were circling in the distance.

Even before the incident there had been indications, intimations, of her career mortality. She had heard (while waiting in a queue in the canteen – there had been one of those sudden lulls when a chance remark that would normally have gone unheard boomed out) someone refer to her as a 'has-been'. She had initially felt like walking up to him, challenging him, but when she had looked at him, twenty-six to her forty, ridiculously fresh-faced, she had thought, Maybe, maybe he is right. Maybe I am. Or maybe the world of policing has changed, and I haven't.

She had slunk away, wounded. Pretended she had forgotten something on her desk.

She had now endured a week of not being at work. She was beginning to feel like a ghost, that she wasn't living in her studio apartment so much as haunting it. Work had always been there, like a drug, to stop her thinking, to stop her brooding. Now it had been taken away. What could she do with her free time? There was only so much physical exercise she could do, she had no other hobbies, she despised the TV, didn't own one, had no interest whatsoever in books or cinema.

She forced her thoughts back to the noisy plane. Let's not think about London. It was low tide and she looked down at the muddy banks of the river Clyde, grey and brown, the red and green buoys marking the channel clearly visible from up here. Cranes standing by the sides of the waterway looked like giant metal herons. The sprawl of greater Glasgow gave way to the wrinkled, matt green of the hills, dark, geometric shapes of the conifer plantations with occasional lochans, small lakes, reflecting the gunmetal-grey of the sky, which mirrored the colour of her own eyes.

Well, it certainly made a change from London, the endless streets, the underground, the people.

Below them now she could see the sweeping gold of the beaches and patches of white where the water was breaking. Her view was framed by the thick white strut holding the wing to the body of the plane, and the air was blurred when she looked forward by the circular agitation of the propeller, invisible as it spun, the air almost visible as it trembled in front of her. The noise of the engines, a powerful droning roar, was mind-numbingly loud.

She watched two ferries far below which looked like bathtime toys for children, gaily painted red funnels, white superstructure and blue hulls.

She gazed almost dreamily at the sea, thirsting to be in it, to feel its cold, clean immensity wash everything away, wash her clean. Hanlon loved wild swimming.

She tried to focus on the view. Her thoughts wouldn't let her. They were leaping around unhelpfully like scalded cats.

She was going to have a psychiatric assessment on her return. Mandatory.

Hanlon believed in preparation. That was why she had paid to see Dr Morgan. She wanted to know the kind of questions that they might ask so she wouldn't stumble into their traps. Know your enemy.

The trouble was, having seen Dr Morgan, she was uncomfortably aware that the doctor might reasonably say, 'But you do have a problem. You can't even get on with people who want to help you. I'm not your enemy, I'm your friend. I'm trying to help you. It's you who is tearing yourself apart.'

She was going to spend some time staying with her old boss, DI Angus Tremayne, now retired on Islay. He ran a guest house, accommodation in a converted barn away from his house. Generally, Hanlon disliked the intimacy of B&Bs. You might have to make conversation. She hated small talk.

But staying with Tremayne would be fine. He knew her. He would leave her undisturbed while she did what she wanted to. He had provided her with detailed running routes, swimmable lochs, good deserted beaches. He had borrowed a mountain bike for her. She had a triathlon competition in three weeks' time. It would be her first time as a veteran. She liked the term, 'veteran'. Someone with experience. Certainly it was a damn sight better than 'has-been'.

She would spend her days in holistic, natural training in the company of some of Scotland's most beautiful scenery.

But then the original plan had had to be modified. Tremayne, not the most organised of men, had cocked up the dates and had people booked into his guest house during Hanlon's slot. She felt she had to get out of London so, until his B & B was free, she had booked herself into a small hotel on the neighbouring island of Jura, the Mackinnon Arms, for a fortnight. It had looked fine on the website.

Now she could see the southern end of the Argyll peninsula. It seemed incredibly neat and tidy from up here. A patchwork of fields and toy tractors and tiny cows and sheep. It was getting cloudy now. The mist and the rain were rolling like smoke over the hills with their muted brown and purple colours with yellow splashes of gorse.

Hanlon gazed bleakly down.

*'I think that you're addicted to violence. I think you like the adrenaline rush, the danger. I think you like losing control.'*

Thank you, Dr Elspeth Morgan, BSc (Hons) Cantab, MSc, CPsychol.

While they had discussed her life history, Dr Morgan had pointed out to her how the violence had started as one-off incidents – policing had been more robust twenty years ago, certainly with men like Tremayne around. Then it had become habitual, she had enjoyed the excitement, the thrill of violence, and then one day she found she had crossed a line, allowed the red mist to descend, and never looked back. She went looking for trouble these days; she was addicted. And she had never tried to do anything about it other than feed the beast. She had sought out dangerous, challenging situations. Dr Morgan had said it was like talking to someone who had become accustomed to breaking into lions' dens and then complaining when she was attacked. Until now. The dawning of a slow sense of self-awareness.

The plane was descending now through wispy banks of cloud, down onto the runway. And she caught a glimpse of high, conical hills in the background, covered in silvery grey scree, the Paps of Jura.

Her journey's end.

* * *

'So you'll be a tourist here?' asked the taxi driver politely as they drove across the island of Islay, where the plane had landed, to the opposite side where Hanlon was due to catch the small ferry that ran back and forth between Port Askaig and the smaller island of Jura.

He studied the woman in the back of his taxi: slim, her face was attractive but hard, grim-looking. Her grey eyes watchful. She had the kind of mouth that wasn't built for smiling. She looked guarded and sad. Maybe a bereavement, maybe a divorce, thought the driver. He liked guessing about the background of his passengers.

'Yes,' she said. Her tone discouraging any conversation. The driver persevered. He was a genial, talkative man.

'Did you know that George Orwell lived on Jura?'

'Yes.' Her voice was flat, dismissive.

'Oh.' He retreated into silence; he felt a bit wounded. Surely politeness cost nothing?

Hanlon looked out of the window of the car at the gorse and the bushes of alder and mossy spindly trees stunted by the wind and spray. Fields full of sheep staring incuriously at the taxi and dry stone walls. Grey rocks covered with light green and yellow-gold lichen rose above heather and fronds of bracken.

*I've seen this so many times before, usually in drugs and alcohol... You're the first person I've met with a violence dependency. Most of my clients are quite pleasant.'* As opposed to me, thought Hanlon. *'But it's like all addictions. Like I said before, starting off as fun, then a steady escalation, there are a well-defined series of stages, until we have total addiction, an inability to live without it.'*

Get out of my head, Dr Morgan, in your chichi Hampstead

study with your repro Giacometti sculptures and cubist art. And your fucking Mondrian rug.

The driver, studying her face in his mirror, saw her scowling furiously; her lips moved occasionally. God, she looks like trouble, he thought.

She wrenched her attention back to Islay. There was a feeling of enormous space and emptiness about the island, which she guessed might partly have explained the taxi driver's garrulousness.

'So you're staying on Jura?'

'Yes.' She finally took pity on the taxi driver and tossed him a crumb of conversation. 'I'm looking forward to swimming. The beaches are lovely, I hear.'

He pulled a face. 'Too cold for me,' he said. 'I'm more of a Mediterranean man.' He laughed, relieved that they were having a normal conversation. He didn't enjoy driving morose, irritable people around. She was probably stressed, he decided. So many people on the mainland were these days.

'Mind you don't swim in the Corryvreckan.'

She frowned. 'The Corryvreckan?'

'Aye. It's a whirlpool, just off the north of Jura.'

'Really? Is it far?' she asked.

He shook his head. 'No, not really. It's at the tip of the island – there's another island to the north and it's halfway between them. It's the third biggest whirlpool in the world, or so they say...'

I'd like to see that, she thought.

The driver added, 'Ye can doubtless hire one of the fishermen to take you. It's kind of impressive, but you would nae want to fall in.'

They drove over the brow of a hill and there was Jura in full glory.

'Wow,' said Hanlon, her troubles momentarily forgotten.

# 4

As the small ferry crossed the narrow strip of water between Islay and Jura, the water an incredible ultramarine blue, the hills on Jura, the Paps, seemed to rise up massively in front of them.

The boat got closer to the Jura side and Hanlon could see a Land Rover with police markings and an ambulance as well as several other vehicles waiting to board. She stood impatiently, her suitcase next to her. Several other foot passengers were waiting; they all seemed to know each other. The bow door on its enormous pistons descended with a muted clang onto the concrete of the landing area. Above the roar of the engines, a member of the crew shouted instructions to the drivers in their vehicles and then waved them down towards the slope that led up to the road above. Three cars and a delivery van disembarked, the metal ramp clattering and clanking below their wheels as they drove off, then it was the passengers' turn to walk off and up to the road.

Hanlon looked curiously at the police standing by their vehicles. Professional interest. Something had happened, you could see from their body language, a tell-tale tension. The Land Rover was driven by a uniform and there was a tall slim man with red

hair standing by the passenger door. He was a commanding presence. She was too far away to see him properly, but he had that
kind of calm self-assurance that the good-looking so often have.

The police presence and the proximity of an ambulance. A
death? Not an accident – nobody seemed in a hurry. She wanted
to go up to them, the tug of curiosity was almost irresistible. But
she didn't.

Various vehicles met her fellow passengers, greetings were
exchanged and car doors slammed. Engines started and cars
drove off. In five minutes, everyone who she'd been on the ferry
with was gone.

Now it was the turn of the police car, the ambulance and the
other vehicles to drive onto the ferry. She looked in through the
passenger window at the red-headed man. He was talking on the
phone, his features fine-chiselled, his mouth full. He was as good-
looking as she had suspected. He looked intently lost in thought
as he terminated the call and said something to the uniform who
was driving. The vehicles were on board, the bow was raised, and
the waters churned white and blue as the CalMac ship reversed
away from the terminal. She watched as it headed back towards
Islay then she turned and looked around impatiently for the car
from the hotel that was supposed to be there to pick her up.

No sign of it. Hanlon felt anger rising inside her. She hated
inefficiency, and this was plain sloppy. She looked at the single-
track road, the absence of vehicles. You could hardly blame traffic
for being late on Jura.

Hanlon took her phone out of her pocket and glanced at it.
No network coverage. The detective who had been on the phone
must be on a different network. She swore in irritation and
looked up at the road just in case the hotel car might be visible.
Nothing.

There was one vehicle still parked there in the ferry car park, an old Volvo. The door opened and its driver got out, a woman who looked to be in her early thirties, short, slim with long dark hair and a thin, pinched face.

'You OK?' she called to Hanlon. Hanlon frowned; she must have been looking lost. She hated showing weakness. She recognised her as one of the people who had been talking to the good-looking detective and the uniform in the Land Rover. She picked her bags up and walked over to her.

'I'm staying at the Mackinnon Arms and they were supposed to pick me up.'

'The Mackinnon Arms?' the woman said in surprise.

'Yes, that's right.'

'Jump in,' said the woman, indicating the Volvo. 'I'll give you a lift, it's not far out of my way.'

Hanlon went over to the Volvo. The back of the estate had a black and white dog inside, a border collie. It was screened off from the car by a metal mesh dog-guard. The woman smiled at her and opened the back door so Hanlon could put her luggage in.

The dog bounded about in its confined space, hoping to be let out, curious as to what was happening, who this stranger was.

Hanlon stood motionless, mentally frowning at the disorder inside. The back seats had become a wide shelf for a variety of clutter. There were crumpled ordnance survey maps, plastic bags, a couple of beanie hats, a pair of muddy walking boots, a police notebook, a scrunched-up cagoule, her personal radio, a half-eaten packet of biscuits, a Thermos flask, and some empty water bottles.

The woman swept everything on one side of the car to the floor behind the driver's seat with a casual hand, making room for Hanlon's luggage. Let's hope she doesn't need that radio, Hanlon thought.

'There you go.'

Hanlon put her bags inside and climbed into the front passenger seat. The foot-well was covered in mud and small stones, bits of gravel.

The woman started the engine.

'I'm Catriona.'

Hanlon shook the proffered hand. Catriona's handshake was firm, her nails were cut short. In person she was a lot cleaner than her Volvo.

She put the car in gear.

'Are you with the police?' Hanlon asked casually.

'Aye, I am, I'm DS McCleod.' She had that gentle west-coast accent that was a feature of the islanders, a far cry from the harsh Glaswegian tones of Tremayne. It sounded barely Scottish, almost Dutch.

'Why the ambulance?' asked Hanlon.

McCleod looked at her in an evaluating kind of way. Hanlon recognised that look, she'd worn it often enough herself – how much should I say?

McCleod said, cagily, 'Unfortunately a girl drowned. She went missing a couple of days ago and we have only just recovered the body.'

'Oh.' Hanlon bit her tongue. It was nothing to do with her, but she couldn't help but ask.

'Was it an accident?'

McCleod gave her an irritated look.

'It's too early to say... probably.' In other words, no, thought Hanlon.

McCleod changed the topic of conversation abruptly. 'Did you know that George Orwell lived on Jura?' she asked.

Hanlon wondered if this was a common question or if she had

inadvertently stumbled across a fan club of the famous writer. First the taxi driver, now the cop.

'Yes.'

'Oh,' said McCleod. Hanlon glanced at her. She looked as if she was beginning to regret her act of kindness in offering this woman a lift. Hanlon turned her attention to the scenery through the car window. Ferns and more stunted birch and alder. A gannet plunged like an arrow into the gunmetal-grey sea. A couple of fishing boats were out in the sound between Jura and the mainland Argyll peninsula, their low raked lines graceful in the afternoon light. Hanlon felt her irritation at the inefficiency of the hotel begin to lift.

Behind everything rose the massive rocky domes of the Paps. Devoid of trees or bushes, just rock and grass, huge and rounded.

Everything lay in their shadow. They dominated the island. They were the kind of feature from which there was no escape. Hanlon gazed up at them, eager to climb them.

McCleod noticed her looking at them. 'Impressive, aren't they?' she said. Hanlon nodded.

'Shit!' swore McCleod, stamping on the brakes as a large, brightly coloured bird with a long tail ran out from the foliage by the side of the road straight in front of the car. She managed to stop in time and the bird turned and looked at the vehicle incuriously. Then a smaller, dowdy brown-grey bird cautiously emerged from the grasses and bracken to join its mate and the two of them disappeared into the trees bordering the sea.

'Pheasants,' McCleod said. 'The estate breeds them for the shoot. These two must have survived the season. Anyway, how long are you staying here on Jura?'

'A couple of weeks.' Hanlon decided to make polite conversation; Dr Morgan would doubtless approve. 'I'm looking forward to swimming – the beaches are lovely, I hear.'

McCleod laughed.

'Aye, well, that they are, more so on the other side.'

Hanlon said, 'There's a whirlpool, isn't there?' She'd gotten quite excited at the thought of it; she'd never seen a whirlpool before.

'Oh aye, the Corryvreckan.' McCleod braked sharply to avoid a rabbit running across the road. 'It's quite the thing. You should go and have a look at it while you're here. You can pay someone to take you out in a boat to see it. In fact, I'm pretty sure that the hotel's got one. They'll take you.'

'Is it dangerous?' The idea of a famous whirlpool conjured up an image of a huge maelstrom, sucking ships down into the depths of the ocean.

'Och, not really,' McCleod said disappointingly. 'I wouldn't swim over it, people have. I think I mind there was a guy with one leg who did it a while ago. It's interesting, in a low-key kind of way.'

So, no maelstrom, thought Hanlon. Not if a one-legged swimmer could cross it.

They drove through a small village.

'Craighouse,' said McCleod. 'There's only a couple of hundred people live here on the island, so this is by way of a metropolis. There's another hotel there, if you get tired of the Mackinnon Arms.'

Hanlon shuddered inwardly. Only two hundred people. She was from London. Intensely solitary, she found the idea that everyone would know your business, as they had to in a place as small as this, a terrible thought. Hanlon had secrets; she didn't want people ever knowing her past. The mistakes she'd made. People she'd hurt, not just physically. Rules bent or broken. Nor would she want people to know about the cloud she was currently under. 'Look, there goes the unstable cop.' Or, 'They're probably going to sack her, you know.' She lapsed into silence. She began to wonder if coming here was such a good idea.

The road ran on. They drove for a good few miles past the village, seeing the occasional house and farm building. They didn't see a single person. She found this slightly unsettling. The road hugged the coastline; occasional forestry tracks ran inland from it and they met no traffic at all until they came to a stop at a cattle grid. After the grid that they rattled across slowly, the dog in the back leaping around in agitation at the noise, the tarmac changed to a different colour and a faded sign said, 'Mackinnon Arms'. The drive to the hotel was long. Rhododendron bushes on both sides obscured the views.

'Why the Mackinnon Arms?' asked McCleod.

'I'm only there by accident really,' Hanlon said. She explained about staying on Islay, the need to find somewhere for a while until her accommodation became free.

McCleod nodded. 'So you don't know much about the Mackinnon Arms?'

'Just the name, really.' She hadn't bothered to read that much about it on its home page. 'What's it like?'

'Oh, it's OK, I believe. The food's good, I hear. It used to be a big private house, way back when,' McCleod said. 'There was some kind of scandal, the wife was having an affair... a lot of that goes on, on an island.' Her voice sounded strangely far away, as if she were talking to herself rather than her passenger. Hanlon wondered if she had someone in mind.

'And the husband killed her, I suppose,' said Hanlon. There was an edge to her voice that made McCleod stare at her questioningly. Hanlon had seen a lot of domestic violence in her time.

McCleod shook her head. 'No, almost the reverse. It broke his heart and he hung himself. Maybe I shouldn't be telling you this, since you're staying there. The hotel is on a psychic trail.'

'A psychic trail?'

McCleod nodded. 'Yeah, people interested in ghosts and haunted places come and stay. It's quite big business, ghost tourism. Anyway... the house got turned into a hotel in the fifties, but recently it must have had about ten different owners in as many years. Out of season we don't get many tourists and it's difficult to make a hotel pay when you've only got those few summer months.'

'Despite the ghost.'

'Despite the ghost.' McCleod grinned; it transformed her face. She had excellent teeth, white and even.

Hanlon nodded. She was beginning to slightly regret booking into somewhere so isolated. Nothing to do with the ghost – she was worried that she would just be left alone with her regrets.

'Here we are,' said McCleod, pulling up in front of a large white building. 'The Mackinnon Arms.'

## 5

From outside, the hotel at first sight looked idyllic. It was a large building, painted white, with symmetrical window stones picked out in black. It overlooked the sea facing the Argyll coast and the Atlantic Ocean towards America if you kept going westwards. To the rear of the hotel was the car park and, rising up behind it, the Paps of Jura.

So far, so good. It was just like the images on the website. However, as Hanlon got closer, a different picture emerged.

The paintwork was cracked and peeling, and the old-fashioned metal drainpipes had been leaking, staining the white paint an unpleasant shade of yellow. There were a couple of flower tubs in front of the hotel made from half-barrels, but the wooden strakes were rotting and the straggly geraniums were choked with weeds.

There was a small beach in front of the hotel and next to it a jetty that ran out to sea, about twenty metres long. A sizeable launch was tied up to the end. She could see the thick white mooring ropes wound around large metal bollards. To the right of the jetty was a large rowing boat moored to an orange buoy and beyond that an eight-metre fibreglass fishing boat with a covered cockpit.

She looked back up to the road. The Volvo was still there. McCleod was looking at her from behind the wheel, as if intent on making sure that Hanlon was really going into the hotel. Hanlon waved and she waved back, then drove off.

As Hanlon walked up to the front door she noticed, frowning, that the tarmac was littered with cigarette ends. There was a sign hanging on a pole outside; it was quite disturbing, a boar's head with a bone between its teeth, below it a length of knotted rope, and the name, the Mackinnon Arms. The sign was dilapidated, the tusks of the boar a sinister yellow and rust-covered stains on the bone where the paint had discoloured looked unpleasantly like blood. She walked into the reception area, the usual configuration of desk walling off a back-room management office section and a framed Admiralty chart on the wall, blue and yellow with depths marked in metres, and sandbanks and rocks shown. In Hanlon's, admittedly limited, experience of small seaside hotels and pubs, this was practically de rigueur lobby decoration. She looked around for a member of staff, but the reception was deserted. There was a framed photo, a montage of hotel staff; Team Mackinnon, it was titled.

She gave it a closer look. Jim Richardson, Owner/Manager; Harriet Reynolds, Food and Beverage Manager; Johanna Helmanis and Eva Balodis, Restaurant Staff; Kai McPherson, Bar Manager and Donald Crawford, Head Chef.

Eva Balodis had a thing for facial piercings: eyebrow, nose and ears. Hanlon looked at the other photos, two very Scottish names, two that looked English and, she guessed, another Eastern European-sounding, like Eva's. A fairly typical staff composition, she guessed, for a hotel in the wilds of Scotland.

There was a plaque on the wall with the boar's head motif

again, with the words, '*Audentes Fortuna Juvat*' and a translation, 'Fortune assists the daring'. There was an explanation of the sign: it was the Mackinnon coat of arms. It referred to an incident when the clan chief had been sheltering in a cave and had been attacked by a savage boar. He had jammed its jaws open with a bone from a deer he was roasting, disabling the homicidal pig, and then killed it.

She looked around. The carpet was scuffed and threadbare, a kind of unpleasant blueish tartan, worn through in patches. The, what she guessed were originally cream skirting boards and paintwork were now an off-yellow.

There was no one around, so leaving her bags behind, something she would never have dreamed of doing in London, she went through into the hall of the hotel in search of staff. Tremayne had warned her about the slow pace of life on the Western Isles, which was sometimes great, but sometimes infuriating, especially to a Londoner. He'd told her the story about the islander who had had the Spanish concept of '*mañana*' explained. 'Oh aye,' he'd said, 'we have a similar expression, but without the sense of urgency.' She guessed that what would have been highly unusual in a hotel in London was more acceptable out here.

A staircase led upwards to the rooms and there were three doors: one was to a small bar, empty, the other to a large, bare function room and the third led into a restaurant. Hanlon went in.

It was nearly 3 p.m. now and it had obviously been a busy lunch. The tables were uncleared, dirty, smeared plates and cutlery still on view. Floating on top of the odour of food was cigarette smoke. This was coming from a shaggy-haired man sitting alone at a table near the back of the restaurant looking blearily at Hanlon.

She felt an instinctive surge of irritation at someone flouting the non-smoking regulations. She stood, framed in the doorway, hands on her hips, staring the guy down.

She guessed he was about sixty, his thick hair salt and pepper in colour, and he had a droopy brown moustache. He had been good-looking once, but those days were long gone. He was wearing a short-sleeved shirt and pale-blue supermarket, dad-style jeans. His build was that of a powerful man gone to seed. The fabric of his shirt that stretched over his belly, which was sizeable, was tight with the strain. His forearms were strong and heavy with faded retro nautical tattoos. He grinned conspiratorially at Hanlon, his cigarette burning between his fingers.

'Afternoon, lass, can I help you?' he asked. His smile was one of unadulterated sleaze and he ran his eyes over her body in a deliberate, provocatively evaluating way. She was glad that she was wearing combat trousers and a Gore-tex cagoule. She certainly couldn't be accused of dressing provocatively.

He obviously wasn't Scottish. The accent, with its short vowel sound, was, to her ears, generic north of England.

'My name's Hanlon. I've got a room booked,' she said. She would have liked to add, unfortunately. Her gaze travelled coldly across the mess in the dining room, lingering on the landlord's half-drunk pint of lager accompanied by a glass of what she guessed was Scotch.

'Someone was supposed to have met me at the ferry.'

'I'm short-staffed at the moment,' he said by way of excuse. 'The girl who normally does that died yesterday.' He shook his head sorrowfully. 'Drowned. They found her body today. Poor lass.'

Hanlon blinked in surprise on two counts: first that it should happen in the hotel that she was staying in; secondly that the landlord would so blithely mention it. It somehow didn't seem hotel protocol to tell a newly arrived guest that a member of staff had just died. Perhaps the landlord was unusually candid, or perhaps he was just very pissed.

So now the hotel had another death in its history. Maybe the girl would become part of the folklore like the long-dead jilted husband. Another ghost for the psychic tourists to look for.

'Busy lunch, we had a coach party...' His voice drifted off; he stared into space as if he had forgotten about her. Then he shook himself awake. 'If you'd like to come with me...' he said, hoisting himself upright.

'Call me Jim, lass, or Big Jim, as the ladies do,' he said to her, with a suggestive leer. His voice lingered suggestively on the word 'ladies'. Hanlon stared at him with horrified fascination. She hadn't met anyone this genuinely repellent in a while. They walked to reception. He was a tall man, a head taller than she was. He unhooked a key from a board, picked up her suitcase with one hand as if it were light as a feather, leaving her the kitbag, and then motioned her to accompany him upstairs.

She followed the broad back and saggy buttocks in their baggy jeans to the first-floor landing, through a fire door and along a corridor. Big Jim puffed in exertion as they walked up the steep stairs but the muscles in his arms were still big and defined, despite his age. He certainly was having no difficulty with her case. He was one of those people with great muscle strength but poor aerobic fitness. Hanlon, a devotee of gyms, was often surprised by discrepancies like that. The most common one was men who exercised their arms with fanatical devotion to the exclusion of everything else, so they ended up with huge biceps and scrawny chicken legs. Big Jim could probably curl thirty kilos with ease but collapse if he did a lap of the car park.

He unlocked one of the rooms and stood partially blocking the door so she would have to squeeze past him. His gut made a formidable obstacle. Their eyes met and he leered at her. Hanlon felt the old, familiar anger rise within herself.

She paused, waiting for him to move aside, which he didn't. He was obviously hoping that she would make body contact as she passed him, having to rub against him. She could imagine him pushing against her saying, 'Now you know why the girls call me Big Jim.'

Hanlon had no intention of touching him. She had her handbag in her right hand and the torpedo-shaped zip-up hold-all in her left. It was heavy, twenty kilos, and she lifted it to groin level and slammed it into Big Jim's crotch as she entered the room. As if by accident, but they both knew it wasn't. He grunted with pain and took a painful step backwards, glaring at her angrily.

'Oh, I'm sorry,' said Hanlon, her tone blatantly unapologetic.

The room, at least, was unexpectedly pleasant. It was at the end of the corridor and of the hotel itself. Clean, airy, with an en-suite bathroom. The room was flooded in clear light from the two windows, one on the end wall, the other on the side wall that overlooked the front of the hotel, the road and the car-park. She walked over to the large window overlooking the sea, which stretched out limitlessly in front of her. Clouds had started to roll in and the Argyll peninsula was now invisible.

Big Jim looked at her expectantly. What does he think I'm going to do? she thought, with increasing irritation. Make a pass at him?

'The room's fine,' she said. He showed no sign of moving away. Then she noticed that he was staring, not at her, but past her out of the window facing the sea at a sizeable boat that was coming into view. He had obviously forgotten temporarily that she was there; the boat absorbed his attention fully.

'About time,' she heard him say. He seemed lost in thought.

She wondered if it was the sight of the boat or if he was just drunk. Either way, she wanted him gone.

'If you'll excuse me.' She started to close the door and he finally got the message.

'Dinner's at eight,' he said flatly. 'Bar opens at five.'

She looked contemptuously at the broken veins in his cheeks, his mottled nose and the slightly yellow tinge to his eyes. I'll bet the bar opens a lot earlier for you, she thought.

'I'll see you later,' he said. He turned and left the room.

I hope not, thought Hanlon.

\* \* \*

A couple of hours later Hanlon was pounding along the road on a five-mile cross-country run. It was less of a run than a mix of jogging along tracks near the beach and some road work. The hotel drive continued way past the Mackinnon Arms itself and the two cottages close by. It became a single-track road that ran towards the northern tip of Jura.

The sun had come out and it was a beautiful afternoon. The sea breeze cooled her as the sweat started to dampen her clothes. She fell into an easy, relaxed stride; her body felt good. The richness of the smell of the island, earth, sea and the sharp tang of pine were strange, new. It was exhilarating. When she bored of the tarmac she went down to the shore and scrambled along the stones and shingle of the beaches and the rocks. She was pleased with her physical condition. Her legs felt tireless and she exulted in the strength in her muscles. She felt she could have continued forever. She was exorcising the ghosts of recent events. This is what I need, she suddenly thought, looking at the grey-blue, limitless sea and the huge sky. The atmosphere of London that had seemed so exhilarating now seemed claustrophobic. She suddenly, for the first time since leaving Heathrow, felt that she had done the right thing in coming here.

As she ran, she wondered which one of the staff had drowned. It had to be one of the two members of staff with Eastern European sounding names. Harriet looked too old to be referred to by Big Jim as 'a girl'.

She reached the two-and-a-half-mile mark, stopped and stretched her body. She did some breathing exercises and noticed again how the air of the island felt amazing: a mix of salt, seaweed from the desiccated, dark fringe of bladder wrack and kelp at high water mark that lined the beaches, and the damp, peaty smell of the land. It was almost intoxicating. It made what she was used to breathing in the city smell dead and recycled, like the air in a passenger jet.

She slowed to a walk, feeling the sweat running down her body and prickling her scalp under her tangled dark hair. She waved her hand to keep away the swarm of tiny midges, only slightly bigger than a pinhead but eager to make up for their lack of size by weight of numbers. She rounded a corner and now, about a kilometre away, she could see the hotel. It no longer looked so picturesque; its silhouette looked tatty and sinister. The rear of the building was temporarily in the shade from a dark cloud and its sign flapped mournfully in the wind. She thought again of the drowned girl. As she drew close, a shaft of sunlight pierced the cloud and caught the piggy eyes of the boar on the sign and it seemed to grin contemptuously at her as she stood looking up at it.

The path by the side of the road took her to the back of the Mackinnon Arms. She walked past an outhouse, some wheelie bins, a large coal bunker and wood store, into a paved court that backed onto the kitchen.

The boat that Big Jim had been staring at out at sea was now moored on the opposite side of the jetty to the launch that she had noticed earlier. The hotel jetty was a substantial straight piece of concrete that ran into the sea. The craft was a sizeable motor yacht flying a red ensign flag.

'*Lorelei. Portsmouth*' was painted on the bows. Hanlon stared at it with curiosity. It was a large boat, rich-man rather than oligarch or Saudi-prince size, maybe ten to fifteen metres long. It exuded an air of expense and professionalism. It was obviously seaworthy enough to make it to the west coast of Scotland from the Channel. As she looked at it, a couple of crewmen in a rudimentary uniform, jeans and white polo shirts, appeared from below and busied themselves on the decks. The Mackinnon Arms seemed a strange choice of berth for such an expensive boat; maybe it was just a question of convenience.

Her gaze turned away from the sea to the building itself. From this angle, facing the sea, it looked even more dilapidated. The black paint on the window frames was almost all gone, the tiles of the roof looked uneven, some of them cracked. Weeds sprouted on the terrace. Big Jim's kingdom, like his face and body, was visibly crumbling.

Hanlon walked around to the front and into the hotel entrance. The forecourt of the hotel now had a couple of Range Rovers parked in it. In the back of one of them, through the rear window, she could see oxygen tanks and other bits of diving gear. She went inside and glanced into the bar as she walked past.

There were three thickset men, jumpers and jeans, presumably the Range Rover owners and divers, sitting chatting with Big Jim at a table. She saw Big Jim pick up a full pint of lager, raise it to his lips and unhurriedly down it in one. He put the glass down with exaggerated care and motioned to the barman for another one. There was another group in there, two men and three girls, talking to a figure in chef's whites, presumably about the menu.

Hanlon guessed that these were the party from the yacht she had just seen.

She went up to her room, showered and changed into trousers and a patterned shirt, lay down on the bed and stared at the ceiling. She noticed a dark brown stain on the plaster near the window – damp, she guessed.

Thoughts ran through her head: Big Jim, McCleod telling her about the history of the hotel, speculation as to what the yacht was doing there. It was all a blessed relief from fretting over the fallout from her assault on the suspect in South London. She yawned. She had been up since five, a flight from Heathrow to Glasgow and then, after hanging around Glasgow airport for a couple of hours, the short hop to Islay. She guessed she must have covered five to six hundred miles. She closed her eyes and fell asleep more or less immediately.

**6**

---

She woke up a couple of hours later. The phone in the room was ringing. She picked it up, was she coming down for dinner? She had phoned down earlier and booked for eight o'clock. She glanced at her phone, it was now nine, the kitchen was closing soon.

Shit, thought Hanlon. She hated being late.

'I'll be straight down.'

She washed her face and dragged a brush through her unruly black hair. She looked at her reflection in the mirror in the bathroom. Her dark, straight eyebrows drew attention to her cold grey eyes, her strong nose with a slight kink in it from where it had been broken in the past and a slight bump on it, another break. Her cheekbones were high, her jaw emphatic. It was a challenging face. Intimidating.

She left her room and walked along the poorly lit corridor – several of the light bulbs had blown and not been replaced – through the fire door and down the main staircase to the dining room. She blinked in surprise as she walked in. All traces of the mess that had greeted her earlier in the day had been expunged.

It was like a completely different room. The cheap wooden tables that she had seen earlier were now covered with starched white tablecloths. There were candles on the tables bathing the room in a soft glow. It was a magical transformation. She was shown to her seat by a quiet Eastern European waitress.

A name badge was pinned onto her blouse: Johanna. So the dead girl was probably Eva, thought Hanlon. Eva Balodis, the girl with the multiple piercings.

There was a woman by the till that she recognised from the group photo she had seen on the noticeboard earlier, Team Mackinnon. The name came back to her: Harriet Reynolds. The divers she had seen earlier were just leaving; one of them spoke to the restaurant manageress. His voice was quiet but his tone was furious. He was obviously extremely angry. Hanlon could hear every word he was saying.

'Thanks for a lovely meal...' the accent educated Home Counties: generic, featureless, self-confident '... you've been fine.' He stressed the you; obviously someone else hadn't been.

I wonder who that might have been, she thought sarcastically.

The man continued, 'The food's great, and we have no complaints about the hotel, but after what that drunken cunt, pardon my French, of a landlord said to me, we're not staying a minute longer.'

'I'm sorry you feel that way.'

Harriet Reynolds was tall and slim with a long face and short-cropped hair. She looked like a teacher from an exclusive girls' school, thought Hanlon. She handled the irate customer with practised coolness.

'Is there nothing I can do to make you change your minds?'

'No,' came the short answer. 'You can reimburse me later. I'll e-mail you my bank details. Tell your boss he's a twat. We're off now, getting the last ferry.'

'Enjoy Islay!' said the manageress, a hint of despair now in her voice.

Perhaps Big Jim made a pass at him too, thought Hanlon.

The food was extremely good. Surprisingly so. The hotel's fine-dining credentials, which they'd made a big deal of on their website, were very much on show. She had carpaccio of lobster, an amuse bouche of a raviolo of scallop and, as a main course, local 'wether', a two-year-old sheep, with a brilliantly green mint jelly and gratin dauphinoise.

As she ate in these comfortable surroundings, she was struck by the ambivalence of the hotel, its odd contrasts. There was the room she was in now, earlier smelling of vinegar and fried food like a cheap café, now a temple to fine dining. The crumbling ruin of the building, the luxury yacht moored nearby. The professionalism of Harriet Reynolds contrasted with the sleaze of Big Jim.

There were ten other people in the restaurant, one couple she'd seen who were staying in the hotel, the others, judging by their accent and conversation, local. Hanlon studied the manageress with detached interest. She was lean and radiated an air of slick professionalism. But when you looked closer, she was tired; the make-up didn't hide the bags under her eyes. Her mouth was a resentful red, compressed, narrow line of lip-balm. She worked the room energetically, refilling glasses, bringing dishes from the kitchen in tandem with Johanna, who had shown Hanlon to her table and was proving a model of exemplary efficiency.

She thought she recognised Harriet's accent from her former boss, Tremayne, who had pilloried a former colleague from Edinburgh about the way he spoke, which Tremayne had claimed was prissy.

She had heard that Edinburgh Morningside way of speaking enshrined in jokes that Tremayne had told her, like:

Q: What's sex in Morningside? A: What you put your rubbish in for the binmen.

Q: What's a crèche in Morningside? A: When two cars collide.

What was this sophisticated Edinburgh woman doing, working for an idiot like Big Jim? For some reason, although Harriet had been both polite and efficient, Hanlon was conscious of disliking her. Hanlon was a naturally prickly person, quick to take offence. She had an uncomfortable feeling that Dr Morgan would have something to say about this. Harriet seemed to be patronising her. Whether or not she was didn't really matter. That was how she felt. And there was something about Harriet that didn't ring true, as if she were pretending to be more sophisticated than she was. Maybe it was a British thing, where people disguise their accents to hide a working-class background. Was it a class thing? She shrugged to herself. It really didn't matter one way or another. Her meal was now nearly over. She finished her pineapple tarte Tatin and Johanna took her plate away.

The manageress came over. 'Can I get you a coffee, tea, a liqueur?' offered Harriet. Her voice lingered on the word 'liqueur'. Hanlon had drunk only water and she had the feeling that Harriet disapproved.

'Coffee. I'll drink it in the bar, if that's OK.'

'By all means. I'll have it brought to you.'

Hanlon stood up and walked out of the dining room, across the hall with its sad, tattered carpet to the bar.

It was small with a commanding view of the sea. At moments like this you could see how the hotel could really work; the potential was certainly there. Its view was breath-taking. In the distance you could make out the hills of the Argyll peninsula. It was still light outside although it was nearly ten at night. The soft, unearthly light, like nothing she had experienced before, almost hallucinatory, bathed the huge calm grey ocean in a strange lambent glow. This more than anything else made her realise just how far north they were. It would be dark back home. A couple of fishing boats passed in the distance, heading in the direction of Islay. Their presence only emphasised how vast the sea was. A seal broke the surface nearby and its sleek, dog-like head stared curiously at the yacht before it sank back beneath the Atlantic waters.

There were a few people in the bar, including a small group who were obviously from the yacht, the *Lorelei*, that could be seen moored outside, its port and starboard lights glowing red and green in the gathering dusk. She guessed its owners were the two men, in their late forties, early fifties, one bald and trim-looking, the other with a comb-over and a sizeable beer belly that an ill-advised polo shirt couldn't contain, spilling over his white chinos. They looked like the kind of men who would own a boat like that. They were accompanied by three girls who were young enough to be their daughters but probably weren't. The two men were British, the girls, judging by their accents, foreign. They were drinking champagne.

Hanlon sat at a table in the corner, took her phone out and toyed with it, not because she had any desire to check messages or look at anything in particular, just so she didn't look out of place and alone.

Comb-over guy said something loudly and the girls laughed hysterically. They looked to be in their mid-twenties, in ripped jeans and T-shirts. Two brunette, one blonde. Comb-over had his hand on one of the blonde girl's thighs, stroking it intently. She patted it absent-mindedly, as you would a dog. He was sniffing loudly at intervals. His eyes were bulging; they glittered alarmingly. Hanlon glanced over disapprovingly and the girl noticed her look and scowled. Hanlon shrugged and went back to looking at the news on her phone. More accurately, pretending to look. There was no signal. She had forgotten to ask about Wi-Fi.

Another gale of laughter. Hanlon looked up, frowning. The blonde girl with a stud in her pierced nose, caught her eye, sneered and, surreptitiously, so only Hanlon would see, gave her the finger. She sighed to herself and shook her head, trying not to let the girl's contempt rile her. But it did. She put the phone down and looked at the bar.

There was an elaborate Gaggia coffee machine, hissing and steaming, and the barman, Kai McPherson, she remembered from the group photos at reception, busied himself with it and brought Hanlon over her coffee. He was young, good-looking and he knew it. There was a mirror on one wall and she could see the blonde girl staring at Kai with undisguised attention. She guessed that Kai was everything that the yacht owner wasn't. Unfortunately, that included poor.

As the barman put her coffee on the table and the yacht group burst into loud laughter again, Hanlon noticed the tattoos on the bar manager's wrists, revealed as his cuffs rode up, a series of dashes running around his wrist like a bracelet, and a pair of scissors poorly inked into the skin. She guessed that on the inside it would say 'cut here'. A home-made tattoo, rudimentary, slightly inept. She wondered if it was institutional, a foster home, a young persons' detainment centre or prison.

She looked at him now with professional interest. Kai was short and slight with blond hair and a hard face. He had blue, watchful eyes and walked with a fighter's swagger. It was the kind of walk that said, Look at me, do you want to have a go? Hanlon had arrested a fair few Kais in her time.

'Here's your coffee,' he said. 'I'm Kai, by the way...' Their eyes met. He looked at her suggestively. With a shock she realised he was flirting with her. She smiled. I'm so out of your league, she thought. She noticed a faint scar, about the length of a finger, three to four centimetres, that ran down the left side of his forehead, finishing at the corner of his eye. She doubted it was the result of an accident.

Kai had seen her smile and misinterpreted it. 'If you need anything... just see me.' His voice lingered on the 'anything'. His accent was different from the west coast lilt; it was harsh Glaswegian.

'Thank you,' she said.

The bald guy got up and went to the bar. He rapped his knuckles on it loudly for attention. The barman caught Hanlon's eye and rolled his own heavenwards. Some people, he seemed to be saying. He went back to the bar, spoke to the man and disappeared out the back, returning with a couple more bottles of champagne.

Harriet appeared in the bar carrying a small plate. She walked up to Hanlon.

'I've brought you some complimentary petits fours, courtesy of the hotel,' she said, placing them reverently on Hanlon's table. Another gale of loud laughter from the far table. Harriet winced and closed her eyes as if wishing they would go away. The things I have to put up with, her expression said. Despite her instinctive dislike of Harriet – maybe it was the short hair, the short sleeves and the brusque attitude that was reminiscent of an in-your-face gym mistress – she felt a twinge of sympathy for her. She knew what it was like to have to be polite to people you hated. Except when you weren't. Except when you drove your elbow into their faces.

'Thank you,' said Hanlon.

'Breakfast is from seven until nine thirty,' Harriet said. 'I do hope you have enjoyed your dinner tonight.'

Hanlon nodded and watched as she disappeared. She didn't want the petits fours but she ate them anyway. They were delicious.

Hanlon suddenly felt a sense of unease, the kind of feeling she got sometimes just before she went into action at work when she realised that things could go terribly wrong. What was it? What was wrong?

She checked her e-mails on her phone – the hotel did have Wi-Fi, she'd discovered – nothing of any importance. The bar was starting to fill up – locals, judging by their accents. But the feeling that something wasn't right wouldn't leave her.

A dozen couples, ages ranging from mid-thirties to late fifties. Nothing unusual, but a sense of strained anticipation. Kai laughing and joking behind the bar. He'd done jail time, she was sure of it now. His ready smile now seemed sinister. In the mirror she caught a glimpse of Big Jim as he ambled past the bar door in the corridor. Their eyes met and he gave her a self-satisfied, hungry smile as he went past. The smile reminded her of the boar on his sign, violent, piggy and self-satisfied.

The yacht party were guzzling their champagne as if it were water, with cocaine-induced thirst. The ageing men and their child-girl prostitutes.

Hanlon drank some coffee. It tasted good. She shook her head. Maybe she had gotten it all wrong. Christ alone knew, her perception of reality was skewed at the best of times. Twenty years of dealing with low lifes, stupidity, cupidity and violence. Not everyone was a criminal. Maybe she was becoming paranoid.

She felt herself sweating. She really did feel peculiar. What the fuck is going on? she thought. She stood up and left the bar and followed the sign to the toilets.

She closed the door behind her and, leaning against it, breathed deeply. Calm down, she told herself. She was feeling

odd – was this some kind of panic attack? First paranoid delu-
sions, now this. Stress from all that unresolved business in
London?

To take her mind off things she forced herself to concentrate
on her surroundings. She looked around the bathroom. Harriet
was doing a good job; they were spotless. There were several
framed pictures on the wall to entertain the customer: a couple of
old photos of crofters on Jura, one of Orwell (inevitably), a framed
front page from a local paper, the *Argyllshire Advertiser*, from the
1950s, about the hotel. There was a vase of fresh flowers artfully
arranged; it was very tasteful. Again, the odd contrast in the
Mackinnon Arms between the ultra-professional and the
amateur.

She walked over to a sink, ran the tap and splashed water over
her face. She began to feel marginally better. I'm just paranoid,
she thought. There's nothing wrong. Everything is fine. They are
all just normal people, having a normal night out. You're the
crazy one.

She heard women's voices and drunken laughter from down
the stone-flagged passageway. Almost certainly the girls from the
yacht. Her heart sank.

She was in no mood to speak to them, or even acknowledge
their existence. She had taken a rooted dislike to them, particularly nose-stud girl, the one who had insulted her.

'...*uncontrollably violent...anger issues.*' Comments made during
the *IOPC* hearing. All the shit that she had seen over the years,
domestic incidents that had escalated to serious assaults and
preventable deaths, the obviously guilty getting off on 'reasonable
doubt' defences, promises made and promises broken, and her
own part in some highly questionable violent events. Things she
had tried to forget she had done, things she was beginning to feel
ashamed of. Now Dr Morgan had cracked open the self-doubt,

the self-recrimination, the self-awareness, and the dam was about to break. She didn't want to be part of another incident.

The year before she had been part of a team that had tracked down and arrested a guy who'd stabbed another man eight times in a Brixton nightclub. It had been a frenzied attack. When Hanlon had interviewed him, he'd shrugged and told her that the guy had looked at him 'in a funny way'. And the terrible thing was, deep down, Hanlon knew exactly how he had felt. She was no stranger to uncontrollable rage.

Hanlon was worried about what she might do. She could picture the scene now, another sneer from the blonde girl, an insult from her. She had a horrible feeling that if an argument developed between her and the girl it would rapidly escalate, and not in a good way. An uppercut to the girl's midriff, short left hook to her head. No, no, no, she thought. No. She was in enough trouble as it was without being arrested for assault in Scotland. *'Just avoid crime...'* That had been Dr Morgan's advice.

She certainly didn't want to commit one.

She retreated into one of the three cubicles, locked the door behind her and sat down on the seat.

'Let it pass...' That's what Dr Morgan would suggest.

Drunken laughter from the other side of the door, then the smell of weed. Hanlon hated the sickly, compost stink of grass at the best of times; she sat in the cubicle, fuming, her temper rising, trapped by her dislike of others and the mistrust of herself.

She ground her teeth listening to the joint-smoking trio, their words punctuated by loud sniffs as they did lines, and shrieks of laughter. Her temper rose. God, they were annoying on so many levels: the arrogance, the in-your-face drug-taking, the noise. The smell of the cannabis. *'Is it because they are young with their lives ahead of them? In contrast with you?'* Shut up, Dr Morgan, Hanlon thought angrily. You're not here to counsel me, you're in millionaires' row in Hampstead with your collectible 1930s Weimar German ceramics. You smug woman.

The conversation was weirdly polyglot; the girls were speaking German with other languages thrown in. Maybe Polish or Czech, with occasional snatches of English, which she guessed was a language they all knew a bit of. She assumed they were from different countries.

'Ist der Koks gut?' Is the coke good? translated Hanlon from behind the door.

'*Koks?* Was ist?'

'Koks... Cocaine... coke.'

'Oh, ja, super-toll...' more loud laughter '... ausgezeichnet, hier... du probierst.'

'Was?' She means it's very good, thought Hanlon. Are you thick or what?

'Super good... you try.'

'Oh, ja... JA! Das ist von Kai, ja.'

In the toilet stall, listening to the conversation floating over the door like the smoke from the weed, she remembered Big Jim's cigarette in the restaurant. The Mackinnon Arms was not overly keen on smoke alarms. Hanlon's ears pricked up as she eavesdropped on the conversation. Kai, *if you need anything, just see me.* Von Kai must mean 'from Kai'. They had bought the coke from the barman; that was what he had been offering her, not sex. Do I look like a cokehead? she thought, annoyed. It was harder to know what was worse: being mistaken for a sex-starved forty-year-old or a drug addict.

On the other side of the door the drug-fuelled conversation continued.

'Mmm, hmm. Ich werde fuck him, sex für coke.' Sex for coke, she thought.

'Er hat eine Girlfriend... in der Ecke.'

'Oh, ja...' sarcastic emphasis on the 'ja' '... das Buttenschleck.'

*Buttenschleck?* she wondered. Judging by the reply, she wasn't the only one.

'Was?'

'The old lesbian in the corner...'

That means me, thought Hanlon, incredulous. The old lesbian. They're talking about me! Her fingers automatically curled into fists.

Her mind went back to Dr Morgan.

*'There's a technical term, Hanlon. In layman's terms it's called pushing the fuck-it button. That's when addicts give in to their chosen addiction big-time. They know it's going to have terrible consequences, but they've ceased to care. They almost seem to relish it.'*

You were right, Dr Morgan, thought Hanlon, standing up. Not that you ever doubted it. Fuck it! she thought to herself. Whatever a *Buttenschleck* is, it's coming to get you! All thoughts of restraint evaporated. Fuck you, IOPC! Fuck you, career! Fuck you, world!

*Old lesbian. In a fucking corner!*

CRASH!

The door to the cubicle smashed against the wall and the three girls turned in unison, jumping out of their skin as an enraged Hanlon emerged to confront them.

Her eyes took in the expected scenario. There was a zip-up bag with white powder inside on the counter by the sink. The joint that she had smelled was being held by the brunette with her hair in plaits. Next to the coke was a small hand-mirror, a curled-up ten-pound note and a credit card that they had obviously been using to chop and line the white powder up with.

Hanlon took a stride forward, grabbed the plastic bag and put it in her pocket. There was a shocked silence but everyone froze, too frightened of Hanlon to do or say anything. Then Nose-stud shouted something in German; the other two girls, seeing the furious look in Hanlon's eyes and the purposeful body language, drew back. They were having no part of it.

Nose-stud wanted her coke back. She grabbed Hanlon's arm. Hanlon shook her off. She swore at her in German and threw an amateur punch at Hanlon's head. Hanlon jerked her head to one side, avoiding the blow easily. She could have straightened up and driven a left hook into Nose-stud's ribs. Then a straight right or an upper-cut to finish her off.

She didn't.

Look at my restraint, Doctor! SATISFIED?

She just stared her down, her very grey eyes boring into the dilated pupils of the German. Nose-stud, furious, threw another punch at Hanlon. This one she blocked with the palm of her hand.

She took a step forward and shoved Nose-stud backwards. Pushed her face close to Nose-stud's. Let her see the fury and violence in her eyes.

'Fuck you.' Hanlon turned around to face the other two girls.

'And you!' she added, white-faced with rage.

Stunned silence and immobility. She turned on her heel and strode out of the toilet. No one followed. They had seen the look in her eyes, the contemptuous and professional way she had dealt with the alpha girl of the group. No one was going to challenge her.

She walked upstairs to her room, shaking with anger.

She unlocked the door and sat down on the bed. Her heart was thundering with adrenaline. She felt better than she had done for weeks. But then she thought about the doctor, her measured tones.

'You can't control yourself, Hanlon – worse, you don't want to.'

Well, Doctor, I did. I did control myself. But, she thought, acknowledging the truth, she hadn't wanted to. It had been a very near thing. Only she knew just how close it had come to unrestrained savagery. She'd wanted to drive her left fist into Nosestud's exposed ribs, repeated blows, and then a savage blow downwards with her straight right. She could see her nose explode, a bloody mess, as Hanlon's knuckles shattered bone and cartilage.

She stood up. Her legs suddenly felt weak. She sat down on the bed. Shit. She began to feel very alarmed indeed. What is wrong with me? Stroke? she thought, starting to panic. Heart attack?

Unexpectedly, she yawned. What the hell was that about? She'd just been in a fight. She suddenly felt extremely tired. What was going on? She stood up and nearly fell over, went to the window and, holding onto the sill with one hand to steady herself, opened it wide. Her thoughts were confused. Momentarily she didn't know where she was. It was 11 p.m. The sky wasn't fully dark yet; it was an amazingly beautiful colour, a very deep blue/black. Now she felt dizzy. Was this some sort of post-traumatic stress? That had never happened before. She could hear the surf crashing on the rocks. She breathed in the smell of the sea and, underlying it, the not unpleasant umami tang of slightly rotting seaweed. The cool breeze from the ocean with its salt tang calmed her slightly.

In front of her was the car park, the single-track road a ghostly grey ribbon in the darkness; above rose the huge mass of a tall hill that the framed map on the wall of her room had told her was something unpronounceable in Gaelic, reaching up into the sky. She yawned again. The car park was surprisingly full, given the fact that there was hardly anyone actually staying in the hotel, and as she looked out another vehicle arrived. Did they have lock-ins? Big Jim would be up for it, that was certain.

She yawned yet again. It must be the sea air, she thought

sleepily, woozily. Blackness beckoned, and then, as her legs threatened to give way beneath her she suddenly thought, Sea air, bullshit.

Like fuck it's the sea air.

The room tilted on its axis and she nearly fell. I've been drugged. The thought was quite clear. Startlingly so.

Then the room started to spin, as if she were drunk. Her legs turned to jelly and she collapsed backwards onto the bed.

Before she blacked out, she thought of Big Jim, the bulge in his trousers, his final words to her, the piggy eyes of the boar ablaze with drink and lust...

'I'll see you later.'

## 7

Don't fall asleep, Hanlon, she told herself. Just don't fall asleep. Easier said than done. She would open her eyes, blink, stare at the ceiling and then forget what she was doing as her mind shut down. She could feel that she was fighting a losing battle against a dark, swirling cloud of unconsciousness.

Don't give in... don't... Big Jim's coming... She thought of his gross flabby body, his budding erection, his sleazy smile. Wake up... WAKE UP!

She put her hand in her jacket pocket and her hand met an unrecognised object. Her fingers closed on it and she pulled out the zip-up bag with the white powder, Nose-stud's coke.

She hauled herself into a sitting position, forcing her body to obey. Every other second she blacked out, so her progress felt like time-lapse photography. A series of freeze-frame stills.

Now she was moving her hand towards the bedside table.

Darkness.

Now she was pulling the bag open.

Darkness.

Now she was staring at it stupidly. Darkness. Now she was

wondering what was in it and what she was trying to do. Darkness.

Now she tipped the contents of the bag out on the glass-topped table by the bed.

Several grams of coke, hundreds of pounds' worth, lay in a snowy heap on the smooth reflective surface. If anything was needed to kick-start her fogged brain, she was now looking at it.

Hanlon blinked at it, zoning in and out of consciousness.

No time to try and find her bag and her purse to locate a note to roll up, she pushed her unruly black hair back out of the way and leaned forward.

She must have blacked out again because her head crashed against the glass as she shifted her weight. She was now sitting on the edge of the bed, bent double, head leaning on the cool glass of the bedside-table surface, staring blankly at the mound of white powder a few centimetres from her eye. From this angle and distance it looked enormous.

The coke high would snap her out of the lethal torpor she was sinking into. Either that or she would OD, her heart unable to cope with the enormous, potentially fatal, boost she was about to give it. Better dead than alive with Big Jim on top of her.

She closed one nostril with the tip of her forefinger, slid the other into the mound of coke and inhaled sharply.

What must have been at least half a gram of coke hit her brain like a sledgehammer. Inside her head a pharma-battle raged as whatever she'd been drugged with collided and fought with the cocaine. Her heart felt as if it were going to explode. It was going like a jackhammer.

She fell back on the bed and stared at the ceiling while her heart raced uncontrollably. I hope I don't have a heart attack, she thought. She laughed in a slightly unhinged way, imagining the news story.

'Disgraced police officer dies in hotel room in drug-fuelled frenzy after angry punch-up in toilet. Enough coke in her body to kill a horse, says medical expert.'

She sat upright on the bed and took stock of her condition. Her heart was still beating like crazy, her eyes were bulging out of their sockets, there was an incredibly bitter taste at the back of her mouth and nose, and she was now pouring with sweat.

She felt wildly elated, unstoppable. Fuck you, Big Jim and your rape plans...

One thing was for sure, she was not going to fall asleep. Victory!

Full of energy now, she stood up and went into the bathroom and looked at herself in the mirror. God, I look a state, she thought. Hanlon was aware she was good-looking in a strong and intimidating fashion. Now she studied her face intently in the mirror as if looking at it for the first time.

She stared at her untidy, very dark, coarse black hair. She put her hands into it and pushed it up, beehive style, and studied the effect. Then she let it fall and turned her attention to her forehead. There were two small, deep scars there. There were fine lines etched on it now, and crow's feet around her very grey eyes when she narrowed and widened them, which she did several times, fascinated by her own face in a way she never had been before.

I must be stoned out of my mind, she thought. She grinned maniacally and crossed her eyes, pulling a face at herself in the mirror.

She moved her attention down to her nose. Her nostril was rimmed with white powder and the odd crystal. She wet the end of a towel and wiped the coke off. She rubbed the bridge of her nose thoughtfully with an index finger. She could feel the familiar small kinks in it, where it had been broken in the past.

She traced the line of her strong jaw with a finger; she could feel two cracks in it on the right, and one on the left. Three healed fractures from where it had been damaged previously. She thought of Laidlaw, her boxing coach and friend. He'd be retiring soon, or dead. A lifetime of boozing was bound to catch up with him at some stage, as it doubtless would with Tremayne. Big Jim wasn't the only one she knew with alcohol issues.

She had no control over her thoughts now, but her mood was one of almost insane optimism. God, I'm so good-looking...

Her mouth, full, sensual, her chin, determined. She ran her exploratory finger along her jaw again. Thank God the fractures didn't show. Her right canine was an implant, the original had been knocked out long ago in a fight. It was a great prosthesis; it had cost a great deal of money.

Then she thought, Shower, that'll wake you up even more.

She pulled her clothes off and examined her body. She could smell the drug sweat on her body, sharp and rank. It was not unpleasant, quite sexy in its own way, she thought. She stared at her stomach, flat, the small black triangle of hair. There was no fat there. She was in superb condition. She pumped her biceps, struck a couple of body-building poses in the mirror, her coked eyes staring wildly at her impressive musculature. The curve of her trapezius, her defined lats, her triceps, no bingo wings, she thought proudly, her small high breasts, her slim hips. She turned around; God, what a great ass. Ten out of ten there.

'You told me you had even managed to find a lover with a similar *laissez faire* attitude to the law. Even though like calls to like, it's quite an achievement.'

Go away, Dr Morgan, she thought irritably. But she did miss Serg. He had a great body too. She was certainly feeling in the mood. She thought to herself, Coke must be an aphrodisiac. For some reason, she suddenly thought of DS McCleod.

She tired of the game of looking at herself; besides, her eyes kept swimming in and out of focus. She showered, hot, cold, then scalding hot again, dried herself and pulled some clothes on.

She sat in the armchair facing the door in the darkness. Waiting like a tiger for its prey. Waiting for Big Jim. There was only one reason that she could think of for drugging her.

Big Jim was the man behind it, that was for sure. She could imagine him as a Rohypnol rapist, targeting single women, defencelessly unconscious. Big Jim ascending the stairs, with an unhurried tread, confident of what he was going to find, pass key in one hand, bottle of Scotch in the other. But who had administered it? It had to have been in the coffee, maybe the petits fours. Harriet? Conceivably. She could imagine her as Big Jim's assistant/accomplice, avenging herself on the despised guests. Or maybe Kai, the suspected jailbird. He had made the coffee; that would be the easiest way to do it.

If Kai had been inside, as she suspected, what had it been for? And was the death of Eva an accident or murder? Had she been drugged and raped too? This couldn't have been the first time that Big Jim had done it. How many single women guests at the Mackinnon Arms had found themselves in a similar situation to her? Few of them would report it even if they were aware when they woke up of what had been done to them.

There could be literally dozens of victims.

She thought about Eva Balodis again. Had she complained, maybe threatened him with the police? Or blackmail? Had she been drugged and thrown off a boat into the whirlpool?

So many questions.

She looked at the green digital numbers of the bedside clock. Whoever it was – she couldn't rule out Kai, he could have been inside for sexual offences, or even, unlikely though it was, Harriet

– would wait for the hotel to settle itself before making their move.

Well, she was ready. They were going to get a surprise, a hell of a surprise. Of that they could be sure.

She rolled up a ten-pound note and helped herself to another line of Nose-stud's coke. She didn't want to fall asleep while she waited. Her eyes gleamed in the moonlight. She was more than ready. Come into my parlour, said the spider to the fly, thought Hanlon, balling her capable hands into hard fists.

## 8

An hour and a half later, nothing had happened. No one had tried to slip unnoticed into her bedroom. Hanlon walked around her room in frustration like a caged animal. What was happening and why?

She thought, Well, if I wasn't drugged so I was easy meat, there has to be another reason. Various hypotheses drifted through her mind. The most compelling one – maybe so I don't notice something. Rohypnol affects memory so you're not necessarily aware if you pass out that you've been drugged. If she'd gone to bed normally, if she hadn't had the encounter with Nose-stud, she would never have been any the wiser. She'd have ascribed that odd feeling she'd had in the bar and the sudden fatigue down to sea air, the journey, maybe even depression.

She'd have just climbed into bed and slept through whatever.

Now she stood up and walked over to the window. She looked down below at the front car park of the hotel. It seemed strangely full; she counted fifteen cars. The boar on the hotel sign stared down at them, swaying slightly in the sea breeze, its red tongue curled around the bone in its mouth. Who did they all belong to?

Hardly anyone was staying at the hotel. She frowned to herself, puzzled.

With Hanlon, to think was to act. She was wide awake and curious. She slipped on a pair of training shoes and a dark fleece and left her room.

She walked along the short corridor and came to the glass fire door that led to the landing. The corridor was in darkness, but enough light was filtering through a window at the end to see. The fire door was locked. At first, she couldn't believe it. She rattled it experimentally. No, no mistake. She frowned. As far as she knew she was the only one who was staying on this floor. It had to be a measure to keep her locked in, in case she had woken up and wanted to come down to the main part of the hotel. She returned to her bedroom.

She closed the door behind her and looked out of the window. It was a quiet night, lit by a half-moon. In the distance she could hear the boom of the Atlantic from the shore. It made her think of the lifeless pale body of Eva Balodis floating like a piece of driftwood on the waves, her hair drifting in the water like seaweed, her arms and legs moving gently by the current in a parody of swimming. It seemed even sadder that this should have happened so far from home, in an alien sea. Did you do that, Big Jim? She felt a surge of hatred towards the sleazy old drunk. I'm going to bring you down if it kills me, she thought.

She was on the first floor and the drop wasn't too extreme, maybe three or four metres. Below her was one of the raised flower beds that she had noticed when she first arrived at the hotel. The huge old wooden barrel cut in half, about waist height, choked with dying flowers and weeds. It would be easy enough to hang from her fingers and drop down into it. One benefit of the hotel's dilapidated state.

She put her phone on silent and into the thigh pocket of the combat trousers she was wearing. She then raised the sash of the window. It didn't go up very far before the aged wood jammed, but it was enough for Hanlon. She slipped her head out and then her body. For a heartbeat, she hung from the windowsill by her powerful fingers and then pushed herself away from the wall, landing with a soft thud into the loose soil of the flower bed, her supple knees absorbing the impact of the landing.

She prowled around the cars in the car park, examining them. They were local, she guessed. Some of them had the Argyll SB number plates, others simply looked as if they belonged in the country, 4 x 4s in need of a wash, and others with stickers advertising garages or a showroom in Oban, this on a big BMW 4 x 4, or Campbeltown. One mud-spattered Mitsubishi Barbarian bore the legend *SWOA Give Good Wood!* She looked back at the hotel, a dark, geometric mass against the lighter sky. The sea was very loud as the surf crashed rhythmically on the rocky beach. Here on the islands the Atlantic was omnipresent. She could feel it on her skin and hair, smell it in her nose, taste it on her lips. Far away on the water she could see the red port light of a fishing boat. The noise of its engine drifted across the water to where she was standing. The yacht moored by the jetty was in darkness apart from its riding lights.

There was a line of light showing at one of the downstairs windows between the curtains and Hanlon slid between a couple of cars and glanced through the gap.

She could see into a room she hadn't really paid that much attention to earlier, the function room. About twenty or so people were sitting, in various stages of undress, watching a widescreen TV with rapt attention. There was a lot of wrinkled flesh on offer. The baby boomers were not going gentle into that good night. She stared at what was going on in horrified disgust. Big Jim's sleaze was bad enough, she hadn't bargained on him being the ringleader of a group of like-minded locals. The Mackinnon Arms hotel was obviously the centre for some sort of ageing island swingers group. She shook her head in distaste.

Then she saw what was on the TV screen. If what was going on in front of her was bad enough, this was off the scale in terms of decency, in terms of what was acceptable. It wasn't so much that the content of the porn film that was being shown on the large flat-screen TV in the function room was particularly gross. Hanlon didn't like porn, but on the few occasions, mainly for professional reasons, she had viewed it, she had seen worse. It was who was in it.

The male star of the film, if star was the word, was Kai. So be it, if that floated his boat or earned him some extra cash – being a barman was not the best-paid job in the world. It was his partner that so enraged and disgusted Hanlon.

No mistaking those piercings. The audience, male and female, shuffling and rubbing, intent and excited by the action taking place, several of them taking their cue from what was happening on screen. Maybe even more excited by the knowledge that the girl in the film was dead. It was Eva Balodis. A mouth open and moaning with real or feigned pleasure. A mouth that would never make a sound again.

Hanlon turned her attention to the watchers. She recognised the couple in their fifties who had been at dinner, despite their lack of clothes. They were doing lines of coke – God, the stuff was everywhere these days – off a small hand mirror. And there, of course, was Big Jim, busy with a woman whose face was invisible to her. Harriet was there, fully clothed, standing by the door, watching what was going on with a look of smug satisfaction. Another service expertly and efficiently organised. The others, Hanlon didn't recognise. She was obscurely relieved that she couldn't see Johanna. Kai was nowhere to be seen either – maybe the reality wouldn't live up to his on-screen athleticism. She had seen enough.

Coldly and angrily efficient, she quickly moved around the car park photographing the car number plates for future reference. They were, on the whole, expensive. These weren't council-estate families, these were, she suspected, the local professional classes: estate agents, teachers, businessmen, trawler owners. Eva was lying in a morgue, her corpse, pumped with preservatives if they'd finished the post-mortem, would be waiting for return to her homeland and her family, and this bunch of baby-boomer sex addicts were getting off on her violated body. Well, she thought, as she took another photo, this time of a Land Rover with a sticker saying 'Argyll For Ever', we'll see about that.

There were maybe copyright issues as to who had ownership of the images of Eva's body after death. Eva was in no position to give permission to allow access to her personal history. Was money changing hands at this event? Hanlon suspected that the answer was yes. Had Big Jim declared it? Had he fuck. Did he have a late licence to be serving alcohol? She could smell weed wafting out from the ill-fitting windows. That and the coke. Allowing drugs to be consumed on the premises.

I'm coming for you, Big Jim, Hanlon thought. I'm going to get your licence revoked and I'm going to leak this to a paper and I'm going to create a real shitstorm such that the Mackinnon Arms will never survive. There'll be another party and the next time it'll be raided. Let's see how these entitled baby boomers, the kind that applaud when I bust a foreign coke dealer, enjoy being nicked for possession of a class A substance. They tut-tut over terrified, trafficked prostitutes in a brothel in back-street Streatham in South London, but they're happy to get off watching a drowned girl young enough to be their daughter being fucked for their entertainment before she died.

And in this community, small and tightly knit, everyone will know. Fingers will be pointed; tongues will wag in the fisherman's co-op.

Good.

She had enough evidence for now. Time to get back to her room. She could hardly ring the doorbell and ask to be let in; there had to be another door. She'd break in if necessary. They were certainly not going to have the alarm switched on.

She walked around the back of the hotel. There were the couple of stone outbuildings, bothies as they called them here, and the paved area with wheelie bins in the kitchen area that she had noticed earlier. She walked up to the kitchen door and peered in. The room was dark, nobody around. As she had guessed, in such an isolated island community, security was lax. The door was unlocked, although even if it hadn't been, she could easily have climbed in through the window.

The silver metal chain-link fly screen jingled softly as she stepped through. The room was lit by a tiny blue corona of gas underneath the corner of a gigantic stockpot full of beef-bones that was ticking away on the stove. It was a sizeable kitchen. Her glance took in the huge stove, the fat fryers, the char-grill, fridges and steel work-surfaces.

Hanlon heard voices coming towards the kitchen. There was a door that was half open; she could see shelves with cans and jars, a dry store.

She slipped in, closing the door behind her as she did so but leaving a gap so she could peer out.

She heard low voices and recognised Nose-stud and Kai.

Both of them were quite business-like in their movements as he bent Nose-stud over a kitchen table. Hanlon tapped her fingers impatiently, waiting for them to finish. It didn't take long.

After they'd rearranged their clothes, he reached his hand

into his shirt pocket, took out a paper wrap and chopped out a couple of lines. Their heads bent, first one, then the other.

Nose-stud stood looking at Kai questioningly.

'Well?' she said.

'Well what?' he sneered.

'Where's my coke?' *Koks für sex*, remembered Hanlon.

'You've had it.' It was clear that she had let him have her in exchange for drugs, and she had been expecting a hell of a lot more than a line. To say that Nose-stud was feeling short-changed and aggrieved would be a huge understatement.

'WHAT?' Furious.

'Go on, off you go.' Kai's tone was curt, dismissive. 'You've had your fun, that's all you're getting. Now, offski!'

'But, we had an agreement... Three grams!'

So that was how much it cost to have sex with her, thought Hanlon.

'Sorry, darling.' The barman's face was a hard sneer. 'That was then, this is now. Anyway, you were nae worth it.'

Hanlon could see the fury on Nose-stud's face lit by the eerie blue flame of the gas. She almost felt sorry for her. What a shit night she'd been having. Coke taken by Hanlon, now ripped off and insulted by Kai. All that sex for nothing.

He was standing with his arms folded staring down the Eastern European girl. Her hands, balled into fists, were resting, knuckles down on the silver-coloured metal of the work table. Her eyes flickered around the room.

Hanlon suddenly thought, She's looking for a weapon. I would get out, Kai, if I were you.

On the wall near where she was standing was a magnetic strip holding several knives. Nose-stud suddenly darted a hand out and grabbed one with a ten-centimetre blade, tapering to a vicious-looking point. She waved the knife menacingly in his direction.

'Give me that coke, you bastard!'

Kai took a step backwards, his left hand held up placatingly. From her hiding place Hanlon wondered whether to intervene. She decided against it. If Nose-Stud saw her in her present ill humour she would probably stab her. If it hadn't been for Hanlon, she wouldn't be in this position anyway.

'Calm down, Franca,' he said soothingly.

'I want my coke, now...' She took a pace towards him, the knife rock-steady in her hand.

Kai was backed up against the work surface. Hanlon saw him reach his right hand behind him. It closed around the handle of a frying pan.

'OK, Franca,' he said submissively, 'I'm sorry... you win.'

Franca smiled in triumph, too soon.

With incredible speed he swung the frying pan from behind him.

You don't do things like that without practice, thought Hanlon. Kai was obviously no stranger to violence.

It struck Franca at the elbow and automatically her hand opened. It sent the knife spinning across the room. She cried out in pain and grabbed her injured arm.

Kai, no gentleman, stepped forward and slapped her viciously across the face with the flat of his hand. Much as she disliked Nose-stud, or Franca as she was apparently called, Hanlon felt another twinge of sympathy for her. She was having a truly dreadful night. Now, on top of everything, she'd been beaten up.

'If you threaten me ever again, I'll kill you, understand!' His face was contorted with rage. 'Now fuck off back to your friends, bitch.'

Anger and pain were imprinted on Franca's face. 'Fuck you,

you fucking pussy!' she snarled. 'I've got friends, they'll cut you bad—'

'Oh, like your sugar daddies,' sneered Kai. 'I'm so scared.'

'I've got friends in Glasgow,' said Franca. 'I used to work for Wee Paul McFarlane, maybe I'll text him.'

'Go ahead. Text him now, see if I care.'

'That's not a maybe... I text him tomorrow. When I get reception on my phone.' Franca marched to the door then turned. 'Take some selfies for the memories, Kai. You won't look so pretty soon.'

She left the kitchen, slamming the door behind her.

'Jesus, fucking women...' He lit a cigarette and stood framed in the kitchen door. He finished it quickly and came back inside. He ran his hands through his hair so it stuck up; he didn't look so confident now. 'Shite... Wee Paulie...' He shook his head. Hanlon realised he was very frightened indeed.

The kitchen light came on, bathing the room in harsh white light.

Hanlon pulled her door shut. She stood there in the darkness. It seemed to be a night of listening behind closed doors.

'I thought it might be you.' A woman's voice. An educated, refined Edinburgh accent.

'Who else would it be?' he said.

'Maybe a couple of guests slipping out, keen to do it in a kitchen. We are catering for fantasies to a certain extent.'

'Is that right, Harriet? Sure you just haven't had enough of the party?' His voice was faintly mocking.

'Don't you be so snotty,' Harriet said wearily. 'Jim's parties help keep this place afloat, you know that. They pay your wages, give you a chance to entertain our guests, as I know you've been doing tonight with that whore from the boat.'

Hanlon stored this information away in her mind.

'Not to mention the coke that you're dealing to the clients,' Harriet added.

'You get your cut,' he muttered.

Harriet laughed. 'Remember which side your bread's buttered, Kai.'

'Come on,' he said. 'It's not just the sex parties. I know what you and Jim are up to with those boys.'

There was a silence. The kind of silence that was meaningful, full of unknown significance. Kai's words obviously meant a great deal to Harriet.

'I'm sorry? Boys? What boys?' Harriet was obviously annoyed by the question, trying and failing to indicate it meant nothing to her. 'What are you on about?'

'Never mind, Harriet, just a rumour...'

A rumour I shall be chasing, Hanlon thought. Boys... underage sex? She heard the well-modulated tones of Dr Morgan in her head, back in the consulting room in North London. *'So just avoid crime, OK... That should be an achievable goal.'* The thing was, it had seemed easy at the time, but not now. Hanlon wanted someone to pay for Eva Balodis' death. Sadly not, Dr Morgan. But I didn't go looking for crime, it found me.

'Anyway,' Harriet said, 'I wanted to find you to tell you to be careful with that woman Hanlon.' Hanlon pricked up her ears.

'Why? What's the story with her?' he asked.

'She's police.'

Hanlon's eyebrows lifted; how could she have known?

'That's why I wanted her drugged for tonight. I don't know why she's here, but I don't want her sniffing around, not when it's a party night. She might be here undercover, the vice unit. So I want you to be very careful. Maybe she's the drugs squad. You wouldn't want that, what with all that nose candy you've got in your cottage.'

'Aye, bearing in mind who some of those people are I'm nae that surprised. People talk. Police, eh... she's not bad-looking, that's for sure. I'd do her.'

'You'd do your granny, Kai.'

'Aye, well, I've done you, Harriet, so I guess I'm capable of anything.'

'You'd better watch your step,' Harriet said. Her voice was level; she didn't sound particularly angered by the insult. Hanlon guessed that it would take a fair bit more than Kai's childish slurs to rattle her cage. 'You are skating on very thin ice.'

'Oh, is that a threat?' he said. 'That I'll end up like Eva?'

'Just watch it, Kai, just watch it,' said Harriet coolly.

'Who did it, Harriet? You or Jim?' he sneered.

'Fuck off.' Now Harriet did sound angry. She didn't sound guilty. Hanlon wondered for the first time if they had actually had something to do with Eva's death. It had seemed obvious to her that they were implicated. Maybe she had just jumped to conclusions, her judgement swayed by her hatred of Big Jim.

'Consider this a final warning.'

'Oh, aye, are you going to put that in writing? I'm not shaking with fear, Harriet.'

'Goodnight, Kai. Don't stay up too late. You've got work in the morning.'

The kitchen light went off and Hanlon heard the door into the dining room swing behind her.

'Auld bitch!' he said. Then she heard the clatter of the fly chains and the bang of the kitchen door as he walked into the night.

Hanlon sat down on the floor of the dry store. She suddenly felt dreadful: her head thumped, her mouth was dry and she felt depressed, exhausted and deflated. A reaction to the cocaine. She looked at her phone.

Three a.m.

She endured another two hours of waiting on the floor of the dry store before she stood up. She felt herself drifting in and out of a weird, gossamer-thin sleep. She let herself out of the kitchen and stood staring up at the morning sky, breathing in the heavy salt air and listening to the crash of the surf on the rocks. In the distance, out at sea, she could hear the throbbing of the powerful engines of a fishing boat. On the far horizon the sky was darkening in the east. It looked as if a storm was on its way.

She made her way round to the front of the hotel. The cars were gone; the party had finished, its participants returned home.

She yawned and went back into the kitchen. She stole through the deserted, dark dining room and into the hall. All the lights were out except for one over the porch. She walked quietly up the stairs. The fire door was now unlocked.

She walked down the corridor and let herself into her room.

Sitting on her bed, Hanlon looked out of the window. She considered Harriet's words to Kai. A hotel propped up financially by revenue generated from sex parties. How much would a participant pay for such a thing? A venue for like-minded couples?

'*Bearing in mind who some of those people are...*' Kai's phrase – pillars of the local community maybe? Was someone seeking to monetise the clients with a spot of blackmail?

Then there was the dead girl. Accident or design? Kai's words: 'Is that a threat? That I'll end up like Eva?'

Had Eva been murdered? Kai clearly thought so.

And Kai's cryptic comment about boys?

The mountain outside, its dark bulk gradually becoming more distinct in the early morning light, was not going to provide any answers. That was for sure.

Hanlon got into bed fully clothed. Just in case.

Sleep was a long time coming.

## 9

The body was discovered the following day.

Earlier, Hanlon had been discovering how changeable the west-coast weather could be. The day before it had been sunny, the colours an impressionist blue of the sky and sea, the amazingly varied shades of green – from brilliant moss to calm bracken and ferns to the sombre darkness of the needle-like leaves of the conifers. Patches of yellow lichen on the rocks and the red plastic balls of buoys in the sea added vivid splashes of colour to the scene. Above everything, the silvery scree covering the tops of the emerald mountains.

Today was predominantly grey. A shade that leached the colour out of everything. Grey skies met gunmetal-grey sea and misty drizzle obscured the views of the Paps. Hanlon shivered in the gusty wind whipping in westerly from the Atlantic. She was wearing black running tights, shorts and a light cagoule over her Lycra vest.

She set off for a run after breakfast up the single-track road northwards, in the direction of the headland.

She was feeling infinitely better than she had when she had

woken at seven. Her body had felt heavy and drugged, her
sinuses were painful, still inflamed from the coke, she guessed. As
she ran along the track that skirted the foothills, her mind clear-
ing, she wondered what course of action to pursue.

She could, of course, call the police. But to say what? That a
sex party had taken place, that she had seen people taking drugs?
If anything, she was probably the weird one, never taking them –
God knows she had seen enough people doing lines – rarely
drinking. Her abstemiousness certainly hadn't added to her
popularity with her colleagues in the police. And being drugged?
Well, no one had tried to assault or rob her. And evidence?

She splashed through muddy puddles on the trail. Streams,
burns as they called them in Scotland, criss-crossed the path, the
water brown with peat. When she left Jura to go and stay with
Tremayne he could make discreet enquiries about the cars she
had photographed in the car park; he maybe knew some of them
himself. It was, after all, a small community.

She rejoined the single-track tarmacked road and ran back
down it until she was near the hotel, then walked along the
beach. Her feet scrunched on the stones of the rocky shore as she
slowly made her way back to the Mackinnon Arms, looking at the
flotsam and jetsam that the sea had washed up: seaweed, wood,
branches, the occasional plastic fish crate, bits of plastic rope, a
dead seagull. The overwhelming presence of the ocean, its heavy
smell in her nostrils, its salt taste on her lips.

She came to the path that ran below the road, a couple of
hundred metres from the hotel, that connected it to two cottages.
They were small, set close to each other, one single storey, the
other with an upstairs, both like their parent hotel, in a shabby
condition, paint peeling from the windows. They were made of
whitewashed stone and the low slate roofs were covered in moss.

She followed the path to the hotel. Large and shabby, the

Mackinnon Arms looked particularly mournful under the lead-grey skies. The sign flapped in the wind; the boar, its jaws clamped around the bone between its teeth, looked at her with porcine malice. She checked her watch. It was nearly 8 a.m. She walked past the two outhouses, into the paved court that backed onto the kitchen.

She looked at the kitchen door, which was open, the same kitchen door that she had walked through earlier that morning, the doorframe blocked by the metal chains of the fly screen. She swatted away some midges that were buzzing around her head. She guessed that the chains might keep flies out, but the midges would sail through them.

Sitting outside on an upturned beer crate, with a couple of buckets in front of him, was a man dressed in chef's whites scrubbing mussels. He was overweight, with a pleasant, capable-looking face. He looked up at Hanlon and smiled. He seemed unaffected by the cloud of midges haloing his head.

'Hi,' he said. 'You're staying here, aren't you?'

'Yes, how did you know?'

He threw his head back and laughed. 'This is Jura, everyone knows everyone's business.'

He was one of those people who was instantly likeable and knew it. Confident, comfortable in his skin, obviously easy-going. Fine by Hanlon – she wanted to get to know the hotel staff, to build up more of a picture of Big Jim, her target.

'Yes. Those on the menu tonight?' She indicated the mussels.

'Aye,' he said as he wiped a hand on a tea towel folded into his apron strings. 'I'm Donald, the chef here.' She guessed from his accent he wasn't local.

'So you're the famous chef,' Hanlon said. She dimly remembered him being praised on the hotel website.

Donald nodded.

'Oh, aye... so famous I'm here, at the world-famous Mackinnon Arms.' He laughed.

'Where did you work before here?' she asked, more to be polite than because she was remotely interested.

He reeled off the names of several places where he had cooked. Hanlon was a good judge of people. She noted to herself how his hands were working with lightning speed and how he would continually glance into the open door of the kitchen where he could see the pass to monitor how breakfast was going.

Hanlon asked what had brought him here to Jura. It seemed an oddly remote place for a good chef to choose. It was the kind of place you ended up in if you were running away from something, some professional disaster, a mass food poisoning, an almighty cock-up, or maybe a scandal. Maybe a broken heart.

Donald scratched his head.

'I am from Fife originally, moved down south to work. I was doing eighteen hours a day in London, Head Chef at a rosetted place in Chelsea, split shifts but working through my break. I'd done twelve days without a day off and all for no extra money and I thought, fuck this.' He paused. 'Do you ever feel like that? About work, I mean?'

So I'm not the only good judge of character here, she thought, slightly alarmed by the relevance of his question.

'Sure,' she said, not volunteering any information.

'So I walked out, came here.'

He laughed. 'I've now ended up doing eighteen hours a day here on Jura, split shifts, working through my breaks for a lot less money... No, seriously, it's a lot more relaxed, and by Christ I'm saving so much more money now I don't have to pay London prices for things. I get my accommodation free. I'm in that cottage up there.' He pointed at the cottages she had passed earlier. 'I've got Kai living next door.' That must be fun for you, thought Hanlon.

'And what do you do?' he asked.

She was going to make some kind of general remark about being a civil servant, but remembered that Harriet somehow knew what she did.

'I'm in the police,' she said.

He smiled at her. 'I'm available for interview at any time you suggest.' He looked at her hopefully, like a dog desperate to be taken for a walk. Hanlon shook her head.

'I don't think so,' she said, but smiling, to show she hadn't been offended by his making a pass at her.

Donald turned his mouth down in mock sadness. 'I'd better get back inside,' he said. 'Fair bit to do today.'

She noticed that the mussels were done, their shells gleaming with a purple iridescence in the bucket.

Suddenly there was the sound of running footsteps crunching on gravel and a figure came flying around the corner. They both turned round. It was the waitress from the previous night. Johanna. She was dressed like Hanlon, for running. But right now she wasn't running for exercise. Her chest was heaving and she was wild-eyed, breathless, her eyes wide and her face pale. Donald jumped to his feet.

'What's the matter, Jo?'

She took a deep breath, pointing towards the front of the hotel, pointing to the sea. 'Help, come, there is girl in water!'

Now the two of them were running after Johanna. Onto the terrace with its rotting wooden furniture, benches with slats missing, rickety tables.

Below was the jetty running straight out into the sea, a strip of sandy beach on one side, a rocky shore on the other.

'Where is she?' shouted Hanlon.

'There,' panted Johanna, pointing to the right of the concrete jetty. The *Lorelei* was moored at the end with no sign of life.

Hanlon sprinted along the jetty, leaving the other two behind. As she ran she noticed that under the wooden slats of the pier, just under the surface of the sea, boulders ran the length of the structure. The tide was in and the rocks were just under water. They were dark grey covered with patches of white barnacles.

When she was halfway along the jetty she could see a body in the sea more clearly. By the orange buoy, a splash of vivid colour in the gunmetal-grey water, she could see a figure floating. Hanlon ripped off her cagoule, kicked off her trainers and leaped into the sea.

The shock of the water hit her like falling into an ice-bath. Although she was fully clothed, Hanlon was a powerful, experienced swimmer and the buoy was only a few metres from where she had hit the water. She reached the body in under a minute. She supported herself with one hand on the hard, cold plastic of the buoy while she looked at the girl. She was floating face down, her blonde hair fanning out in the water, gently rising and falling with the swell of the sea. As she swam up to her, Hanlon could see a contusion and broken skin on the right side of her forehead near the hairline. She gently trod water feeling the pull of the current. The girl's waterlogged sleeve had got caught on the shackle that secured the mooring buoy to the chain just below the surface of the water. Otherwise she would have been carried out to sea.

Hanlon freed the material from the metal protrusion and swam back to the shore on her back with one arm cradling the dead girl's head. She pulled the body onto the beach and turned her over.

'Oh, shit,' she said.

Franca's sightless eyes stared up to the cold grey Scottish sky, her gold nose stud a sad reminder of her once forceful personality. Donald was waiting for her.

He looked bleakly down at the drowned girl.

'She's dead?'

Hanlon nodded. 'She's dead.'

She looked down at the still face. She had only known Franca in high-octane mode. Images of the girl, laughing loudly, pointing and jeering at her in the bar, throwing a punch at her, screaming at Kai. None of them ways in which you would want to be remembered, but all of them undeniably full of life at full throttle, partying, drugging, fighting, sex, violence. All in a five-hour time frame.

And now this.

First Eva Balodis, now Franca. Two drownings in just a few days.

Donald looked thoughtfully at the jetty.

'She must have slipped when she was going back to the boat.'

Hanlon looked at the jetty, the large rocks breaking the water just underneath the boards. If you fell head first into the water you could smash your head against one. But she was sceptical.

'Kai said she was quite out of it,' Donald said.

Hanlon looked at him in surprise.

'You spoke to Kai last night?'

'Oh aye. I was at home having a wee dram or two. We chefs don't usually go to bed early.' He grinned. 'I keep late hours. Kai saw my light was on, he came in, said he'd been doing Charlie with one of the girls from the boat. He did nae stay long, said he was tired.'

I bet he was, thought Hanlon.

'Have you called the police?'

'Aye.' He tapped the mobile in his breast pocket.

'Where's Johanna?' she asked. She had only just realised that the girl wasn't around.

'She's gone back to my place,' Donald said. 'I told her tae go to the hotel, tell them what was going on, but she refused. She's frightened of Harriet and Big Jim. She was crying. I guess it's shock. I told her to wait at my cottage for the police.'

Hanlon nodded. She could hardly blame Johanna for not wanting to go back to the hotel. She wondered how Johanna had spotted the body. Well, that would be a matter for the local police, not her. She turned and stared at the Mackinnon Arms. Its dilapidated shape no longer seemed forlorn, it seemed sinister. She shivered uncontrollably. She realised that she was incredibly cold. Donald noticed.

'You'd better go in and get some dry clothes on. You must be freezing.'

'Will you stay with her?' Hanlon looked down at Franca.

'Aye, I will.' He looked back at the jetty. 'Must have slipped and hit her head on the rocks,' he repeated to himself, like a man willing himself to believe that it was true.

Hanlon nodded. 'I guess so.'

She turned and walked back to the hotel.

She thought of Nose-stud's face, inscrutable in death. Whatever had happened, Hanlon thought, she did not believe that it was an accident. Nose-stud was not the kind of girl to leave this world by falling off a walkway. No matter how stoned she was.

Dr Morgan's voice surfaced again in her head.

*'No, you don't trust people, do you? Don't you think that's part of your problem, an inability to trust?'*

No, Doctor, thought Hanlon, glancing back at the burly figure of Donald in his chef's whites, standing patiently by Nose-stud and gazing out to sea. No, I don't trust people. And it's not my problem, it's their problem.

She walked into the hotel, meeting Harriet as she did so. Harriet stared at her in disbelief, the wet clothes and hair, damp footprints on the just-hoovered carpet.

'What the hell is going on?' Harriet looked furious. Another inconsiderate person adding to her managerial problems. She obviously had no idea of what had happened.

'There's a drowned girl out there,' Hanlon snapped. Quite apart from her obvious reasons for disliking Harriet, the sex parties, being drugged, the manageress was living up to Hanlon's view of her as a first-class bitch. She had had enough of her. 'At least it's not a member of your staff this time.'

## 10

The local police were taking statements in Harriet's office at the hotel. Hanlon was sitting across the desk from DI Campbell, McCleod was in a chair in the corner.

'I believe that you had an argument with the deceased last night?'

'I'm sorry?' Hanlon raised an enquiring eyebrow.

She looked at DI Murdo Campbell and wondered why she disliked him so much. Was it his slightly arrogant, condescending attitude? Was it the fact that he obviously disliked her? Was it his slightly affected drawling voice? She couldn't place the accent, but she was sure that it would translate into expensive schooling, a relatively privileged background and a desirable university. Posh Scottish. Or was it just his youth that she envied?

Campbell studied some notes in front of him. His red hair was very fine, not like her own coarse locks. His eyes were grey-green. It was kind of hard to tell what colour they were. Sometimes they looked blue. His skin was pale with a few freckles on his cheek-bones. He read from his notes.

'"A crazy woman burst out of the toilet cubicle and attacked

Franca. I don't know what we did to upset her. It was like she was possessed...We were terrified.'"

He emphasised the words crazy, possessed, terrified.

His green eyes, definitely green, she thought, flicked upwards to Hanlon.

'Well?'

She could hardly deny it. She said nothing. Campbell continued.

'That was the testimony of Ms Silberhorn. It's not exact – her English is quite good but obviously she needed a bit of help. Luckily I speak German.'

I bet you do, she thought.

'"Possessed" was tricky...' mused Campbell.

'Luckily Ms Silberhorn had seen *The Exorcist*,' put in DS McCleod from the end of the table.

Hanlon stared at her in incredulity. What had that got to do with anything?

McCleod looked washed out and dull beside her colleague, colourless. The two of them reminded Hanlon of the pheasants she had seen – was it only yesterday? When she had been with the policewoman in her Volvo. The male of the species, Campbell, eye-catching with his red and green plumage, the hen, McCleod, dowdy, insignificant.

'I was involved in an altercation with the woman I now know to be Franca Gebauer, that much is true,' admitted Hanlon, picking her words carefully. She was tempted to just say, 'No comment,' like most of the suspects that she interviewed. But this would be too hostile, she felt. She had no wish to antagonise Campbell. She carried on. 'Ms Gebauer and her friends were smoking cannabis in the toilets and doing cocaine, a situation I felt unable to ignore.'

'Ah, yes, DCI Hanlon.' Campbell's voice was sharp. 'I gather you have quite a history of "robust" interventions.'

Hanlon rolled her eyes. So Campbell had been speaking to colleagues in London, he had to have been. Donald's words came back to her memory. 'This is Jura, everyone knows everyone's business.'

'Are you accusing me of anything?' she said, leaning forward across the table and staring hard into Campbell's green eyes. 'I mean, am I under suspicion of involvement in this girl's death?'

Campbell sighed. 'Look, DCI Hanlon, we're here to try to find out what happened to an unfortunate dead young woman, not fight. This is not a formal interview, as well you know. We don't even know if a crime has been committed and that will not be for me to decide. So, in your opinion, was Gebauer the worse for wear with drugs and drink?'

'When I saw her she was probably drunk, technically, but perfectly lucid,' she replied.

'And this was the last time that you saw Franca Gebauer alive?'

This was the question that she had been dreading. She had no wish to get drawn into Campbell's investigation, not even as a witness. She assumed that Franca's companions hadn't mentioned her coke theft and she certainly was not keen to bring that up. She suspected that she was already persona non grata in London, reports that she had been involved while on holiday in a fist fight in a toilet, followed by stealing a large bag of a Class A drug...

An image of Dr Morgan: '*The trouble is, Hanlon, you know your own history, you know what you've done and what you're capable of, and you project that onto others. They don't know all the dubious things you've done over the years. You've got a guilty conscience, and rightly so.*'

Hanlon looked Campbell in the eyes.

'Yes.'

And immediately hated herself for lying. For a horrible moment she felt utterly transparent, that Campbell was going to call her out. It was a horrible situation to be in. Campbell would be unaware of the fight between Kai and Franca, not to mention the orgy in the hotel, the drug taking, Kai supplying coke. But any mention of any of this would necessitate talking about the bathroom fight, and word would get back to London about her unorthodox activities. That would probably be the final nail in the coffin. This officer cannot be trusted.

The moment seemed to extend indefinitely. Campbell dropped his gaze first.

'Well, that's that, then. Thank you very much for your cooperation. What did you say your plans were?'

Hanlon hadn't said anything. So, I've got away with it, then. She decided to actually be cooperative.

'I'm staying here for a couple of weeks, then I'm on Islay for another week.'

'Good.' Campbell's phone rang. He glanced down at the caller ID and said to McCleod, 'I'll take this on my own, if you don't mind.'

McCleod nodded and signalled to Hanlon to stand up. They left the room together and stood in the hallway of the hotel.

Hanlon looked at McCleod, appraising her in her new role as police rather than as kindly citizen giving her a lift.

She was wearing a white blouse, black jacket and matching skirt. Her hair was tied back in a ponytail and she was wearing very little make-up. Although she was smartly dressed her face was thin, waif-like, half starved. She did look as if she had stepped out of a poster highlighting poverty or drug addiction. It was surprisingly easy to imagine McCleod slumped in a doorway or standing on an ill-lit street corner bending down to peer into car windows. She looked at Hanlon.

'So, we meet again.' She smiled warmly; it transformed her face.

Hanlon nodded.

'Coffee?' McCleod suggested.

Hanlon nodded again and they went into the bar. Kai was stacking the depleted shelves. She studied him speculatively. He had gelled his short blond hair this morning and a gold earring gleamed in the sun. He looked tired but perfectly at peace with the world. If Franca had been murdered, and it was a big if, he certainly didn't look over-burdened with guilt. What am I doing? she thought. McCleod was oblivious of the fact that Kai had starred in a home-made porno with one drowned girl and had had sexual relations, done drugs and had a fight with a second drowned girl. What am I going to do with this information that I'm holding back?

'Can we have a couple of coffees?' McCleod asked.

He smiled at her; he had a certain easy charm. 'Surely can... you'll have tae gi'me a few minutes. I need tae switch things on.' His harsh Glaswegian accent an unlovely contrast to McCleod's soft tones.

Kai busied himself behind the bar and McCleod and Hanlon sat in a bay by the window looking out at the sea.

'What's the story with the boat?' Hanlon asked.

'It's owned by a couple of businessmen, the Hart brothers...' Baldy and comb-over, thought Hanlon '...who have got a portfolio of hotels in England and are up here looking to buy into Scotland. The market's depressed, prices are low, they reckon it's a good time to invest.' McCleod yawned. 'Sorry, I went to bed late last night. Anyway, they were interested in buying the Mackinnon Arms.'

'So Big Jim's got it on the market?'

'I believe so, or he's certainly open to offers.' She looked around. The bar, so welcoming in the evening, looked decidedly tatty in the cold light of day.

'And the girls? The three of them with the Hart brothers. What's the story there?'

McCleod grimaced.

'They told me that they had recruited the girls as sex workers from mylittlearmcandy.com. It's a Glasgow-based company which provides, "female companionship" for the lonely, but they don't seem to be hiring locally, for which I'm profoundly grateful.'

'Sex workers?' said Hanlon.

'Well, technically "escorts" and "personal masseurs". However, I think we all know the score. But it's all legit. The girls are EU citizens, they're not underage, they're not being coerced. I can't say I envy them their jobs.'

They both looked at each other and simultaneously pulled faces.

'It's not a murder inquiry, so they're free to go.'

Hanlon looked out of the window. The sea was calm now; the yacht, the *Lorelei*, had indeed gone. It was hard to believe that a girl had died out there.

'What's your feeling on this death?' Hanlon asked, 'It seems a bit strange, two women dying in the sea from one hotel, in such a short time frame.'

McCleod made a kind of equivocal gesture with her hands.

'Well, I asked myself that question. I checked the figures. On average fifty people die each year in Scotland from drowning. In Tarbert...' she nodded '... over there in Argyll, six people drowned in a couple of boat accidents in a relatively short time frame. That's in a small village. You know, shit happens, the sea is dangerous. It looks as if Franca Gebauer might have just fallen off the jetty while out of it. Just another statistic. I don't know. We'll wait for the post-mortem results. As for Eva, I can't comment officially but a friend of mine says drugs and alcohol were present, but who knows...?'

McCleod looked around the bar. 'Perhaps the hotel is cursed.'

Hanlon snorted. 'You don't really believe that, surely!'

McCleod shrugged; her tone was serious. 'I suppose I mean unlucky. Nothing good has ever happened here since the place was built – that guy killing himself, it's never been successfully run. I've met unlucky people, why not a building?'

She stopped talking as Kai brought them their coffees. Hanlon noticed a strip of sticking plaster covering the first two knuckles of his right hand.

'Been in the wars, Kai?'

The bar manager gave Hanlon a strained smile.

'I grazed it in the cellar, moving a beer barrel. Now,' he said briskly, signifying that the conversational topic was closed, 'can I get you anything else?'

'No, thank you,' said McCleod. They both looked at Kai thoughtfully as he returned to the bar. I wonder what he would say if I told him he had a really shit tattoo on his ass, thought Hanlon.

'Do you mind if I fetch Weems?' McCleod asked.

Hanlon looked at her, puzzled. Was this some sort of Scottish expression? Fetching Weems? McCleod noticed her confusion, threw back her head and laughed. It transformed her face, vivacious, fun-loving, and as her shoulders moved back, straining her blouse, Hanlon suddenly noticed what a great figure she had. She might have a starved-looking face, her body certainly wasn't.

'My dog,' she explained. 'He's called Wemyss. He's a rescue – he was found in Wemyss castle, in the grounds. That's in Fife. But he gets separation anxiety.'

'By all means,' said Hanlon. McCleod went and spoke to the bar manager.

'Aye, provided the dog does nae bite.'

'He does nae bite, he's nae stupit,' said McCleod, mimicking Kai's heavy accent. She turned and grinned at Hanlon. As she left the room, Hanlon thought, surprised, I've made a friend. She was more pleased than she cared to admit. It didn't happen that often.

Shortly afterwards, McCleod returned with Wemyss. The border collie stared up at Hanlon with adoration and nuzzled her hand.

'He likes you,' said McCleod, sounding surprised. 'He's not normally all that friendly with people.'

Hanlon stared at the dog expressionlessly. She wasn't all that keen on animals. Dogs seemed overly needy to her.

'So what are you doing exactly, about Franca?'

'There'll be an autopsy. It won't be up to us, but Murdo...' McCleod noticed the look on Hanlon's face '... he's actually not that bad, once you get to know him. I know he comes across as a bit of a smart-ass, but I think that's insecurity.'

'Really?' Hanlon's tone was incredulous. She had little time for what she thought of as 'shrink speak', which she immediately thought was ironic since she was seeing one.

'Well, anyway... His grandmother lives on Jura and he happened to be here anyway. When I was called about the incident, I got in touch with him. We're just doing a preliminary round of interviews, just in case there's more to the death than meets the eye. We'll know more later, but, right now, I think it'll be put down as an accident. Of course, that'll be up to the coroner, but all things considered...'

'An accident?' Hanlon's tone bordered on the incredulous.

'Who would want to kill her?' asked McCleod simply.

I can think of someone, thought Hanlon, recalling Kai's casual, practised brutality as he swung the pan into Franca's arm.

McCleod continued, 'She was the worse for wear, there are no lights out on that jetty, it was pouring with rain, the planks were slippery. There are rocks underneath the walkway, just below and above the waterline, and on the side she fell in there is no rail.'

Silence fell as the two women contemplated Franca's fate. Hanlon's eyes flickered to the man behind the bar. She wondered if maybe Franca had returned with revenge on her mind. Kai's comment, 'I'll kill you.' A throwaway line or a statement of intent? She dismissed the thought. Franca was almost certainly a realist. She hadn't come after her, or turned up at her bedroom door begging for, or demanding, her coke back.

Perhaps Kai had simply scraped his knuckles on the rough walls of the beer cellar as he said. Maybe it was Big Jim, wanting sex, being refused and losing his temper. That was probably just wishful thinking on her part. But she was curious about him. She looked at McCleod, who was following her gaze.

'What are you thinking?' she asked.

'I was just wondering if Kai had ever been inside, and if so, what for,' Hanlon said. McCleod scratched her pointed chin. Her face was so at odds with her body.

'Do you know what? I think I'll find out,' said McCleod judiciously. She finished her coffee and looked at her watch. 'I'd better go.' She smiled apologetically. 'You know how it is...'

Hanlon smiled back. 'Don't worry... It was nice meeting you again Catriona.'

'Likewise...' McCleod hesitated. 'Look, why don't we meet up for a drink, say not tomorrow evening but the night after that? In Craighouse, at the hotel there. Not here.'

'God, no! Not here,' said Hanlon, with feeling. 'But yes, I'd love to meet you for a drink.'

'I'll fill you in on how things are going. The post-mortem will be prioritised, that much I know. And I'll tell you what I've learnt about our friend over there.'

'I'd like that,' Hanlon said.

'I'll bring Wemyss.'

'Oh, good,' said Hanlon, insincerely. The dog's tail swished on the carpet.

'See you Thursday, then, 8 p.m. Oh,' she said, 'what's your number? Coverage on the island's really patchy, it's a bit weird, sometimes you seem to get it, sometimes you can't.'

They exchanged numbers. 'Don't be late!' McCleod added.

'I'm never late,' said Hanlon, somewhat stiffly.

McCleod grinned. 'I kind of knew you'd say that.'

Hanlon returned the smile, turned and left the bar. McCleod stood up and was on her phone. Wemyss stared at Hanlon's back, unrequited love shining in his intelligent brown eyes.

She walked up the stairs to her room and lay on the bed, staring at the ceiling. She didn't know what she wanted to do. Nose-stud was dead. She remembered how she had cradled the girl's head in the crook of her arm as she had slowly swum her back to shore. The cold, clean chill of the water surrounding her. What a waste of a life.

She idly stared out of the larger window overlooking the car-park as she stretched out on top of the duvet. There was a buzzard circling the mountain behind the hotel. Hanlon stood up and went to the window to get a better view of the bird. She watched it effortlessly wheeling in the grey sky, then she heard voices in the car park. She looked down. McCleod was talking to Campbell. As Campbell opened the driver's door of his car she saw McCleod look at him and shake her head with what looked like irritated disbelief. There was something about his car that drew her attention. As McCleod was getting into her old Volvo Hanlon realised what it was and her heart started beating fast.

She realised she had seen the vehicle before. She watched as it reversed away from the low wall. A long-wheelbase Land Rover. 'Argyll For Ever', read the sticker on the back as Campbell drove out of the Mackinnon Arms car park.

A car park he had been in the night before.

## 11

'Iveta Balodis, from Jurmala in Latvia, that was her name. She called herself Eva.' It was the next day and Donald poured Hanlon a cup of tea and gave her one of the rolls he'd made that were cooling on a wire rack. He opened the fridge and took out a plate of thin sliced gravadlax, flecked green with finely chopped dill.

'Thanks,' said Hanlon. She put a piece of the smoked salmon on the warm bread and took a bite. It was excellent.

'This is very good,' she said. She pushed her rain-and-sweat-sodden hair back.

She had been returning from a run up the foothills of the mountain. The one that she could see from the larger bedroom window at the rear of the hotel.

It had taken her nearly an hour to get to the top. Once there, the views were fantastic. She could see Islay to the south, west, the endless Atlantic, a silver sheet of light to the far horizon. To the north, more small islands, splashes of green and black and grey in the blue of the lochs, and to the east, the Kintyre peninsula. And below, like a malignant tumour, the Mackinnon Hotel.

She stared at it. She could have left, but she wanted to stay, simply to get some leverage on Big Jim, leverage that she could use to bring him down. Once Hanlon started on something, she was remorseless, unstoppable, hard and obdurate as the quartzite that made up the Paps.

When she was on the way back to the hotel, running past the cottage, Donald had glimpsed her through the window and invited her in.

Although she suspected his motives – he exuded lechery – it had been too good an opportunity to miss.

'Of course it is.' He grinned. 'I made it.'

Hanlon smiled back. 'Have you got a picture of Eva?'

Donald nodded and got out his mobile. He found what he was looking for and passed the Samsung to Hanlon. She looked at the image: blonde and dumpy, with a mole to the left of her nose, her aggressive earrings, derms and studs somehow at odds with her rather homely face. Nose-stud had instinctively known how to rock facial piercings; Eva looked as if she was dressing up for a bet or a dare.

McCleod had texted her that the preliminary report had suggested death by drowning, nothing overly suspicious. She'd called her back and McCleod had added more to the story. Harriet had given a statement that Eva had told her that she was going to swim out to the Corryvreckan. When she'd asked her why, Eva had said it was to test herself, that she was a girl who liked to live life to extremes. She had told Harriet that was why she was so pierced. To push the envelope back, to approach the limits of the possible. Hanlon suspected this was bullshit.

'What was this story about Eva and the Corryvreckan?' She told Donald about Harriet's statement. 'Was it true?'

'Aye, it's right enough,' confirmed the chef. 'Eva had mentioned it several times. Thing is with that whirlpool it can vary in strength like crazy, depending on the tides, the time of year, it's hellish changeable.'

'So it's possible that she could have underestimated it?' asked Hanlon.

Donald nodded. 'Easily. And it's true what Harriet said, she did bang on about how she liked to push herself to the limits...' He laughed. 'Although not at work – I never saw any signs of pushing any limits there! Lazy bitch. But she did like sea swimming, that is actually true. She was a good swimmer.'

Well, thought Hanlon, slightly disappointed, be that as it may, she still suspected Big Jim and Harriet of having had a hand in the death.

'You weren't fond of her then?'

'Christ no!' Donald stood up and stretched; his gut rose a couple of inches upwards as he did so, and then slid back down to its comforting resting place over the broad belt holding up his jeans. He walked over to the fridge, opened it and got out a beer.

'Want one?' he asked Hanlon.

She shook her head. 'I'm fine with tea.'

'It's my day off,' said Donald by way of explanation, and sat down. Hanlon looked at the clock: 10 a.m. He pulled the ring on the can and tipped half of it down his throat.

'No, I was not fond of her.' His voice was emphatic.

'Why not?' said Hanlon.

Donald shrugged. 'She was a pain in the arse, that girl. I know that. Like I said, she was lazy, stuff would go missing. She had the nerve to try to pin it on Johanna – that girl wouldn't say boo to a goose. Big Jim wanted to sack her, but she was threatening to take him to an industrial tribunal. She threatened me with that too, come to that.'

Hanlon looked at him questioningly.

He grinned shiftily, guiltily. 'She told me that she was pierced all over... I said I would nae mind a look... och, well, you can only ask...'

Repeatedly, I bet, thought Hanlon.

Donald continued, 'And she had two lawsuits from those no-win no-fee lawyers going, one against the council for hurting her ankle in a pothole and one against the taxi driver, Davey Lennox, for alleged whiplash after he braked hard when a deer jumped out in front of him.' He shook his head. 'What the fuck was he supposed to do? Drive into it?'

'She wasn't popular then?' asked Hanlon. A picture was definitely emerging: a sly, manipulative person, not many friends. Generally disliked.

Donald shook his head. 'No, when she died a fair few folks heaved a wee sigh of relief. But she was no fool either, and this town she was from, Jurmala, it's by the sea. If you're brought up by the sea you tend to respect it, you don't go swimming near a whirlpool.' He looked at her keenly. 'The sea's the sea whether it's the Baltic or the Atlantic.'

'So what do you think?'

Donald shrugged again. 'Shit happens,' he said, 'but let's just say I bet Big Jim was delighted when she never came back from her swim.'

I knew it, she thought.

'Why all the questions?' he asked. 'I thought the police had it down as an accident.'

'I'm sure they're right,' said Hanlon. 'I suppose old habits die hard.' Silence fell for a minute or so, then, 'Does the hotel have a boat?' she asked.

'Two,' he said. 'You'll have seen them moored at the jetty. One's a fourteen-foot rowing boat Big Jim uses for fishing, the other's a twenty-footer. It's open with a small wheelhouse. He uses that for diving.'

'He dives?'

'Aye,' said Donald. 'He was a professional, very much in demand, I believe, specialist stuff. He was on North Sea rigs for years. He had an idea that he could get divers to use the hotel. He could take them to places that were good for dives, wrecks and suchlike. We had some here the other day, but he got pissed and was rude to them, and off they fucked.' He shook his head in disgust. 'Why?'

'Oh, no reason.'

'I heard someone say you were staying a week or two. What are you going to do to occupy yourself?'

'I was told that I should go and see the Corryvreckan, while I'm here.' She felt a sudden urge to see the place where Eva died.

'My brother's got a fishing boat. If you don't want to ask Big Jim, get him to take you.'

Hanlon looked at him in surprise. 'I thought you were from Fife?'

'Aye, we are, but John moved here a couple of years ago, lives on Islay. It's why I moved up here. We've got plans to open our own place. I was talking to the Hart brothers about it. The guys with the boat. They're keen to invest.'

'Is that why they were here? To check you out?'

'Aye, well, partly. I knew them from London. They part-owned a place I worked in. I've cooked for them quite often. They ken me well.'

'They told Big Jim they were interested in buying the place?' Hanlon remembered what McCleod had said.

'That's what they said,' Donald agreed.

'Whereabouts are you thinking of a restaurant?'

Donald looked shifty. 'You're staying in it. I want to buy the hotel off Big Jim.'

Hanlon nodded. 'So not the Harts, then?'

'No, it was just to get an idea of what he would want for it. He wouldn't want to sell it to me, he'd rather die. He hates me.'

'You think it's viable?'

'It would be for me,' Donald said smugly. 'Out of season I would make it pay as a residential cookery school. There's good money in that these days. I've done the market research, done the costings.'

Hanlon thought, That does sound plausible.

'What's Big Jim's problem with you?' she asked.

Donald frowned. 'I don't really know – jealousy? Because I'm a success and he isn't? I don't care, but if he knew, he'd go crazy. He's got a hell of a temper, let me warn you now. And he's handy with his fists. I saw him knock a drunk fisherman out a while ago in the bar. No, he thought the Harts wanted to pump money into the place. Nobody would be stupid enough to do that – the guy's a mess.'

'What makes you think that he'll sell up?'

The chef smiled; it wasn't a nice smile. 'When I hand my notice in, which I plan to do any day now, he'll be fucked. The business will go tits up. He'll be desperate.'

Hanlon nodded. Then changed her line of questioning.

'What's Kai's story?' she asked. 'He doesn't look like he belongs in a hotel.'

Donald laughed. 'I ken what you mean. I was a wee bit puzzled too. But Kai came from a really good restaurant in Glasgow, The Sleeket Mouse.'

'Funny name for a restaurant,' she said.

'Not if you're Scottish,' said Donald, shaking his head. 'You should read your Burns.' He nodded at his bookcase, which was mainly filled with cookery books. 'I've got a book of his poems over there. You can borrow it.'

No, thanks, thought Hanlon.

'Anyway, they just missed out on a Michelin star. He worked there, Assistant Bar Manager.'

'Really?' Hanlon was mildly incredulous. Kai seemed perfectly efficient but not that good, OK for the Mackinnon Arms but not the kind of man you'd employ in a high-class, metropolitan restaurant.

'I know what you mean,' Donald agreed, recognising the tone in her voice. 'I was suspicious myself. I know a couple of chefs in Glasgow, mates. I got one of them to check, just in case Kai was being a wee bit creative with his CV. But, no, he was definitely there, shite tattoo and all.'

I'd quite like to have a look at that restaurant, Hanlon thought. Kai was seriously interesting to her. She liked him very much in the role of a suspect in the death of Franca.

Donald looked at the clock on the wall. 'Anyway...' It was clear from his tone that she was being asked politely to leave.

Hanlon stood up. 'Well, it was nice talking to you.'

'You're police, aren't you?' Donald said.

'Yes, why?'

'Well, since I am seriously thinking of buying the Mackinnon Arms with my brother, I could do with this business having the drownings cleared up. Maybe it was just an accident, but if not...' he suddenly looked serious '... I really want to help you, if I can, to get to the bottom of how those girls died.'

Hanlon frowned. 'Donald, it's nothing to do with me.'

'Of course it isn't...' He sounded as if he didn't believe her, that somehow she was part of the investigation. 'People won't want to eat in a place that's associated with murder.'

'Even the psychics?' she teased.

'Oh, God, we had a party of eight of them over the other weekend, don't remind me... no. They want a historic ghost from way back. They don't want anything to do with current murders.'

'No one has said that it's murder, yet.'

Donald gave her a look that said, really?

'Well, remember the offer's there. You need any help, I'm your boy.'

'Thanks,' she said. 'I won't forget.'

Hanlon opened the door and stepped outside. It had stopped raining, but the weather was still blustery.

'At least it's stopped stotting down,' said Donald, looking up at the sky.

There was a bicycle, a man's off-road bike, under a tarp.

'Is that bike yours?'

She looked at Donald; he grinned shiftily. He had a peculiar charm all of his own. She looked at his gut hanging over his belt. She doubted he'd get very far on the bike up one of the forestry trails.

'Aye, I use it when I go drinking in Craighouse.'

'Could I borrow it some time?'

'Surely, whenever, just ask. I've got a kayak too, if you want that as well.'

'A kayak?' If it was hard to imagine Donald on a bike, it was even harder to picture him in that. Would he fit in? Or get wedged like a cork in a bottle?

'Aye, a sea kayak, well, it's my brother's, to be precise, but, as I told you, he's got a boat. He sees enough of the Atlantic these days for work. Anyway, it's there, round the back.'

He scratched his stomach and belched gently.

'Oh, and I'd eat out tomorrow if I were you,' he said.

'Why?'

'I'm off and so's the sous. Harriet's cooking.'

'Oh.' That settled things immediately. And obviously not just for any possible lack of culinary expertise. Hanlon wasn't going to eat anything that woman might have come near. She'd been drugged once, she didn't want to risk a second occurrence. Or be poisoned.

'Get the ferry to Port Askaig on Islay. You can eat at the hotel there, the food's fine.'

'Thanks for letting me know.'

She closed the door and walked slowly back to the hotel. Islay. She wondered if McCleod would be free to change their drink to a dinner date.

## 12

'Two cautions and a suspended sentence for drug possession.' Kai was the topic of discussion.

'Intent to supply?'

McCleod nodded and sipped her coffee. It was Thursday night and they were in the lounge of the Jura Sound hotel, the one that Donald had recommended. Wemyss was not allowed in, a no-dog policy in the restaurant, and was sulking in the back of McCleod's car. Hanlon had enjoyed her meal; she had been voraciously hungry and, more to the point, she was enjoying McCleod's company. It was a rare thing for her to be able to relax with someone fully or to find somebody interesting. McCleod ticked both boxes. She was also, it turned out, a fitness nut, which gave them common ground and something to talk about. Hanlon's troubles were not referred to.

But now, with the end of the evening in sight, Hanlon had brought up the subject of the barman.

'So he's never done jail time?'

McCleod shook her head. 'He came very close to it, but no. The cautions were for violence – he broke some guy's jaw in a fight and the other one was for something similar. Maybe drugs were involved too.' She grinned. 'But that happened in Paisley. They're quite used to stuff like that there.'

Well, that was enough about Kai, thought Hanlon.

'Tell me about Campbell,' she asked. Most of the participants at the orgy had been at least fifty. How old was the DI, she wondered, thirty? Campbell would have been much sought after by the ladies there, she guessed. Maybe he had odd tastes.

McCleod looked at her in surprise.

'Well, he's no fae here, as Kai would put it, he's a Glasgow boy. Did French and German at Edinburgh, joined the police under a graduate training scheme... He's fine, a wee bit stuck-up, a bit up his own arse, but he's OK.'

'And his gran lives on Jura?'

'Aye, that's right. He more or less lives there when he can. He has a place on the mainland, I believe, in Dumbarton, just outside Glasgow. But he loves it out here. Murdo knows this place like the back of his hand, and he's a keen sailor too. Fishes a lot. He knows the coast around here really well.'

McCleod finished her coffee. 'He's ambitious, but not crazily so. I don't know why he asked to be transferred out here. I heard he could have had Edinburgh – that's a plum posting. But no, he prefers it out here in the wilds. Who knows why? Maybe he's close to his gran.'

'What's his gran like?' Hanlon asked.

McCleod looked suitably mystified at the question. 'I've got no idea. She's a Wee Free, they're ultra-religious, no singing in church except psalms, the Bible is the direct word of the Lord. You get the picture.'

Hanlon laughed, casually. 'So not the kind of woman you'd bump into at an orgy?'

'God, no. But she'd be too old for that anyway, or do they do orgies differently in London?'

'I wouldn't know,' Hanlon said simply. 'I've never been to one.' She brought the conversation back to Campbell.

'Does he have a girlfriend?'

McCleod laughed. 'She'd have to join the queue. Murdo keeps quiet on that side of things, but I have heard stories. He's very popular with the ladies.'

Probably more popular than you could imagine, thought Hanlon.

'He likes to put it about, or so people say. Anyway, that's enough about the DI, let's talk about you. Tell me about yourself...'

Hanlon smiled. I'll give you the edited version, she thought.

* * *

They paid the bill and walked back to McCleod's old Volvo. Wemyss, in the back, greeted them frantically. McCleod opened the hatch and he ran around the car, leaping up at Hanlon while McCleod looked on like a proud parent whose child was doing something clever.

'He really does like you!' she said admiringly.

'And he can really find people lost in the hills?' Wemyss sniffed her ecstatically.

McCleod nodded. 'Aye, he's done it four or five times. Folk leave the hotels to go and climb up the Paps. From the road it looks no distance at all, but you just try it!'

I have, thought Hanlon, I ran up. But she held her tongue. McCleod continued, 'Benn an Oir is a Corbett, that means it's over seven hundred and sixty metres high. And it's hard going. We've had to go out for broken ankles, a couple got lost on the other side of the island when the mist came down. People are just so unprepared, you wouldn't believe it!'

She bent down and ruffled the dog's fur.

'But Wemyss found them, didn't you, boy? He's got a great nose.'

Wemyss nuzzled Hanlon's hand and then leapt athletically into the back of the estate when McCleod pointed. She closed the hatch and the two women got in the car.

'There's a circuit class on the day after tomorrow in Craig-house, 8 p.m. Want to come?' asked McCleod. 'You'd enjoy it.'

'That'll be great,' said Hanlon. Solitary exercise was all well and good, but she was deeply competitive, she thought. I like beating people. She suddenly realised that she wanted to impress McCleod. God, I'm childish, she thought. 'I'd like that.'

'Good,' McCleod said. 'I'll pick you up.'

* * *

The following morning, Hanlon was back on the ferry, this time heading for the airport. It was the same plane that she had flown in on but now she could see nothing out of the window after they had taken off except for the milky white swirl of the clouds. Occasionally they would part and she would catch a momentary glimpse of gunmetal-grey sea or dark green hills.

They landed at Glasgow Airport and she caught the bus from there into Buchanan Street and found The Sleeket Mouse without too much trouble. She was in Glasgow to check up on Kai. Something about the barman did not ring true. There was no reason why an ex-con shouldn't have worked in a not quite Michelin-starred restaurant, provided he fitted the bill, and lots of people loved a reformed character, particularly if they had a sexily criminal past. Kai's chequered history fitted that bill; he hadn't done anything too outrageous. But he wasn't smooth enough, competent enough, professional enough to have warranted being employed by a classy place. Donald had felt the same and he'd worked in Michelin-starred establishments. Well, she'd pull on this thread and see what unravelled.

The restaurant was centrally located in one of the dark red Victorian sandstone buildings that make up the West End of the city. A blue façade with a stylised silhouette of a scurrying mouse ran above the doorway. The name of the restaurant was printed in small, lower-case letters. It was the confident assertion of a place that did not need to advertise its presence too heavily.

Hanlon sat in the window of a Starbucks opposite and had a coffee while she waited for 12 p.m., opening time.

She walked inside at noon on the dot. Did she have a reservation? asked the charming girl on the desk. No. Frowns, checks on a computer screen while Hanlon looked around. It was classic, muted restaurant chic, greys, browns, white tablecloths, the waiting staff in black trousers, white shirts and black waistcoats. Hanlon noticed that the buttons had little mouse designs embossed on them. It was a look and décor that said no expense spared. Smiles now. Yes, they did have a table, could they have it back by 1 p.m.? Hanlon – certainly. She was led to her table by a tall, Glaswegian hipster with an ornate beard, a pierced eyebrow and exquisite grace. From the bottom of his cropped tartan trews to the top of his topknot, he exuded style. That was what Kai was lacking, thought Hanlon. Kai had no style.

The menu was modern French and at least twice as expensive as the Mackinnon Arms. Hanlon ordered a seared scallop on cauliflower puree followed by guinea fowl with a Sauternes jus.

Her eye was drawn to the manageress, a short, dark-haired woman who seemed highly efficient, as she would have to be in a place like this. She looked strangely familiar. Hanlon wondered why – maybe she just resembled someone well known. She could tell by the wary body language of the staff that they were all slightly scared of her.

Attentive, polite waiting staff brought her bread, olives, an amuse bouche made of pastry and seaweed, a bottle of water. They were fresh-faced and keen. She wondered again how Kai had managed to get a job here.

Hanlon had looked at their website before, now she re-checked it on her phone while she waited for the starter. She studied its information with more attention than she had previously. She read about its philosophy – Scottish classics (really? Guinea fowl? Was that Scottish? Sauternes? How Scottish were Pommes Anna?), its awards – numerous – and its team. Head Chef, Gisela Lennox and Sous Chef, Daniel McCullough, who had come from one of the Galvin restaurants in London a year ago. She had eaten at that particular restaurant three times; it had been a favourite with her former boss.

And then, out of the blue, there it was. The connection that she had half suspected, half known about between The Sleeket Mouse and the Isle of Jura. It was present in the attractive, smiling face of the manageress, and her name, Ishbel Campbell. Now Hanlon knew why the face had looked familiar. Campbell.

By quarter past twelve the tables were starting to fill up. Campbell was making her rounds of the tables, then she was standing, smiling down at Hanlon. A lot more welcoming than her brother had been.

'I hope everything is all right with your meal...'

Hanlon smiled. 'It's delicious. Are you by any chance Murdo's sister?'

She noticed Ishbel's eyes widen slightly in surprise. 'We're colleagues... of sorts,' Hanlon said.

Ishbel Campbell said, warily, 'Yes, he's my brother. Are you Glasgow CID?'

Hanlon shook her head. 'Neither, I'm from London. I just met your brother a while back, by chance. I just wondered... you look very alike.'

Ishbel laughed. 'People do say that, but he's much better-looking... He's got the Campbell hair, mine's just boring old brunette.'

'He certainly does have remarkable hair,' Hanlon said. 'I'm sorry, I'm holding you up.'

'Och, don't worry. Anyway, lovely meeting you...'

Ishbel moved off, exuding charm, efficiency and ability in equal quantities to attend to the other tables. When Hanlon paid and left, she noticed Ishbel on her phone, watching her leave and talking in that guarded way people have when they don't want others to overhear. Perhaps I'm just overly sensitive, thought Hanlon.

An hour later Hanlon was back at the Starbucks opposite The Sleeket Mouse. Sitting in the window at a long counter, her eyes fixed on the restaurant. Her flight wasn't until seven, so she had plenty of time before she was due at the airport.

So, Kai's former employer was Campbell's sister. Murdo Campbell – was he a bent copper? Certainly attendance at a swingers' party where class A drugs were being freely consumed would be gross misconduct. Bringing the force into disrepute. And any friend of Big Jim's was an enemy of Hanlon's.

She thought of Wemyss, his keen nose for a scent. Kindred spirits, she thought. And I can smell something that stinks to high heaven. Come on, she thought, drumming her fingers on the counter top.

She had drunk two cups of coffee and read her e-mails twice over before she saw what she was looking for. Daniel McCullough, the sous chef. He emerged from the main door of the restaurant and looked around. Fortunately, there had been several good photos of him on the website.

Like Ishbel Campbell, McCullough was small, efficient-looking and handsome. She put her coffee down and hurried after him.

**13**

She followed McCullough along Sauchiehall Street in the centre of Glasgow, the monumental dark red sandstone buildings as powerfully confident as his strutting walk. Hanlon hurried after him. She caught up with him as he waited to cross the road.

'Excuse me, Daniel McCullough?'

He turned and looked at her.

'Yes?' He was good-looking, neat, regular features, intelligent, calm eyes. He was the personification of efficiency, she thought.

'DCI Hanlon, police. Can I have a quick word? It's nothing serious,' she added, reassuring him.

'Sure.' He was puzzled but not alarmed, a man whose conscience was clear.

The lights changed and they crossed the road together. There was a pedestrianised area with several benches. Hanlon pointed to an empty one.

'This will do fine.'

They sat down; he looked at her with curiosity. Passers-by eddied and flowed around them. It was a hot sunny day and the mood in the centre of the city was relaxed and genial.

'How can I help?' he asked.

'I just wanted to ask a few questions about one of your former colleagues, Kai McPherson.'

McCullough shook his head at the mention of the name. He looked at the sunny street area with its shirt-sleeved businessmen and women in summer dresses. Like most chefs, rarely seeing the light of day, he was very pale.

'So what's Kai been up to?' he said.

'Nothing, really.' Hanlon shook her head. 'His name came up in the course of an investigation. I was wondering what you could tell me about him.'

McCullough rubbed his chin thoughtfully. 'Not a great deal, he was only with us for a couple of months. He was competent enough, but... well...'

'But?'

McCullough sighed. 'He wasn't really, I don't know what the right word would be, suitable, I suppose. Posh isn't the right word.' He looked Hanlon in the eyes. 'If you're shelling out sixty to a hundred quid for lunch, you want to be served by someone with a bit of class. I don't mean upper class, I'm not a snob, I mean "class". Davey, who's a waiter, he's from some shit-hole part of Glasgow but he's "*simpatico*", like the Italians say.'

'And Kai wasn't,' said Hanlon. She knew exactly what the chef meant; it mirrored her own thoughts.

'No, don't get me wrong,' said McCullough, 'he was polite, never caused trouble, but his face didn't fit.'

Hanlon came to the question that she really wanted answering. 'So why was he given the job?'

McCullough smiled. 'That's actually more or less what I asked Ish.' He paused. 'That's Ishbel Campbell, she's in charge. Why the fuck would she want to employ Kai? If we advertise for staff, we're inundated.' He shook his head, baffled. 'She didn't really answer my question. I kind of got the impression that she gave him the job to do someone else a favour. But it would have been her decision. I mean, she part owns the place after all.'

'Wow,' Hanlon said, thinking of the lavish expense on fixtures and fittings, 'she must have some money.'

'I'll say,' said McCullough with feeling. 'She bought one of the partners out a year ago. Half a million. Wish I could get my hands on that kind of money.'

He fell silent, maybe thinking of what he would do if he had got such wealth.

'Any more questions?' he asked.

'No, that should do.'

'Tell you what,' said McCullough suddenly, 'Kai was from Paisley. He used to work at a pub called the Rob Roy. You could always ask there, his home turf.'

'Thanks,' said Hanlon. 'The Rob Roy...' She made a note of it on her phone, checking the address with McCullough. 'I think I will.'

'That's OK,' said McCullough. He looked at her. 'Now, if that's everything, I'll be off. I'm on a split.' He looked at his watch. 'I'm back on at five.'

'What are you going to do for two hours?' she asked, suddenly curious.

'Couple of pints...' McCullough yawned '... then a couple of lines. Shouldn't really say that to you, should I?'

'I'm a discreet person, Mr McCullough,' Hanlon said. She thought it was a measure of how widespread drug use had become in society that McCullough was cheerfully admitting this to the police, but then again, maybe it was just him. You don't get to be sous-chef in a rosette restaurant without a certain amount of ego. She recalled her own coke experience a few nights before; the stuff seemed to be everywhere these days. It seemed at times she was fighting a losing battle. People like McCullough didn't seem to realise that the cost of coke wasn't just fifty pounds a gram or whatever the street price happened to be, its cost was measured in violence and corruption.

He said, 'Well, I don't particularly miss Kai as a person or a colleague, but he always had a shit-load of coke on him.'

I can well believe that, she thought.

'Thank you for your time, Mr McCullough.'

'Dan, please.'

She stood up. 'If ever you eat at the Mouse again, ask if I'm working,' McCullough said. 'I'll upgrade your meal.'

'Thank you, Dan,' she said. 'I will.'

She left him on the bench and walked thoughtfully back to the bus station. Time to go to Paisley and check out Kai's home turf.

* * *

An hour later Hanlon was studying the outside of the Rob Roy. Paisley had seen better days, in her opinion, that much was for sure. Like many high streets, its centre was full of boarded-up shops and there was an air of sad desperation about the place. Its locals looked pallid and depressed. But it was not all bad news. She walked past the abbey, which was beautiful, and the imposing Catholic bulk of St Mirin's Cathedral.

If Paisley had seen better days, the Rob Roy had probably never had a good day in its life. Unlike The Sleeket Mouse, it was exactly the kind of pub that she could well imagine Kai working in. Unlike The Sleeket Mouse, it didn't have a website but was listed in a website of Paisley pubs. Possibly there was nothing to recommend about it other than it being a pub. As she stood outside it certainly looked that way.

It stood on a street corner as a tired old prostitute might, soliciting trade, and not doing very well. Its sign was peeling; a chalkboard advertised 'Exotic Dancers' on Saturday afternoons. A poster said, 'Food available'. In the Rob Roy that sounded more like a warning than a promise. It also had live football and a pool table.

The windows were three quarters covered in a metal grill, so you couldn't throw a brick through them, and painted over with advertising for Tennent's lager, so you couldn't see through them. Only the top strip was clear glass. Cigarette butts littered the pavement by the door. Over the lintel it said, 'Emmanuel Johnson, licensed to sell beer and spirits.'

It didn't say anything about ambience.

Hanlon walked in.

It wasn't as bad as she had feared from the outside. The pub was high-ceilinged and spacious. A large flat-screen TV was angled at the rear, high up on the wall so you could see it over the heads of the customers.

The furniture was chunky dark brown tables and upholstered, heavy chairs. They looked as if you could take a sledgehammer to them and they wouldn't break. Almost certainly why they were chosen, not for their aesthetic but their durability in a pub brawl. The floor was lino in a brown and yellow tile effect. There were three small, old men standing by the bar with their backs to Hanlon, drinking half-pints of beer with whisky chasers.

They didn't turn around.

There was a table by the door with three young guys that appeared to be in their twenties. They looked as if they could have been part of Kai's extended family. Perhaps they were. Two of them wore trainers, nylon tracksuit bottoms and hoodies, the third, with his back to Hanlon, had dyed blond hair, a blue nylon tracksuit with Partick Thistle logoed on the back and trainers.

One of the hoodies said something to him and he turned in his seat and stared at Hanlon. A tough, thin street face, gold necklace, a couple of gold teeth and heavy sovereign rings on his fingers.

She knew without looking that his trainers would be top of the range, that his phone would be the latest model. She knew that he would be the local coke dealer. She also knew that he would have recognised her immediately as police. Well, anyone would. What sane woman would be in this pub otherwise? Unless he mistook her for a down-on-her-luck exotic dancer.

She walked up to the bar.

'Yes, can I help you?' said the barman. He too was small and slim with a small moustache and brown hair in a kind of a quiff. He had a good-humoured face. He was certainly the single most pleasant feature of the place. The old men stared at her with outright dislike, a woman, invading their space.

'Lap dancing's on Saturday, hen.' The voice came from behind her. It was harsh and aggressive. It was tracksuit boy. Hanlon rolled her eyes. Ignored him.

'Can I have a word with the landlord?' she asked.

The barman nodded,

'Aye, I'll go and fetch him.'

He walked to the far end of the bar.

'Dinnae fancy yours much, Frank,' called out tracksuit boy loudly to the friendly barman and burst out laughing, pleased with his wit. Frank half turned, caught Hanlon's gaze and rolled his eyes heavenwards. He disappeared through a door marked 'Private'.

Muttering and sniggers from the table.

Hanlon felt something hit her hair. She turned to face them. A scrunched-up beer mat. Tracksuit had moved his chair round so he was facing her.

'Whit? Whit youse looking at?' he sneered.

Hanlon walked over to him. She felt she had no choice. If she didn't, it would prey on her mind for ever. The day she backed down from an aggressive yob. She didn't back down. She heard a quiet, intelligent voice from a chic Hampstead flat saying, '*You deliberately put yourself in positions of extreme danger...*'

Hanlon ignored Dr Morgan, stared into the hate-filled eyes of the youth half her age on his chair. Is today the day I get knifed? she wondered. Well, only one way to find out.

'Can I make a suggestion?' she said politely.

'A suggestion? A suggestion?' His voice rose mockingly, parodying her accent, putting on a strangled faux-English posh accent. 'Oh, aye, by all means... suggest away...'

'Here's my suggestion.' Hanlon's voice was level; she moved slightly closer, leaned her face close in, invading his body space, intimidating, stared into his slightly glazed blue eyes. He smelled faintly of cheap aftershave, cigarettes, weed and rank sweat. 'Why don't you fuck off?'

The kid blinked, staring up at her in disbelief. 'Sonny,' added Hanlon, for insulting good measure.

'You auld bitch...' he snarled.

He leapt to his feet, fists clenched. Now that it had kicked off, she felt good. She felt confident, light on her feet, fast and strong. She was super-fit. More to the point she was spoiling for a fight.

Most people didn't know how to punch hard; Hanlon did. Twenty years of boxing, two decades of sparring. Years ago her then trainer had urged her to turn pro.

She took a step back with her right foot, weight on the left. Her left shoulder was forward, her body angled to make it less of a target, back foot angled on the ball of the foot, ready to spring forward. Her fists were clenched too, head high, protecting her face. I'm going to hurt you so bad, she exulted.

'Leave it, Tam.' A man's voice, from behind her. Authoritative, warning.

Tam immediately sat back down in his chair, a sulky look on his face, like a kid told to sit down by his teacher. It was astonishing.

Hanlon kept her eyes firmly on Tam. Then she retreated a step and looked round. The voice belonged to an ageing punk, a guy about forty, with a gymnast's physique in a sleeveless workout vest and torn jeans. His shoulders and arms and the top of his chest, between his massive pecs, were a swirling mass of colourful tattoos, his eyebrow and lip were pierced. He had sandy hair shaved into a floppy Mohican and his ears too were multiply pierced. His very blue eyes rested on Hanlon; they were bulging in their sockets. He looked much the worse for wear for drugs, mentally at least. Physically he seemed to be doing just fine. His expression seemed quite crazy and a peculiar smile, half welcoming, half threatening flickered across his lips.

'Youse,' he said, pointing to Hanlon, 'come wi'me.'

She dropped her fists. Sanity prevailed. The rational part of her brain reminded her why she was here – to find out more about Kai and what was going on at the Mackinnon Arms, so she could achieve justice for the deaths of two girls. Not prove to herself how hard she was.

She studied the ageing punk more closely. There was certainly a lot to look at. There was a circle tattooed on his sternum, visible over the low-cut vest, with the word 'Leo' in heavy blue gothic lettering, nestling between his heavy pectoral muscles, bookended between two stylised lion's heads.

Leo beckoned at her impatiently.

She walked up to him and inspected the chest tattoo. She looked up and into his crazy eyes.

'Is that your star sign?' she asked.

Leo stared at her in disbelief then laughed uproariously.

'I like you!' he said, and clapped her on the back. 'Come on, come on through.'

At last, someone who can give me answers about Kai, she thought. They walked to the end of the bar and she followed him through a door marked 'Private'. This led into the backstage hall of the pub, a large, dark and gloomy place. There was a staircase running upstairs, a back door to the Rob Roy's yard and a couple of other doors.

Leo turned to her, frowning, all trace of good humour gone. There was an undercurrent of violence about him; she was glad that she wasn't here to ask him any searching questions. Leo looked as if he might kick off at the slightest provocation.

'Now that we're alone, you'd better tell me what you want.'

'I'm police,' Hanlon said.

Leo nodded. 'I guessed that. You're not local, are you?'

She shook her head. 'No, I'm not here because of anything happening in this pub. I just have a few questions about a former employee of yours, a Kai McPherson.'

His face cleared. McPherson was obviously regarded as non-controversial.

'Kai, eh... nothing serious, then. In that case, the boss'll see youse.'

Leo knocked on one door and opened it. They walked into a spacious office where an elderly man was sitting behind a desk overflowing with papers. He was wearing a cheap blue suit and a yellow shirt with a black tie. He was smoking a cigarette and the room smelled strongly of stale smoke. Despite this, and despite the month being June, the window was tightly shut. The smoke from the cigarette curled around the windows and a shaft of sunlight turned it blue.

The walls were wallpapered with a dark green flock design,

the ceiling was magnolia but the section above the guy's head was stained a dark yellow from the smoke that had drifted upward from his cigarette.

'I'm Manny,' he said, and gave a wheezing cough. 'Frank said there was a police woman wanting to see me. Take a seat. You can wait outside, kid.' The last remark was addressed to Leo.

Leo nodded and closed the door behind him. Manny puffed at his cigarette and looked shrewdly at Hanlon. She sat down in the chair in front of the desk.

He was about seventy, she guessed, and in terrible shape, overweight, double-chinned. He took a big sip from a glass of pale whisky; she could smell it from where she sat.

'How can I help you? You are the police, I take it?'

It was as she suspected – what woman other than a police-woman or a stripper would be here?

'Yes,' said Hanlon without elaborating or offering him ID. Manny stubbed out his cigarette and lit a fresh one.

'So, to whit dae I owe this honour?' His expression was sardonic, good-humoured.

'Kai McPherson – I am told that he used to work here.' She wasn't going to say that the information had come from The Sleeket Mouse. 'Could you give me some background informa-tion about him?'

Manny pondered the question; he looked shrewdly at Hanlon and puffed his cigarette. The tip glowed red. Manny coughed gently. The fingers of his right hand were stained almost orange.

'And why would you be interested in Kai, I wonder?' he asked, pleasantly enough.

'He is connected to an investigation that is currently ongoing,' she said.

'What would that be aboot?'

'I'm not at liberty to say.'

Manny looked at her for what felt like a long time, evidently evaluating whether or not to talk to her; evidently the answer was yes.

'Aye, he did work here.' Manny sighed. 'For a while.'

'What was he like?'

'Oh, he was fine,' said Manny, 'a guid enough barman.'

'Why did he leave?' Hanlon asked.

Manny puffed on his cigarette and wheezed slightly. 'Well, Kai's a bright boy but unfortunately he had a bit of a stooshie wi' Tam, who you've met.' She must have looked surprised; Manny smiled. 'Frank told me.'

'I have.' She didn't elaborate.

Manny frowned. 'Tam's a wee shite. He's a druggie. I'm not in favour, I don't like drugs, but whit can ye dae?' He shrugged. 'You might say, bar him, but in general he behaves. This is Paisley. Better the devil you know.' He extinguished his cigarette and lit another one. 'Shites like Tam are a fact of life. Anyway, there was friction.'

'Friction?'

'Tam and Kai had an argument. Kai came off worst. He had to leave after that.'

'What was the dispute over?' Hanlon asked.

'There was a lassie involved. Tam's ex. Lee Anne. She took up with Kai.' Manny gave a wheezy laugh and said, 'Boy, she sure can pick them. Anyhow, she and Kai had an argument and Kai started whaling on her. She ended up in the Royal Alex. Broken cheek-bones, missing teeth, Christ, she was black and blue.'

So, thought Hanlon, Kai has form for assaulting women.

'He has issues with women then?' she asked.

'Kai has issues, as you put it, with everyone. It's lucky he didnae kill Lee Anne. He's a wee pluke.'

'What's her full name?'

Manny looked at her questioningly.

'Just in case I need to know.'

He shrugged. 'Gillespie, Lee Anne Gillespie. She's a bam – anyone going oot wi' Kai needs their heid seeing to.'

There was obviously little love lost between Manny and Kai. He added, 'If you interview him, I'd take everything he says with a pinch of salt. He's nae the most honest of boys. I hope that's helped give you your background.'

So, violent towards women and an untrustworthy liar. The landlord puffed away at his Regal Blue; he wagged a warning finger at Hanlon. 'This is Paisley, like I said. It can get kind of rough round here, but I'm too auld to move now. I can control what happens in this pub, but not outside. When you leave it'll be out the back with Leo to chum you doon the road. I heard you made Tam look stupit – he willnae take kindly to that. He's impulsive.'

Impulsive, she thought, that's one way of putting it.

'Thank you.'

Manny waved away her thanks with a pudgy, unhealthy hand. 'It's my guid deed for the day. I don't want anything bad happening to you from one of my customers. Anyway, one last word about Kai. I'd heard he'd gone straight, but I dinnae really believe it. He's as bad as Tam.'

'Thank you, Manny, you've been very helpful,' Hanlon said. She had expected him to be a lot more close-mouthed, certainly not cooperative.

Manny lit another cigarette and topped his whisky up with a bottle he took out from a drawer in a filing cabinet behind his desk.

'I'm seventy; I am fucked medically.' He coughed as if to underline the point. It was a very long coughing fit and at the end he was gasping for breath. 'As you may have guessed.' He produced an inhaler and sucked hard on it.

'If it wasnae for this wee puffer...' he waved the inhaler '... I'd be deid, but I'm no terribly long for this world. I just want to create trouble for Tam, Kai and all their kin. Drugs are ripping, have ripped, the heart out of this community. Not just here, all over Scotland.' He sighed. 'But I'm not going to do anything that constructive personally. My action days are over. I heard that Kai had made a big-time connection with a Scottish coke importer. I heard too that he was paying the police off tae look the other way.'

He looked at her in a warning way. 'This is, of course, off the record. Now I've told you quite a bit, you can do the rest. Now, time for you to go.'

Hanlon stood up.

'Thanks again.'

'Dinnae thank me, just inconvenience Tam and Kai. The sad truth is, even if you put them away, someone else will take their place. As well you know...' he picked his phone up and laboriously texted '... but those two are wee bastards, they deserve to go down. Hopefully they'll end up in the same jail, kill each other. Do us all a favour.'

Leo opened the door.

'Yes, Manny?'

'Take this young lady to wherever she wants, Leo.'

'Where to?' He looked at Hanlon with his eager, crazy eyes.

'The airport, Leo.'

The door closed on Manny. The last she saw of him he was lighting another cigarette from the still-glowing butt of the old one.

Leo chuckled and their eyes met.

'Star sign, that's a guid one.'

# 14

Hanlon climbed out of the small plane and breathed in the heavy salt air with a sense of relief. Back on Islay. Even the airstrip, the tarmac running across very vivid green grass, looked welcoming after the huge concrete apron of Glasgow airport. A stiff breeze tugged at her dark hair and she patted the metal of the plane's fuselage with an almost proprietorial hand.

She had run over the events of the day on the flight back, trying to make some sense of what she had learned.

Kai had indeed been employed at a Michelin-starred (well, almost) restaurant. She had been slightly surprised that this should have actually been the case. From the little she knew of such places, she had gathered it wasn't easy to get a job in one. It was quite a leap from the Rob Roy to put it mildly. McCullough, the chef, had been of the same opinion. The consensus was that Kai didn't fit in, that he should never have been employed there in the first place.

This inevitably led to the question, why? It was a big question.

Responsibility for giving Kai the job lay at the door of The Sleeket Mouse's manageress, the sister of the detective in charge of investigating two deaths on Jura, both deaths involving foreign young women, both deaths drownings and both deaths linked to the hotel where Kai now worked. Had Campbell leaned on his sister to employ Kai, and if so, why?

Ishbel Campbell had become the co-owner of The Sleeket Mouse. She had managed to find a great deal of money in a relatively short time.

Kai McPherson was unscrupulous, intelligent, and had a history of drug dealing and opportunistic actions. He was still dealing drugs – she had seen it with her own eyes – trading drugs for sex, cheating people out of what they were due (Nose-stud and her coke), more than capable of violence to women (although admittedly what she had witnessed was in self-defence) and very much a man with an eye on the main chance.

Murdo Campbell had been an attendee at one of the Mackinnon Arms sex parties. Bringing the force into disrepute, possibly leaving him open to blackmail or coercion. And why had Murdo buried himself away in island obscurity?

Manny had claimed that someone in the force was helping Kai with his drug dealing. Hanlon feared that this was only too possible.

She suspected that Murdo and Kai were involved in drug-trafficking, maybe with Murdo supplying and Kai selling, or possibly Kai doing both and Murdo acting as his eyes and ears on the police force for a substantial fee or cut, the profits of which he had laundered via his sister.

Kai was dirty, Murdo probably.

\* \* \*

She got the same taxi driver as she had when she had first arrived, a few days before.

'Oh, it's you again! How are you liking Jura?' He seemed pleased to see her; she was more relaxed than when she'd first arrived, that was for sure.

'It's very nice,' Hanlon said. The strange thing was, she meant it. She liked the silence when she ran, she liked the smell of the place, as opposed to car fumes, food, rubbish, grit, people and the weird, not unpleasant sooty underground smells that she was used to in London. Jura smelled of pine, of ferns, of damp and decay, of water and peat, elemental. It smelled of stone and water, salt and burn. Ten years ago she would have hated it; today, no. She had thought Tremayne was crazy when he had decided to retire here, now she could begin to understand. She had called him once or twice since she'd been on Jura but she'd been reluctant to let him know what she was up to. Part of that was her natural desire to compartmentalise and her habit of not confiding in people. Part of it too was that Tremayne, her old boss, would have wanted to take control; he had never really relinquished that part of their relationship. He liked to be in charge. She smiled. It was as if she were some kind of daughter to him; she supposed he was the nearest to family that she had.

A thought suddenly struck her: I've had enough of London. It was a kind of revelation. She had always defined herself as a Londoner, but the unsullied beauty of the west coast had made her rethink. Then a follow-up thought: I would like to move here. She sat back in her seat, slightly amazed by this.

'Aye, that it is,' the driver said. 'And the Mackinnon Arms hotel, how do you find that?'

'The food's very good,' Hanlon said diplomatically. She looked out of the window, green fields and grey dry-stone walls. A buzzard wheeled lazily overhead in the evening sun, the feathers at the ends of its wings sticking out like fingers. She wondered if it was the same one that she had seen when she had discovered that Murdo Campbell was not all that he seemed.

'Aye, Donald is a good chef and no mistake.'

Silence fell and he dropped her off at the ferry terminal. She paid and thanked him.

'I'll doubtless see you soon,' he said. 'The name is Ruaridh.'

'Thank you,' she said. 'I look forward to it.' And, strangely, she did.

The Paps rose up, huge and grey, bathed in golden light. Hanlon swatted a cloud of midges away from her head. The water between the two islands, the Sound of Islay, looked very blue in this light. But above all, for the first time in her life, she experienced a sense of coming home.

* * *

The following day, Hanlon had a light breakfast. She noticed that there were only a smattering of other guests at the tables. She went back upstairs, changed into her running gear and walked out of the hotel.

The boar on the sign gazed at her with a contemptuous expression.

She upped her pace as she jogged up the single-track road. Its grey surface was in reasonable condition. She guessed that hardly any traffic used it – she hadn't seen a single house yet. Today she thought she would run up into the hills. She was going north now, towards the tip of the island. From there you could see another island, Scarba, across a narrow strip of water, the Gulf of Corryvreckan, named after the whirlpool, or possibly vice versa. Anyway, that was the place that Eva had allegedly drowned, her body carried back to Jura by the currents where it had been discovered by a shepherd, McCleod had told her, washed up on the shore.

The sun was struggling to break through the clouds; occasionally it would succeed, and shafts of brilliant white light would shine through the greyness overhead and play on the grey-blue water like searchlights or spotlights in a theatre. Despite the threat hanging over her head in London that excessive use of force would be a dismissible offence, she felt remarkably light-hearted. London seemed very far away, slightly unreal, as if what was happening there was not connected with her. She was far more interested in what was going on here. Kai was a firm suspect in her mind for the death of Franca. Big Jim for Eva's demise. She was confident that someone was going to pay for the girls' deaths, in one way or another.

In the far distance, across the water, she could see the low hills of the Kintyre peninsula. She decided that she was going to stop thinking about her case. Concentrate on the here and now. She turned off the road, following a footpath she hadn't been up before that headed into the hills. She guessed it would run more or less parallel to the forestry road that she had used previously.

The path was damp underfoot and she had to skirt patches of brilliant green mossy bog. She loved the colours of the island. So many varied greens. Sedge-like light green spiky grasses grew in clumps and there were big tussocks of dark green heather occasionally blocking the way. She jumped over oozing black peaty muddy soil, which the path periodically ran into. Off the trail the going would have been ridiculously tough; the ground was mainly heather and bracken with occasional birch trees and outcroppings of impenetrable, sharp-spiked gorse and tangles of bog myrtle.

And dominating everything, the huge grey stone swell of the Paps.

It was completely silent apart from the wind in the foliage, the ubiquitous sound of running water, and the occasional cry of a bird.

Below her, to her right, the forestry road made of hard impacted stones wound its way into the hills. She had been told that if she followed it, it would lead her to the far side of the island, the western side.

She ran on, ever upwards, her running shoes now sodden with peaty water. The path was occasionally crossed by several small burns, their water icy despite the summer sun, as they ran towards the sea.

She followed the track until it ended at a small loch, not much bigger than a football pitch. Its brown peaty water reflected the sky, and reeds waved mournfully in the breeze. There was a rocky outcrop to the side of the hill, and she climbed up it to get a better view.

It was worth it. Behind her towered the Paps, now much nearer, and she could see how hard it would be to scramble up them. Their rocky slopes, although not needing climbing, would require a slow, painstaking ascent. You would have to clamber up and over countless boulders to reach the summit.

Not today, thought Hanlon.

In front of her she could see just how high she had climbed. She could see the Mackinnon Arms far away now to the right and the cottages where Donald and Kai stayed. From up here, the hotel was a dark, foreboding mass, squatting on the shoreline, guarding its malign secrets. Out in the loch she could see two fishing boats, and in the distance, an enormous ferry, sailing back from Islay.

She jogged back down the path, occasionally taking wild leaps across the boggy patches, disappearing into the black, peaty mud almost up to her knees when she landed with a satisfying squelch, exulting in the fitness of her body. You didn't get this running around Hammersmith, she thought.

She carried on down towards the road then, as she rounded a twist in the path, she suddenly saw Kai through a gap in the alder trees that grew between the path and the forestry track.

What was he doing here? She crouched down in a clump of bracken that reached as high as her chin and watched through the fronds as he walked up the slope. She wondered where he was going. It seemed impossibly out of keeping with what she had seen of Kai for him to decide to go for a stroll, much less a heavy-duty hike into the hills. Kai was a Paisley boy. He hadn't embraced the country life; exercise was alien to him.

Kai was only in his early twenties, tough and strong, she had seen that, but he was not in good shape. She could hear him fighting for breath as he walked up the steep slope into the hills. He certainly wasn't enjoying his walk. He stopped a couple of metres away from her and she could see his forehead slick with sweat, his dyed blond hair flat against his head from perspiration. He was wearing a pair of baggy jeans and a bomber jacket, not a good choice for a hill walk.

He put his hands in his pockets and took out a joint, which he lit, puffing away; the sweet, cloying smoke, that to Hanlon always smelled like compost, billowed around his head. He closed his eyes as he inhaled deeply. He pulled the bomber jacket off; his T-shirt was wet with sweat. He took several more deep drags on his joint.

That'll help your fitness levels, thought Hanlon.

She watched as he finished his joint, which he tossed into the deep drainage ditch that ran alongside the road, took a deep breath and set off once again.

Hanlon turned around and followed him, keeping parallel on the path that she had just run up.

Twenty minutes later she had reached the loch again. She was now ahead of Kai by her reckoning. She climbed up the rock to the right of the loch, stretched out on it and looked down at the view below.

The hillside fell away below her. The trees that had grown between here and the road had been felled. Occasionally a grey, dead pine, useless for timber, still stood. The woodland floor was carpeted in dead pine needles, sawdust and twigs. Very little could grow here now. It looked as if a nuclear bomb had been dropped nearby, destroying the landscape. Or maybe like a World War One battlefield. It was a dying and devastated landscape, desolate and eerily quiet.

She had a perfect view of the road that dropped down into the valley, bearing away to the right. Eventually she saw the plodding figure of Kai, walking slowly along, carrying his balled-up bomber jacket. His head was bent; he looked thoroughly miserable. You need to get out more, boy, she thought.

She waited until he had walked past where she was concealed and then hurried down as best she could to the track. It was hard going, clambering over the tree detritus that was a kind of woody obstacle course. To make matters worse, the land had been ploughed into ridges upon which the trees had been originally planted, and the gullies had filled up with twigs and branches and the occasional log. It was nightmarish but she got to the road in time to see Kai disappearing over a rise in the track in the distance.

She broke into a loose, comfortable run as she pursued him. No danger of Kai doing that, she thought.

Then she heard a car coming up the track heading straight towards her. Shit, she thought.

Hanlon glanced around for cover. The ditch by the side of the road was her best bet. The bare hillside where the trees had been cut down was no good – there was no hiding place and she would be immediately visible. The right-hand side had an unclimbable bank about two metres high where the road had been cut into the hillside.

The ditch was surprisingly deep, as Hanlon discovered when she jumped into it and immediately sank into mud, ooze and water. Her shoulder was level with the road and she crouched down low, pressing her body into the side of the trench. She would be invisible to anyone looking out of a car window.

The car was very close now. She heard it change gear as it jolted its way along. She felt, rather than saw, it pass above her and she risked putting her head up to have a quick look. It was a light blue BMW 4 x 4.

She waited a minute or so, then clambered out. Whoever was driving had to be meeting Kai. He wouldn't be up here unless he had a reason. She had to find out who it was. She started jogging again up the track. Half a mile or so further, the road started to dip down towards a valley with a wide burn running along its floor. There was a cottage or bothy, a small whitewashed stone-built place with a red corrugated-iron roof. The BMW was parked in front of it; there was now no sign of Kai. Whoever was driving the 4 x 4 would be inside with him.

She studied the situation for a few minutes and decided to approach the bothy via the stream bed. Its banks should, with luck, hide her from view. Hanlon turned off the track and cut a diagonal across the fallen branches and timber so she would arrive at the burn a few hundred metres upstream from the cottage.

Closer to the burn there were tall rhododendron bushes, yet more of the ubiquitous alder trees and the occasional silver birch. Hanlon hoped that these would screen her if either of the two people inside looked out of the small window.

Traversing the ground was every bit as unpleasant as it had been before, made worse by the need to keep a low profile. Moving in a kind of half-crouch to reduce her silhouette, scraping her skin on sharp bits of wood, plagued, and bitten several times by horseflies, she eventually made it to the stream and slid down its steep bank, so she was now invisible from the cottage a hundred metres or so downstream.

Hanlon walked carefully and quietly down the stream bed towards the bothy. The peat-brown water came up to her knees and was bitterly cold. The bottom of the burn was covered with stones that were treacherously slippery – she nearly lost her footing several times – and every so often there were large, smooth boulders that she had to skirt.

She was pleased with the route she had chosen. Down here, in the gully, she was below the sight of Kai or the other person even if they looked out of the window. Idly she wondered what they would do if they saw her. Who was it with Kai? Her money would have been on Big Jim, but why would he want to meet Kai away up here? Why not in his office? Ditto Harriet. Maybe it was his dealer, his coke supplier.

If they saw her, it could be dangerous. Kai was a volatile man, she'd both heard and seen it, Big Jim violent by repute. And, if she was right, one of them was a killer. She knew exactly what she would do if that happened: run. Hanlon ran marathons; she had seen Kai struggle to walk up the road. She would set off across the acres of ruined hillside, back to the path that led from the loch to the road. Catch me if you can. But she thought there was little chance of that happening, if she was careful. Ten minutes later she was level with the house. The stream ran within a couple of metres of its walls. She scrambled halfway up the bank and looked over the edge.

As she had guessed, the wall of the cottage was just a few

metres away. The window, its surrounding stone lintels picked out in black, was open. Hanlon pulled herself up out of the stream onto the level ground and ran lightly to shelter behind a pile of logs that had been cut for the fire, stacked up by the wall and partially covered by a tarpaulin. She was now only a metre or so from the open window.

The bar manager was smoking another number. Voices from inside carried to her along with Kai's weed smoke that drifted out, polluting the pristine hillside air. Kai's guttural, harsh Glaswegian accent and another whose educated, west-coast tones she knew well. You! she thought, a sharp satisfaction welling up inside her, I knew it.

'When is the next delivery due?'

'Next Friday. Three kilos of Charlie... So you let the Hart brothers go?'

'Sure. We had no reason to hold them, more importantly, don't want to frighten the horses, eh? What about Big Jim?'

'He's cool, Murdo.'

In her imagination she could see Murdo's handsome face facing Kai's across a table as they talked. '*I heard that Kai had made a big-time connection with a Scottish coke importer. I heard too that he was paying the police off tae look the other way.*' That was what Manny had told her. It looked as if he was bang on the money. Kai in partnership with Murdo.

The conversation carried on, then she heard her own name mentioned.

'You told me he's got a bee in his bonnet about Hanlon. He's sure she's onto what's happening. He's pretty desperate.'

'He' being Big Jim, she guessed.

'Relax, Murdo, ye're like an auld woman.'

'Two deaths, Kai, that's not good. I don't want a third. Hanlon is police. It could ruin everything.'

Oh, yes, Murdo, she thought, you're so right, not in the way that you meant, but I *am* going to ruin everything.

'Look, I'm onto it. Nae bother.'

'OK, but keep an eye on Big Jim. He's an unpredictable alcoholic. He may not even know what he's doing half the time. He's a loose cannon.'

'I'll be here Thursday afternoon, 4 p.m., Murdo. It's my day off. I'll have everything you need. Then we'll both be happy.'

'Good, when I go, I'll put the key where you can find it. I'll leave it next to the water butt.'

'Sure.'

'Oh, and Kai?'

'Yes, Murdo.'

'Don't fuck up, OK.'

'Don't worry, I won't fuck up.'

Oh, but you have, Kai, Hanlon thought as, silent as a ghost, she made her way back to the burn. You have.

She slipped back into the gully and headed northward, watched by the buzzard high in the sky and the implacable, silent bulk of the mountain.

## 15

Filthy, muddy and wet, Hanlon jogged back to the hotel along the main road. Her mind was racing. So there it was, definitive proof that Murdo Campbell was engaged in drug smuggling with Kai McPherson. Three kilos. By the sound of it, Big Jim was also involved. And he disliked her intensely. Good, she thought. She was delighted. The feeling was entirely mutual.

She ran on. What to do with her new-found information? Go to the police? Campbell *was* the police. Her word against his. Hanlon, an officer suspended from duty and under investigation from the IOPC; Campbell, a respected and upstanding young officer. Who would be believed? They'd think it was some crazy plan dreamed up by a disgraced detective to try and salvage an unsalvageable career.

Hanlon's excellent memory kicked in as she gracefully leaped over a puddle.

She remembered verbatim what her psychologist had said about her relationship with her colleagues.

*'Your colleagues have as well. Complained about you... Bit unusual, isn't it? You normally close ranks. When it's the police*

*worrying about police violence, surely alarm bells should be ringing in your head.'*

Whatever she did wouldn't be right. She had to get someone else to act. She herself was hopelessly compromised.

Tainted.

As she rounded a corner, she saw an old Land Rover driving towards her. It slowed down and stopped, blocking the road, its engine idling.

When she got closer she saw that its driver was Big Jim. She hadn't spoken to him since their first meeting; she had seen him in the hotel, here and there. He sat immobile behind the wheel, staring at her, a massive figure in the cab of the vehicle, his powerful forearms with their faded tattoos grasping the wheel. She could well believe that he'd knocked a drunken fisherman out – he had the build for it, as well as the attitude. As she approached he wound the window down.

'Morning,' he said, faux friendly.

She slowed and walked up to the window. She wrinkled her nose; she could smell the whisky from here.

Campbell's words.

*'He's got a bee in his bonnet about Hanlon. He's sure she's onto what's happening. He's pretty desperate.'*

Be careful, she warned herself. Big Jim might be old and out of shape, but he was formidable. Today he was dressed in working clothes: check shirt, old padded gilet. His silvery stubble – he hadn't shaved – contrasted with his red face, making it even more scarlet. His eyes looked at her, slightly out of focus.

'Good morning,' Hanlon said. He looked at her blankly. She had her mobile on her, and she toyed with the idea of calling the police, reporting him for drink driving, then gave up on the idea. The chances of there being a policeman on Jura (excluding DI Campbell, just up the road with his drug-dealer friend) at this precise moment were slim, unless McCleod was working from home, and Hanlon doubted that she would have a breathalyser on her.

'Have you been drinking?' would have been an utterly pointless question. He obviously had. He reeked of booze. But he would hardly have said, 'Well, now you mention it...' Hanlon reached a decision. She was not going to allow him to carry on driving in his current state. She didn't care if he killed himself, but there were others to think of, even though the only people around were probably a woman-beating drug dealer, a corrupt policeman and a few sheep.

'You know you've got a flat tyre?' Hanlon said, innocuously.

'A flat tyre?' Big Jim ran the two words into one. 'Ffflatire?'

'Yes.'

He frowned, trying to process the information through the fog of alcohol.

'Have I bollocks,' he finally said.

'Get out and see,' Hanlon said.

He did so, getting out of the Land Rover stiffly, leaving the engine running and the door open. To Hanlon's incredulity, he reached inside his gilet and took out a flat quarter-bottle of The Famous Grouse whisky, unscrewed the top, took a couple of swigs before replacing the cap and putting it back carefully in his inside pocket.

He really doesn't give a fuck, does he? she thought.

She pointed towards the nearside rear of the vehicle.

'Rear one.'

He didn't speak but walked round the Land-Rover.

'There's nothing...'

Hanlon had taken the opportunity. As he started to walk round the vehicle, shaking his head and grumbling, disappearing round the back, she put one foot on the metal step of the vehicle, and lightly jumped inside. Hardly daring to breathe, she checked the side mirror; Big Jim crouched down staring in perplexity at the wheel. She put the vehicle in gear and stamped hard on the pedal, accelerating away down the road, the driver's door flapping as she did so. She looked over her shoulder through the rear window. His face was a pantomime of angry disbelief as he stood in the centre of the road, arms raised as if he could somehow stop her with psychic force.

'Oi...' shouted Big Jim. He set off in pursuit, a kind of plodding, lumbering run. He was almost comically slow. Hanlon could have got away from him sitting behind the wheel in a child's pedal car, much less a Defender.

She could see him in the mirror, furious-faced. She noticed that he kept one hand firmly on the whisky bottle in the gilet pocket just in case it bounced out as he ran and smashed on the road. Wouldn't want that to happen, God forbid!

She drove about a hundred metres and parked in a layby. She turned the engine off, put the handbrake on, jumped out, pocketed the keys and stood there waiting for Big Jim to pant up to her.

He was insanely angry. His face, after the unaccustomed exercise, was even more crimson than before, a heady mix of anger, exertion and broken veins.

'What the fuck do you think you're doing?' he panted.

'Stopping you from harming yourself and others,' Hanlon said. She smiled sweetly.

'Give me back those car keys or else, you fucking bitch.'

He advanced menacingly on Hanlon, breathing heavily.

'Or else what?' she taunted.

'BITCH!'

Big Jim was now in front of her. Just as she was expecting, maybe even just as she was hoping – at last, a legitimate excuse to hit him – he threw a clumsy punch at Hanlon's head. She bent at the knees, rolling her body and twisting to the left as Big Jim's fist passed harmlessly over her head. He looked at her in angry disbelief; how could he have missed? My turn, she thought. She jack-knifed upright and, using the momentum from her legs and twisting her shoulder, drove a left hook as hard as she possibly could into Big Jim's stomach.

Her fist sank deep into flab. It was like punching a heavy bag in the gym. He staggered back from the unexpected force of the blow, winded, and his legs gave way. He sat down heavily in a muddy puddle by the side of the road. He struggled to say something, but he couldn't speak. His mouth opened and shut like a beached fish as he struggled to breathe.

'Your keys will be back at the hotel,' Hanlon said curtly. She turned and jogged away down the road in the direction of the Mackinnon Arms.

She felt very pleased with herself at having left no visible evidence of hitting Big Jim. No suspect bleating about a broken nose and police brutality today.

A hundred metres or so away from Big Jim, she glanced over her shoulder. He was still sitting where she had left him, in the puddle of water. She stopped in disbelief. She saw the sun, which was coming out from behind a cloud, glint on the bottle as he raised it to his lips. There was an answer to everything for Big Jim. Well, she thought to herself, slowing to a walk, no risk of imminent pursuit.

Hanlon got back to the hotel about half an hour later. There were no cars in the car park; she guessed that she was possibly the only guest staying that day. She wondered if Big Jim would insist that she leave. She really didn't want to; she wanted more time there, gathering evidence. She went into the manager's office. Harriet looked up at Hanlon standing framed in the entrance. There was a mirror behind her and Hanlon caught a glimpse of her own reflection.

Her hair was a dark, tangled mess, her leggings and running shoes were covered in mud, dark sweat circles under the arms of her running top, which was also streaked with more mud and dirt.

Harriet looked at her with an expression of intense dislike. 'Look what the cat dragged in,' might well have been floating above her head in a think bubble.

Hanlon dropped the Land Rover keys on her desk. They landed with a loud clatter. Harriet looked at the keys, then at Hanlon. Her expression changed from supercilious dislike to one of alarm. She obviously recognised them for what they were.

'Big Jim's car keys,' Hanlon said curtly.

'Where did you find them?' asked Harriet. She stared in dread at the keys attached to a greasy leather fob as if they were some exhibit in a crime reconstruction.

'In the ignition,' said Hanlon. 'I took them. He shouldn't be driving.'

Harriet sighed. 'Please take a seat.'

Hanlon did so, in one of those Regency striped upholstered chairs that seem ubiquitous in hotel reception offices.

'How drunk was he?' Harriet asked. Her face looked drawn and tired. She rested her head in her hands.

Hanlon looked more closely at the manageress. She seemed suddenly much older, careworn. Her short dark hair had streaks of grey in it and Hanlon could see the bags under her eyes. Running the Mackinnon Arms was not an easy gig, single-handed. Tidying up after Big Jim. And now, yet another disaster on her hands, by the looks of things.

'Very,' she said. 'I left him with the Land Rover up the road.'

'Did he... did he do anything stupid?' asked Harriet. By that,

Hanlon guessed that she didn't mean drink-driving. She guessed it was a euphemism for either assault or sexual assault or possibly both.

'He tried to hit me. I defended myself,' she added, getting her side of the story in.

'Look,' Harriet said. There was an air of heavy desperation hanging over her. 'I'm really sorry... He's not a bad man... He's been under a lot of stress. Please don't judge him too unkindly.'

Hanlon looked at her. 'I don't care if he drinks himself to death by Sunday, he's a menace to other road users.'

'It's very unusual for him to drink and drive,' Harriet said.

Inwardly Hanlon snorted. She doubted if Big Jim had drawn a sober breath for years.

'He had to leave the rigs because of health issues – that's when the trouble started. He was a highly respected diver, but when he lost his licence, well, part of him died. He put his money into this place, but the season is so short.' She looked pleadingly at Hanlon. 'He's done everything possible. We have tried marketing the place as a diving attraction. That didn't work.'

No, thought Hanlon, I saw Big Jim busy screwing that up with those divers leaving early.

'We tried getting shooting and fishing parties in. That didn't work. Now we are trying the gourmet food approach, and that's not working.'

Hanlon looked at her, hard-faced. You haven't mentioned sex parties or coke smuggling on your list, she thought.

Tears filled Harriet's eyes.

'I'm sorry,' she said. 'It's all been a bit much, Eva dying, Jim cracking up... then that poor girl the other day... I don't know how much longer I can go on...'

Hanlon thought to herself, You must be in a bad way if you're so open with me, but then she reflected, maybe it wasn't so surprising, Hanlon not only knew what she was going through but she was also a stranger; it's often easier to unburden oneself onto someone they respect but don't really know. All the more so as, after she left, Harriet would never see her again.

And now your head chef is planning to pull the rug out from under your feet, thought Hanlon. Presumably there were bookings for the summer months predicated on Donald's Michelin-star-level cooking skills. Without those – and how could they ever replace him at such short notice? – disaster loomed.

She looked at Harriet's pleading face. She doubtless thought that Hanlon might well be able to get Big Jim arrested for drink-driving. Or trying to assault a police officer.

'Just keep him under control,' Hanlon said.

Harriet nodded her head sadly. 'I've tried but he's getting worse. I don't think he even knows what he's doing these days, and he can be violent.' She took a tissue from a box and blew her nose vigorously. 'I'm sorry, I'm actually frightened. I think he's going to hurt someone or himself.'

'That's evident. Where was he going anyway?' she asked, suddenly curious. 'That road doesn't lead anywhere, does it?'

'Oh, God only knows where he was headed for,' Harriet said impatiently, 'and you're right, the road only goes to the end of the island. I know it doesn't alter how bad his behaviour was, but he was unlikely to meet any traffic.'

'Well,' Hanlon said, 'if I were you, I'd leave him.'

At least I'm not being thrown out, she thought. That would disturb my plans.

Harriet shook her head. 'He's a good man, it's just that he's got a problem.'

'Well,' Hanlon said, standing up, 'if he gets in my way again, he'll have another problem, a massive one.'

She walked up the stairs to her room.

# 16

Hanlon had showered and changed her clothes; now she lay on her bed checking her e-mails on her phone.

Nothing concerning the investigation against her.

Well, no news was maybe good news. Various possible scenarios, all unpleasant, all too sadly realistic, bobbed around in her consciousness. To take her mind off things she ran through the morning's events.

Kai and Murdo: the delivery was on for the following week. Three kilos of cocaine. Maybe a hundred and fifty thousand pounds' worth. If it was pure it would then be cut, so maybe double that amount. And Kai was going to meet up with Murdo on the Thursday to discuss it. Kai, with his Glasgow/Paisley contacts, probably money laundered through The Sleeket Mouse. She could probably, as the manageress, put a couple of grand a night through the till as non-existent sales of high-end wine and champagne. At say two hundred pounds a bottle, that would just be ten bottles on a fifty-cover night. It wouldn't raise anyone's eyebrows. Or fifty-pound glasses of whisky or cognac. Easy. Then invoices for non-existent sales of goods, black truffles, turbot, hand-dived scallops – it was probably easy to get quite a lot of money shifted that way.

Then there was the issue of Big Jim. Had he killed the German girl, Franca Gebauer? Hanlon still thought of her as Nose-stud. An attempt to have sex with her, Franca refusing, Big Jim lashing out as he had done at Hanlon. In the morning he might not have remembered. Or possibly Harriet had covered up for him as she had his drink-driving, the power behind the throne.

She found Harriet an oddly compelling character. She was obviously both competent and intelligent, so why was she in this backwater? Donald had every reason to be here, a rest from the stresses of working in London kitchens and his own plans to get a place of his own, but what was her reason?

Most of the criminals that she had met in her career hadn't been particularly evil. But there were exceptions. Was she one of these? Hanlon could easily see Harriet as a Lady Macbeth figure, directing Big Jim's actions. She was probably the one who had organised the sex parties. She had probably filmed Kai and Eva's porn film. It was hard to imagine Big Jim doing it. And if things went wrong, it would be Big Jim who would carry the can. And Harriet would be managing the finances; he'd sign anything she gave him, in all probability.

Where had he been going when Hanlon had met him on the road? The thought of Harriet as Lady Macbeth had triggered the image of the three witches: 'when shall we three meet again?' She wondered if it was to discuss something with Murdo and Kai. Would Big Jim be there on Thursday?

Well, she'd be there in one form or another, that was for sure.

After lunch, Hanlon wandered around the back of the hotel to look for Donald.

He was sitting outside the kitchen on an upturned plastic mixer-crate drinking a pint of lager.

'Hi, pull up a crate,' he said, nodding at a stack of them. Although she'd been at his cottage before, she had never really looked at Donald properly. She'd been more concerned with pumping him for information. Now, in the cold light of day, she did so, sitting down and studying him with interest. He was in his early thirties, tall, powerfully built but carrying a fair amount of surplus weight around his middle. He had a slightly jowly face – if he didn't do something soon about his weight he'd be in trouble in later years. His eyes were very bright, shrewd.

'Hang on,' he said to her. 'Oi, Kai!'

The bar manager came out of the kitchen with a plate of food in his hand. He nodded politely at Hanlon, his mouth obviously full. Hanlon studied him carefully too. He was looking tired and drawn today, distracted. As well he might, Hanlon thought. After that exhausting walk earlier in the day. She wondered if he had met Big Jim on the way home.

He swallowed down whatever he had been eating.

'I heard about your run-in with Big Jim,' he said. He smiled. 'That man is guy raj.'

'I'm sorry?' said Hanlon.

'Raj means crazy,' explained Donald. 'He is a fucking arse-hole. Now, Kai, make yourself useful and go and get my friend here a drink...'

'Sure.' He looked at Hanlon. 'What would you like?'

'She'll have a Beck's,' said Donald, decisively.

'I'll have a Beck's,' Hanlon agreed. It seemed simpler than saying no.

Kai disappeared back into the kitchen.

'So how did your conversation with the Harts go?'

Donald grinned wolfishly.

'It went very well. I've got my backing confirmed. I think the Hart brothers like the idea of owning a place here. I think poor auld Big Jim is toast. Kai's told me that there's been a slew of cancellations after that girl died. People might have accepted one death in a hotel, but two? It's like the place is cursed.'

'And that won't affect you?'

'Och no. We'll close for a refurb. The Harts have committed to doing the place properly. Redo the rooms and kitchen. We'll reopen in the autumn and get everything bedded in for the new year. It'll be fine.'

Hanlon nodded. It was hardly a surprise that Big Jim had run the place into the ground.

'Could I borrow your kayak tomorrow morning?' she asked. She wanted to go out and have a look at the Corryvreckan, keeping a safe distance. The idea of asking Big Jim to take her in the hotel boat had long ago lost its appeal.

'Aye, sure. It's all in guid order. Come round about half nine and I'll help you carry it down to the shore. It's not heavy, but it's awkward.'

Kai returned with the Beck's.

'Thank you, Kai,' she said.

'Nae bother.' He grinned conspiratorially at her. 'Donald been filling youse in on his plans for the future?'

She nodded.

'Aye, weel, I'll be staying on.'

'Only if you play your cards right, Kai,' said Donald.

'I always play my cards right, as well you know, Donald,' he said, then, nodding to them, 'I'd best get back to the bar. Thanks fae the lunch.'

He disappeared back inside. Hanlon drank her Beck's.

'Why are you hiring him?'

'Och, he's OK. He's a known quantity. He can work the bar,' Donald said dismissively. 'He's too chavvy for the restaurant.'

'So it's all working out well for you, then?'

'Yes,' Donald said thoughtfully, 'It's all going to plan.'

\* \* \*

That evening McCleod picked Hanlon up from the car park at half six for the exercise class and they were at the village hall near Craighouse about ten minutes later. McCleod parked the Volvo and Wemyss moved around impatiently in the back, prowling around in the restricted space, anxious to be let out. Hanlon guessed it was separation anxiety. The dog wasn't the only one feeling worried. She had come to the conclusion that she would have to tell McCleod about what had been happening. All of it. Her run-in with Franca, the party at the hotel, Campbell's involvement, what she knew about Kai, the whole nine yards. She suspected that McCleod was going to explode, she probably would if the positions were reversed, but she had to go to the police with what she knew, and McCleod was certainly that.

'No, you'll have to stay,' McCleod said sternly. Wemyss looked at her sadly and lay down disconsolately on his towel.

Hanlon looked at the loving tenderness on McCleod's face as she stroked her dog's head. I'll tell her later, she thought, after the class.

Inside the hall there were about a dozen people standing in a row behind grey rubber exercise mats. The class instructor – McCleod had mentioned he was ex-army and he looked it, very short hair, mid-thirties, ripped and covered in tattoos – greeted them and handed them their mats.

Hanlon was standing next to McCleod and a bald, overweight

man wearing ill-advised Lycra. The instructor spoke, issuing instructions.

Hanlon glanced over at the other people in the class, who were all in the twenty-to-forty age range, except the bald guy. Apart from him and the instructor, they were all women.

McCleod took off her tracksuit top. Hanlon's eyes widened. McCleod had a superb body. Her face might have looked thin, almost sunken (at times Hanlon thought that if she let her hair get greasy the DS would look rather like someone in a poster warning against heroin abuse). But in tight Lycra, black pedal pushers and a white top, her hair tied back in a ponytail, McCleod was not only formidably fit-looking but sexy. Voluptuously so.

It was like in a cheesy film when the gawky, unattractive girl removes her glasses/braces/unflattering hat and ('My God... you're beautiful...') is revealed as stunningly lovely.

Hanlon laughed. McCleod looked at her, puzzled.

'What's so funny?'

'Nothing really...' She certainly wasn't going to share that thought with the detective sergeant.

The instructor put the music on, heavy house and trance, which thundered through the small hall as they warmed up to the beat, star jumps, knee-to-opposite-elbow bounces, before a countdown to the exercises.

Hanlon had been doing this kind of thing more or less daily for twenty-five years. She loved the sensation of pushing her muscles until they shrieked in pain and she was a formidable triathlete as well as a boxer at an almost professional level.

She confidently expected to be by far the most capable in the room. It was not, of course, a competition. But Hanlon, innately driven, couldn't help but make it so.

McCleod, a decade younger than Hanlon, was keeping up

with her. Hanlon was impressed. Impressed and annoyed. The other woman hadn't got Hanlon's upper-body strength; she was far better than her at push-ups, dumb-bell shoulder raises and triceps dips, but even at these, the detective did well. She saw McCleod glance at her sharply defined triceps with rueful envy.

On and on it went, punishing, muscle-searing effort and pain. The two of them led the field and, to Hanlon's fury, the younger woman kept pace with her. The last set of exercises was timed against the clock. Hanlon dug deep and managed to finish about thirty seconds before McCleod.

'My, you're awfie fit,' McCleod gasped. They looked at each other, McCleod leaning forward, hands on her knees, clothes glued to her body with sweat, and grinned.

'I walk to the shops regularly,' Hanlon said. Her hair hung like dank rats' tails, the veins stood out in her toned biceps, her body radiating heat.

'You look great,' said McCleod. They were innocuous words but when their eyes met it was as if a tacit agreement had been reached.

'Thanks,' said Hanlon and smiled.

* * *

After the class, the two of them climbed into McCleod's Volvo. Wemyss leapt around excitedly in the back.

'He really does like you,' McCleod said. Hanlon made a non-committal noise. Although she was not a dog person, not an animal person, Wemyss was beginning to grow on her. Perhaps it was his obvious delight at her company, not something that too many others felt.

McCleod pulled up near the hotel.

'Well, thank you for tonight,' Hanlon said. The inside of the car smelled of their sweat and McCleod's residual perfume.

McCleod's eyes met hers.

'Thank you, you were fantastic.'

Hanlon smiled. 'I've got—'

McCleod spoke at the same time. 'Would you like a drink?'

Hanlon had been going to say, finishing her sentence, '— something I need to tell you.' The prelude to her confession. A drink sounded a much better idea and she gave in to temptation. McCleod was smiling at her encouragingly. Hanlon hooked a finger in the sodden, sweat-stained neck of her top.

'I think I'm a bit smelly for the bar.'

'I meant at my place.' McCleod's voice was low, serious. There was no mistaking the meaning in the words.

'Now?' Hanlon half turned towards her in her seat. The air in the car seemed suddenly charged with electricity and possibility. Hanlon felt slightly faint, light-headed. She hadn't been expecting anything like this, but she thought of McCleod's Lycra-clad body, she thought of her fist thudding into Big Jim's body... she thought...

McCleod put her hand over Hanlon's. It was very warm. Hanlon opened her fingers slowly and turned her wrist, so their fingers interlocked.

'Now,' McCleod said. Their eyes met. McCleod stared into Hanlon's very grey eyes. Inscrutable. She inclined her head towards Hanlon's.

Their mouths met.

'Yes...' breathed Hanlon.

## 17

Hanlon and McCleod lay side by side in the DS's large, comfortable bed.

'What are you thinking?' asked McCleod, rolling onto her stomach and looking at Hanlon's imperious face, slightly sinister in the shadows. She ran a finger gently over Hanlon's high cheekbones. Hanlon had a fantastic face, she thought, as changeable as the light on the loch – tender, passionate, angry, right now beautiful, but slightly frightening.

'I've got something to tell you,' Hanlon said.

'That sounds ominous,' said McCleod. 'Will I need a drink?'

'Quite possibly.' Hanlon put her hands behind her head and watched as a naked McCleod swung her legs out of bed, walked across the bedroom, through the open door into the kitchen and Hanlon heard the fridge door open and close. McCleod came back with two glasses of white wine. She saw Hanlon looking at her and she exaggerated her walk, swaying her hips before bending down and kissing Hanlon slowly, voluptuously.

She got back into bed. Hanlon took a sip of her wine and told McCleod about the attempt to drug her, the sex party at the hotel.

Then she moved on to her seeing Kai with Franca and the conversation with Harriet.

'So, drugging a hotel guest, use of premises for undeclared monetary gain involving sexual activity, supplying drugs... anything else?' said McCleod sarcastically.

'Yeah,' said Hanlon, 'I'm afraid so.'

'Oh, God, there's more,' groaned McCleod.

'I'd had a run-in with Franca earlier that evening. It was in the ladies' bathroom...'

'Well, thank God you didn't hit her,' McCleod said, once Hanlon had finished.

Hanlon sat up. She rather wished she hadn't. Sitting up gave her a better view of McCleod's bedroom. It was not an attractive sight. The room was as untidy as her car. Clothes lay strewn around; you could barely see the floor. She drank some wine. The place needed Marie Kondo. Earlier, on their way to bed, there had been a nasty crunching sound as Hanlon had trodden on a laptop that had been concealed by a denim jacket. The only touch of order in the room was Hanlon's gym wear, which she had neatly folded when she'd got out of bed earlier.

The curtains were drawn but, although it was half past nine, it was still light outside. Hanlon could see the alarm and concern clearly expressed on McCleod's face. Remorselessly she ploughed on. It felt so good to be able to pour out these secrets that she had been concealing to someone who would be able to do something constructive with the information.

The discovery that Campbell's car had been there at the party that night. The trip to Paisley, the fact that the woman who co-owned the restaurant in Glasgow that Kai had come from was Murdo Campbell's sister. Ishbel's purchase of The Sleeket Mouse with an unexplained windfall, Kai's history of drug dealing and violence to women.

McCleod tried to remain unimpressed.

'None of us are our brother's keeper. Murdo doesn't control Ishbel's finances, and so what if Murdo had been involved in some swingers' party at the hotel? It shows a terrible lack of taste, poor judgement, but look at us, we're in bed together...'

'That's not poor judgement is it?' asked Hanlon, leaning her head down. Their mouths met again hungrily, and she ran her hands over McCleod's amazingly curved, soft body, feeling her respond to her touch.

* * *

When they were finished, McCleod was lying in the crook of her arm. Hanlon felt warm, drowsy and content. She stroked the other woman's long, fine hair and stared up at the ceiling, one of the few places that wasn't untidy. It felt wonderful to be sharing a bed with someone. She brought her mind back to duty and resumed where she had left off earlier.

'Big Jim is involved, even if innocently, in the deaths of two women. What was the post-mortem report on Franca, by the way?'

'Death by drowning... she had enough cocaine in her to fell a horse as well. It's not entirely surprising she fell off the jetty.'

'So that's going down as an accident too?'

'Yes,' McCleod said.

Hmm, thought Hanlon acidly. Funny that. I wonder why Murdo Campbell wants to close down any investigation that might involve the Mackinnon Arms. As if I didn't know.

'Anyway. Back to Murdo. Kai has a connection in the police—'

'According to a Paisley publican!' McCleod's voice was scornful. 'Murdo is a pain in the arse, but I cannot believe he's on the take. You're havering!'

Hanlon noticed that McCleod's accent got stronger when she was cross. She delivered the last nail in the coffin as far as Campbell's innocence went. The events of earlier that day up in the hills.

'And today, I saw Murdo meet with Kai...'

She explained how she had followed the bar manager to the croft, the conversation that she had overheard.

McCleod's face grew more and more sombre. She could ignore Manny's claims about a policeman on the take, she could ignore a sex party, but this couldn't be explained away.

'Jesus,' muttered McCleod, 'it looks like you might be right... I would never have believed it of Murdo, never... He's so clean-cut.'

'Clean-cut!' Hanlon said. 'He hangs out at Big Jim's sex parties!'

'It just goes to show how little you know people,' McCleod said sorrowfully. Hanlon shrugged.

'I never liked him,' she said.

'I did,' countered McCleod. 'And I knew him,' then she softly added, 'or thought I did. I just can't imagine him at a sex party...'

'Anyway, this next meeting prior to the drugs delivery. The meeting is on Thursday – hopefully they'll discuss where and how. The delivery, which is Friday, is your chance to make arrests. I know it'll be tricky going behind his back...'

'Tricky? It'll be a nightmare... Can you imagine that conversation with the Assistant Chief Constable?' She shook her head.

'Could you not hide a recording device in the bothy?' Hanlon said. 'He's meeting Kai there on Thursday, we know that. Then we would know for sure what was happening.'

'No, I could not,' said McCleod, 'you should know that, not on this evidence, which is all pretty circumstantial.' She sat up in bed and took a large mouthful of wine. 'And if you think I'm going to my superiors with this... It's career suicide. They won't just want to shoot the messenger, they'll want to fucking eviscerate me. I'll be posted to Tiree.'

'What if,' Hanlon said slowly, 'what if *I* recorded their conversation? Three kilos of cocaine are coming ashore on Jura soon, Catriona, three kilos. Three thousand grams at, say, fifty to seventy pounds a gram, maybe double that if the coke is pure and it can be heavily cut. It's not a little coke deal in a back alley.'

'Go on,' McCleod said thoughtfully.

'Well,' said Hanlon, 'I'll place the recording device, pick it up in the evening, and tell you the gist of it. Then you can go to your superiors, a tip-off from a reliable informant, you'll think of something... and organise a bust, bypassing Murdo.'

'Well...' McCleod said thoughtfully, 'It can't do any harm. It doesn't leave much time...'

Hanlon was getting annoyed. 'Jesus, you can't have everything. Besides, it won't require much in the way of resources; maybe a boat, maybe a helicopter.'

McCleod nodded. 'Well, we'll see.'

Hanlon continued, 'Kai will talk if you lean on him. His lawyer will advise he cooperate. Murdo doesn't strike me as a frightening man. Kai won't be shit scared of consequences if he rats him out, I'm sure, in return for reduced charges.'

'What if they don't go into details at the meeting?' McCleod said.

Hanlon was beginning to get annoyed by all these objections, McCleod's pessimism.

'They're meeting specifically *to* discuss details. They don't want to risk phones or e-mails. Good old-fashioned, untraceable, deniable conversations. They're not going up into the hills for a picnic.' She looked into McCleod's narrow brown eyes. 'And OK, let's say they say nothing of any use, they talk about the weather, or fishing, or sex, or football, well, we're none the worse off, are we? You'll just have to keep an eye on your corrupt boss until he gives you another chance. Or Kai attacks another woman.'

'OK, OK.' McCleod said, 'We'll do it your way. But I still find it hard to believe that Murdo Campbell is on the take. Although, from what you say, it is beginning to look that way.'

'What other explanation can you give, then?' She drank some more wine.

'Good point. So, what do you think exactly has been happening?'

Hanlon ignored the question. Instead, she asked, 'Can you find out who the arresting officer for Kai's Paisley busts were?'

'Surely,' McCleod said.

She got her laptop from where it lay on the floor under the denim jacket and some socks, the one Hanlon had stepped on earlier, and switched it on. Fortunately, it was still working.

'I'll e-mail a friend of mine in Paisley Area Command. He can find out.'

'Anyway,' Hanlon said while McCleod's fingers ran over the keyboard, 'here's what I think happened. I think that Kai was dealing coke in Paisley and got chased out by Tam and his crew. Kai was badly injured in a fight, ostensibly over a girl, but I don't think that Kai and Tam are that romantic. I think it was a turf war. It was then I think he crossed the Clyde. Round about this time, this is speculation, Campbell started protecting him and began laundering Kai's coke profits, in return for a reasonable percentage, via his sister, into The Sleeket Mouse.'

'OK, but why did Kai ask for a job there? What was the point?'

'So he'd make a plausible bar manager at the Mackinnon Arms,' Hanlon said. 'I think that the cocaine shipments centre around the hotel and I think Big Jim is up to his miserable, pissed neck in it, probably backed up by Harriet. He's desperate to save his hotel. He's got a boat. I would imagine he meets someone out at sea, takes the coke off them so they don't need to worry about customs searches or any shit from Border Force or HMRC. The boat would then be clean. It could use any UK harbour with impunity.'

She paused. 'Now, whether Big Jim knows that Kai works with Murdo Campbell or if Murdo just wants an insider keeping track of things, I don't know. I'm hoping to find that out on Thursday.'

'And Eva? Where does her death fit into this? And Franca, come to that?'

'I've heard that Eva was a nuisance, a pain in the arse,' Hanlon said. 'She was the kind of girl who always had an eye on the main chance. Donald, the head chef, told me she was going to sue Big Jim for sexual harassment, one reason to get rid of her, but she was sly, she could have got wind of the drug smuggling. It would be hard to keep secrets in a place as small as the Mackinnon Arms. I think she was blackmailing someone. I also think once we have Kai and Big Jim in custody, we will find out who did kill her. Someone will talk. Neither of those two looks like the strong, silent type to me. They'll almost certainly want to finger the other one.'

McCleod glanced down at her laptop. Wemyss was the screensaver photo. Inevitably.

'Hang on, Alasdair's messaged me.' She looked up at Hanlon. 'Murdo Campbell was the arresting officer on Kai McPherson's last drug bust... yeah, McPherson was R.U.I'd, not charged.'

'There you go,' Hanlon said triumphantly. Officially, McPherson was still being investigated, with Campbell in charge.

'I'll get you that voice-activated recorder,' McCleod said. 'I'm working out of Campbeltown tomorrow. I'll get one there.'

'Thank you,' Hanlon said.

'Do you want to go back to the hotel or stay somewhere else?' McCleod asked. 'Do you think that place is too dangerous? Big

Jim has obviously got it in for you. There's already two dead women, I don't want a third.'

'I don't want to alarm anyone,' Hanlon said. 'They already know I'm a police officer. I'd better go back.'

She sat up and faced McCleod, wrapped her legs around her waist; she leaned forward and their mouths met.

'But not just yet,' whispered Hanlon.

## 18

The following morning, as arranged, Hanlon was round at Donald's house at nine thirty. It took a while of banging on the door to raise any signs of life. Donald, wearing a blue dressing gown, unshaven, smelling strongly of stale alcohol, looked bleary and hungover, but he brightened up when he saw Hanlon.

'Hi, how are you today?' she asked.

Donald grinned. 'A wee bit hungover. I gave my notice in to Big Jim last night. He did not take it very well.' He laughed heartily. The thought of Big Jim miserable obviously cheered him up considerably.

'What are you going to do?' asked Hanlon. Donald's departure would be ruinous for the hotel, even a really drunk Big Jim would be able to work that one out. She wondered how long Harriet would stay on. The writing was well and truly on the wall now.

'I gave him a month's notice, which is very generous of me. I could just walk. So I'm here in this place until then, then I'll probably stay at my brother's – he's got a place near the ferry. I'll just wait for the Mackinnon Arms to come on the market and then buy it. I've got the money lined up both from the bank and from the Harts. They're certainly good for it. I'll be in by Christmas.'

'What did Big Jim say?'

Donald laughed. 'It's unrepeatable. He went raj. He'll be spending today getting absolutely pished, weeping into his drink. I'd avoid him if I were you. Probably blame you.' He paused, looked at her. 'You know, he really hates you. I'd be careful. He's gone really fucking weird these days.'

'I always avoid him,' Hanlon said.

'Aye well... look, if he gets too much, you can always stay here. There's a spare room.' Hanlon looked at him with open suspicion. Donald put his hands up in mock surrender. 'I won't hassle you, promise, but, just for the record, if you're feeling horny... my door's always open.'

'Just for the record, Donald,' Hanlon said judiciously, 'you're not my type. Now you can get some clothes on and give me a hand with that kayak.'

\* \* \*

It had been a while since she had been in a kayak but she was relieved to find she hadn't forgotten how they worked. The knowledge and the motor skills quickly returned.

An hour and a half later, Hanlon was nearing a line of small orange buoys that marked the position of some lobster pots. She suddenly remembered Kai's remark to Harriet that she had overheard when she'd been hiding in the dry store.

*'It's not just the sex parties. I know what you and Jim are up to with those boys.'*

It suddenly came to her with the force of a revelation. It was obvious now. It hadn't been '*boys*' he'd meant, but '*buoys*'.

Was she looking at where the coke would be dropped off the following week? You could package the drugs in watertight containers and just attach them at night to the cables of the pots, below the waterline. Then Big Jim could collect them at his leisure.

Manny's voice in her memory: *'I heard too that he was paying the police off tae look the other way.'*

Murdo Campbell making sure that they stayed one step ahead of the drug squad. Their get-out-of-jail-free card.

She moved the long, slim craft through the water with ease, taking long, slow strokes with her double-ended paddle, not losing momentum so the muscle usage on her arms was kept to the minimum, steering the kayak with firm but gentle pressure from her legs on the foot rests.

She found her heart lifting with pleasure. She was feeling happy. It wasn't something that happened a great deal. It wasn't that she was temperamentally depressed or bowed down by the weight of the world, she just rarely experienced joy. It didn't worry her; it was one of those things. But right now, she was enjoying the kayak tremendously. She suddenly realised for the second time that she loved being out here in the wilds, that she had had more than enough of London. Here with rock, water, sea and air, she could be content. I've had enough of people, she thought. I need places like this.

There was a disturbance in the water. At first she thought it was a rock, some underwater outcrop that the sea was breaking on, but then a sleek grey head, round as a football, appeared, a seal, curious as to what was happening. She looked at its whiskers and eyes, whose doggy look recalled Wemyss. The seal stared at her, then gracefully dived; she watched its streamlined body power under her boat.

You don't get that in Hampstead Bathing Ponds, she thought.

She recalled her night with McCleod. It had not only been highly enjoyable, it had made her realise how lonely she had been. To doze off and wake up next to another human being was something very pleasurable that she hadn't experienced for a long time.

Then part of her mind whispered, 'Don't get too close, don't invest too much, it'll end in grief.' Shut up, she told her mind. Am I not entitled to some happiness?

Now she could sense the current starting to tug at the kayak. She could feel the powerful muscles in her shoulders work as she moved parallel to the current. She felt a momentary twinge of unease at the fact she'd come out without a buoyancy aid. Donald had offered her his life jacket. But he weighed about eighteen stone. Fat bastard, she thought, and smiled again. Donald: sleazy, avaricious, eye perpetually on the main chance, was strangely endearing. His life jacket was far too big for Hanlon, so she'd left it behind. She was beginning to feel maybe she had been over-confident, always one of her weaknesses. Now she was starting to regret it.

You don't mess around with the sea. Eva had found that out, so had Franca. She didn't want to end up like them, fished out of the cold, fatal embrace of the Atlantic. I'd better not get too close to the whirlpool, she thought.

She could feel a breeze starting, scudding across the surface of the loch and agitating the water. She put the skeg, the dagger-board for the kayak, down, to give her greater control. The sleeve of her cagoule caught in the loch and cold water splashed down over her as her arm came up to paddle. It was a reminder, had she needed it, of how chilly the seawater was. In the kayak, the plastic apron taut over the cockpit, she was warm and dry. Let's keep it that way, she thought to herself.

Now she could see the three buoys that marked the hotel

lobster pots more clearly. Donald had told her they would help as a marker, as a pointer, in the direction of where the Corryvreckan was. Seemingly there was an undersea shelf around here before the bottom of the sea abruptly plunged to two hundred metres or so underneath the surface of the whirlpool. The thought of the vertiginous drop beneath her was dizzying, unsettling. So much water!

She paddled alongside the nearest bright orange buoy and held onto its mooring rope with one hand as she rested, stationary on the sea. On the horizon she could see a large yacht, its white sail taut. It reminded her of the smuggled cocaine that Kai and Murdo had been discussing. She had hazarded a guess at either yachts crossing the Atlantic from the Caribbean or drugs imported into the Republic of Ireland, shipped north and then a quick hop across the sea to Jura. Drop the drugs off at the buoys. You could then transfer them to a local boat, a boat like Big Jim's. The smuggler's craft could sail on with no cargo aboard, as clean as a whistle. HMRC alerted by harbourmasters, kept a keen eye on yachts sailing in from abroad. It would be a neat way to go about things.

It was then that she heard the engine.

She turned her head and saw the blunt bow of a small boat heading towards her. Her eyes picked out the JA letters visible on the white fibreglass hull, a local boat from Jura. She let go of the buoy and paddled away from it.

The sound of the engine grew nearer, ominous, throbbing. She could smell its fumes on the breeze, noticeable in the pure sea air.

She looked around and her heart sank. Big Jim standing by the side of the boat and Harriet at the wheel.

She remembered Donald's words.

*'He went raj. He'll be spending today getting absolutely pished... I'd avoid him if I were you.'*

Big Jim had been aggressive enough when all she had done was relieve him of his car keys. He had an ugly temper, fuelled by alcohol. God alone knew what he would be like now that his head chef had left him in what would be the middle of the season. He'd probably blame her for it – she doubted if logic was his strong point. There was certainly no avoiding him now, that was for sure. She couldn't outrun them, not in the kayak. Her only hope was that Harriet would manage to calm him down, or that he wouldn't want to do anything in front of a witness.

She wheeled the boat around with her paddle and faced them. Big Jim, standing on the bow like some kind of terrible figurehead, had a boat hook in his hand, the metal tip dull grey, mirroring the colour of the sea. It looked ominously like a harpoon. Harriet brought the boat close. Shit, thought Hanlon, she's helping the bastard.

She felt a surge of rage against Harriet. To think she'd been on the verge of actually feeling sorry for her. Maybe she was complicit in the drugs-collection business, assuming Hanlon's theory was correct.

Things were looking black for her.

And sure enough, now Big Jim leaned forward and caught the grab loop on the top of the kayak with the tip of the boat hook. She was like a fish on the end of a line.

Hanlon was broadside to the sea now and the choppy water started to splash over the waterproof apron that sealed her in the cockpit of the kayak.

'What do you think you're doing?' she shouted. 'Let go!'

'You think you're so clever, don't you, you bitch!' shouted Big Jim, leaning over the coaming of the boat. His maddened eyes glared at her. He gave the kayak a vicious tug with the hook. It rocked alarmingly and a wave broke over the cockpit rim.

She said nothing but stared at him grimly.

'I know what you've been up to!' His unshaven chin was flecked with spittle. He reached inside his jacket and brought out a half-bottle of Scotch. It was a third full. He put it to his lips and drained it, then flung the bottle at Hanlon. Drunk he might have been, but his aim was surprisingly good. If she hadn't ducked it would have hit her head. It splashed into the sea not far from the kayak.

'Bitch!' His eyes were practically popping out of their sockets. 'You made Donald leave...'

Oh, God, thought Hanlon. The chef had been right. He really had gone crazy. How on earth had he come to that conclusion? She guessed that he had grown to hate her so much that her evil influence knew no limits. Anything bad would be her fault.

'Leave her alone, Jim,' Harriet shouted. Even Harriet, it seemed, thought he was going too far.

'Shut up, woman,' snarled Big Jim. He reached down to pick something off the deck. Hanlon braced herself for another missile to come flying at her head. But when he straightened up it was far worse than she could have imagined.

He had a shotgun in his hand. She stared in disbelief and alarm. Anything could happen; he was furious, drunk, out of control and he hated her.

'Put that down, Jim!' ordered Harriet.

Hanlon was seriously frightened now. Two or three times in her career she had seen the result of a close-quarters shotgun discharge on a body. It was horrific. There was nothing she could do. The kayak was attached to the boat hook, as if he'd gaffed some kind of huge fish, and that was held by Big Jim's powerful meaty hand.

You've got to escape, she thought, but how? The boat was immobile, and she was trapped.

Big Jim ignored Harriet. The front of the kayak its prow, was now secured to the end of the pole that he held. At one end, in the sea, the kayak, at the other, on board the boat, Big Jim. He leant forward and, using his huge strength and the weight of his heavy bulk, pushed the bow of the kayak down into the water with the boat hook. It was perilously close to capsizing and she steadied it with the paddle.

The other hand held the gun, its twin barrels pointing ominously at Hanlon. He was only a couple of metres away; she could see his eyes, glassy and unfocussed. He doesn't know where he is or what he's doing, she thought to herself. That gun could easily go off by accident.

'Jim!' Harriet shouted again, real panic in her voice. She was Hanlon's only chance. At least, she thought, Harriet was trying to stop him from shooting her.

This time he jerked his head as if being woken from a sleep. He stared at Hanlon, then at the gun in his hand as if he was wondering how it had got there.

Harriet was looking out to starboard. 'There's a boat coming, Jim, put the gun down! Do it now!'

Hanlon could see it too, a large fishing boat of traditional design, graceful and lean with its raked lines designed to cut through the Atlantic waves. She could see its wheelhouse clearly and the superstructure of antennae and radar. She felt hope rise in her heart. Another five minutes and it would be here, and she'd be safe.

To Hanlon's unspoken and huge relief, Big Jim laid the gun down at his feet. She exhaled and breathed in deeply; she'd been holding her breath, she realised, tensing her body, convinced he was going to blow her to pieces. Thank God, thank God, she thought. She wasn't religious but she offered up a prayer of thanks to an unknown deity.

Then Big Jim turned his attention back to Hanlon.

Their eyes locked and she could see the implacable hatred and fixity of purpose in his baleful gaze. There was no mercy there. Any doubts about his guilt in the death of Eva disappeared. They were the eyes of a killer.

'Swim, bitch!' he spat at her.

She was now more than ever convinced this was how Eva had died, drowned out here at the hands of Big Jim. Maybe taken out here on this boat, lured by some pretext.

'Jim!' said Harriet angrily. Big Jim leant forward with all his weight and the bow of the boat sank beneath the water as he twisted on the grab loop using the boat hook with inexorable pressure.

Hanlon felt the kayak moving until the momentum became unstoppable and then with a lurch it tipped sideways. As he kept pushing downwards, it rolled over and capsized. She had let go of the paddle and she breathed in deeply before the kayak went fully over.

The cold of the water hit her with an almost physical force. She was trapped under the boat. She only had seconds. She frantically tore the plastic apron away, pulling her feet out of the hull, and she forced herself out of the cockpit. Her sodden clothes felt like lead weights. She opened her eyes, the salt water stinging them, above her the upside body of the kayak, beneath her the darkness, hundreds of metres of water shading to black, the gleaming white of the hull of the boat almost within touching distance.

As she pulled herself free of the kayak, she could feel vibrations in the plastic of the hull, powerful shock waves. Her head broke upwards from the water and now she could see Big Jim leaning out from the motorboat and driving the reinforced steel point of the boat hook into the upturned kayak like a man harpooning a whale. It was floating upside down and he attacked it frenziedly, punching holes into its hull.

She could see several jagged tears in the fibreglass of the body of the kayak. It probably wouldn't sink, but equally it would be useless as a floatation device, she wouldn't be able to cling onto it and, of course, it was unusable as a boat.

For a second she thought that Big Jim might turn the boat hook on her or simply drive the boat over her, shredding her body with the propeller. The kayak banged against the hull of the craft; Big Jim's face was crimson with drink, effort and rage.

Surely the fishing boat would be here soon? She was too low in the water to see it, or maybe her view was blocked by Big Jim's boat. Hanlon tried to think of some way to scramble up onto Big Jim's boat, take the fight to him and Harriet rather than float helplessly around, a sitting target.

She heard the roar of its engines and Harriet turned the bow away from her in a tight arc and headed westwards towards Jura, away from the fishing boat. Harriet wasn't going to risk being caught red-handed by the trawler with a drunk, uncontrollable Jim armed with a shotgun.

As she watched them go, Hanlon felt a sense of overwhelming relief flood through her. Right now, she didn't mind taking her chances with the sea. At least it was neutral, unlike Big Jim, who she knew was hoping she would go the way of Eva Balodis and drown. As she trod water she wondered about Harriet. Had she left her out here because that was the lesser of two evils – she would have a chance with the sea but not if Big Jim decided to attack her? Or was she complicit, confident she would die a natural death rather than have her chewed-up remains spark an investigation? Let the whirlpool take the blame.

She paused to evaluate her situation. The sea was cold but not that cold, she guessed between ten to fifteen degrees centigrade. It wasn't a problem yet, but it would be. What was, though, was the inexorable force she could feel from the Corryvreckan, tugging at her tired body, pulling her into its deadly, watery grasp.

It would only be a matter of time, when, not if, it won.

## 19

Hanlon breathed deeply, treading water, willing her heart to slow. God knows what her pulse rate was.

She fought down panic. There was a lot to feel thankful for. She was still alive; she hadn't been drowned by Big Jim; he hadn't pulled the trigger and blown her to kingdom come. He hadn't driven the launch toward her, smashing its bow into her body. She hadn't been chewed up by its propellers. She was still alive. She would survive and she would have her revenge.

She could see the fishing boat clearly, but it was too far away from her to attract their attention and she was too low in the water for them to see her. It was moving slowly along, maybe dragging a net; she would never be able to reach it. She turned her attention to the current.

McCleod, what seemed like months ago when she had first met her, had derided the Corryvreckan. The story of the one-legged man swimming it. But it was one thing to choose the time and do it on a calm day with a support vessel and when you were psyched up for it, quite another when you were already tired, unprepared, on your own, stressed out of your mind, in a choppy sea and fully clothed.

The pull from the whirlpool was frighteningly strong and hanging onto the kayak now practically below the sea level as the air pockets inside filled with water, was no longer sensible. She quickly pulled off her shoes and clothing except for underwear, let go of the kayak and started swimming for Jura. She was unsure of the distance, maybe one mile, maybe two. Certainly she should be capable of doing it.

Hanlon was a good swimmer but not exceptional. Of the three disciplines in the triathlon, her sport of choice, it was probably her weakest, except when the weather was bad and the water choppy or rough. She had several competitors who would thrash her if the surface of the water they were in was smooth, but Hanlon's tenacious, dogged personality, her ability to dig deep when troubles arose, gave her the edge when it came to adverse conditions. And she loved wild swimming, she liked to feel weed against her skin, to smell the tang of salt in the sea or taste the faint hint of earth and vegetation in a lake. To see the clouds in the sky or the mini explosions of raindrops strafing the water.

So now, to be in the sea in poor weather was not an exceptional experience. She knew what to do. Her arms and legs engaged in a slow, powerful measured crawl, her breathing regular and controlled, she made slow headway against the water that was trying to pull her out to sea, to lie forever in its cold, wet embrace. Hanlon did what she was good at, refusing to give in, keeping on going.

But it was an exhausting struggle. She was tired, emotionally drained and the sea was cold. The wind was getting up now, whipping the surface into choppy waves; once or twice she had to fight down panic as she swallowed water and coughed and spluttered. At times the task seemed hopeless; she was putting all her effort into swimming, but to no effect. The pull of the whirlpool was strong and remorseless, and unlike her it would never weaken, never tire, never cease.

The mountainous form of Jura was there in sharp clarity, but it seemed to be getting no nearer. There were moments she thought she was actually going backwards, being pulled slowly but surely into the relentless maw of the vortex.

She emptied her mind as she swam. There was no past, no future, only now. To have thought of the distance facing her, to have thought of the current pulling at her body, would have been to give in to fear and that would have been the start of the end. For her it was just the eternal present as the iron muscles of her shoulders and legs working in harmony powered her through the sea.

And slowly, imperceptibly, the pull of the current lessened, and slowly her hope flickered and burned more brightly, and the centimetres became metres and the metres became hundreds of metres and then a kilometre and then more, and Hanlon kept grimly swimming. The bulk of Ben Garrisdale visible in the far distance grew larger and larger. With her shoulders burning and forcing her legs to move, she kept on, occasionally inhaling water but refusing to allow any panic, for there was only the now... and now she could make out the stony summit strewn with grey scree. Blurry details resolved themselves, greenery became trees, shrubs and ferns, and she allowed herself the luxury of certainty. She began to feel bootlace weed against her legs, seaweed had never felt so good, and then the tough brown bladder wrack with its bubbles of air trapped in its leathery leaves between her fingers, and there was the blessed black, boulder-strewn shore.

Hanlon slowly clambered out of the water. She had no clear idea how long she had been swimming; she had lost all sense of time. Her legs were trembling and her arms barely able to move.

She sat, briefly, on a rock, and she leaned forward with her head between her knees, breathing deeply, feeling its cold, barnacled roughness with her fingers, entranced by the sensation. Solid, unyielding rock. She was alive. She was alive! She looked back across the horizon; far away in the distance she could still see the lonely form of the fishing boat ploughing the seas.

She lifted her head. With a flap of wings, a herring gull landed on a rock not far away from her and stared at her balefully. It opened its beak and gave an unmelodious caw. Hanlon returned its unfriendly gaze. She knew just how close she had come to being food for the gulls, her naked washed-up body a mini banquet for the voracious seabirds. The vicious, sharp, strong yellow beak scything down into the soft tissue of her dead grey eyes.

I'M ALIVE!

She pushed her sodden hair, hanging in black rats' tails, away from her face and her eyes gleamed with a sinister light as they reflected the silver of the sea and the answering grey of the leaden skies.

Big Jim, she thought grimly, I'm coming for you.

Hanlon stood up and stretched. Well, she thought, she couldn't stay where she was indefinitely. Another wave of gratitude hit her. Despite the bitter cold that she was feeling, she was alive.

Inland she noticed a plume of thin grey smoke rising up into the skies. A fire, probably from one of the isolated crofts that periodically dotted the island.

She shivered again, and this time it took a while for it to pass. Shivering was now too mild a term; her body was shaking with cold. She was abruptly conscious that she had to get some covering over herself, and quickly. She stood up and set off up the beach towards the treeline. The worst of it was not so much being practically naked, it was that she was barefoot. Moving slowly, the rocks painful on her bare skin, she was conscious of every barnacle on every stone, wincing with pain every time she put her weight down on the soles of her feet.

She stood on the foreshore, breathed deeply and headed towards the house where the smoke was coming from.

## 20

Morag Jamieson, a fifty-year-old, divorced forestry manager, quietened her dog, Bridie, and opened her front door to the unexpected ring on the bell. She stared in astonishment at the sight in front of her. Momentarily she wondered if she was hallucinating. A woman wearing practically nothing, dripping wet, barefoot – black mud coating her legs up to her calves. Her arms and legs were covered with vicious red scratches from where she'd had to force her way through brambles and undergrowth that had obscured the path from the beach to the track and there was a long smear of dried blood on one of her thighs. Her skin was very pale against the black of her underwear.

Despite the state she was in, despite surviving God alone knew what, there was no sense of desperation or helplessness. She stood with her arms folded, grey eyes commanding under a mane of tangled dark hair, very much in control.

'My boat sank,' she said sardonically. 'Can I come in?'

Wordlessly, Morag nodded. Imperiously Hanlon entered the house.

Half an hour later, showered and wearing borrowed jeans, socks and a jumper, Hanlon was sitting drinking scalding sweet tea in Morag's spacious, comfortable kitchen. The clothes were two sizes too big on Hanlon; her host was a tall and large woman. She had a pretty face, lined and weathered by the wind and rain of the islands, her body strong and supple from the heavy graft of her job.

'What happened out there on the loch?' she asked. Boats didn't just sink.

Hanlon stared momentarily at her tea. She had no evidence of anything; it was her word against Big Jim's and Harriet's. And right now, she did not want to be drawn into a complex retelling of events.

'I underestimated things,' she said. 'My boat capsized. Stupid of me.'

'What kind of boat were you in?' Morag asked. A sudden thought struck her. 'Were you alone?'

Hanlon nodded. 'Yeah, I was in a kayak; I wanted to go and see the Corryvreckan. I got a bit more than I bargained for.'

Morag shook her head. 'Well, that was...' Bloody stupid, she was going to say.

'I know,' said Hanlon, 'but someone told me that a one-legged man had swum over it so...'

'Well, yes, but it's the sea, it's changeable – you can get thirty-foot waves out there.' She sighed at the stupidity of tourists. 'Anyway, you're alive.'

'Yes,' said Hanlon.

Morag scratched her dog's ears. She had the feeling that the woman opposite was holding something back. There was obviously a great deal more than just a casual kayak ride going on, but she sensed that was all she was going to get. 'Good girl, Bridie,' she said. 'Where are you staying?'

'The Mackinnon Arms,' said Hanlon, then, 'Do you know Big Jim and Harriet?'

Morag shrugged. 'Everyone knows Big Jim,' she said. Hanlon thought she detected a note of wariness in her voice. 'But I don't get out much. When you have to get up at five in the morning, you tend to just stay in and have an early night.'

Hanlon nodded. Morag said, 'Would you like a lift back to the hotel? It'll only take a quarter of an hour.'

There was no way she was ever going back to that place, Hanlon thought. She shook her head.

'I'd better tell the owner I've managed to lose his boat first,' she said. 'Do you know Ardnamurchann Cottage?'

'Aye, I do,' said Morag. 'Did Donald lend it to you, then?'

'Yes,' said Hanlon. 'So you know Donald.'

Morag nodded. 'Och yes, I know him well.'

Bridie yawned loudly and nudged her mistress; she gave a kind of demanding whine.

'I'll just take her out for a wee while – she hasn't had her walk yet,' said Morag, scratching the dog's ears. 'I'll be about half an hour. When I get back, I'll drive you down to Donald's.'

She walked to the kitchen door, kicked her slippers off, pulled on a pair of walking boots and laced them up, the dog panting in anticipation. Hanlon smiled at the animal. It reminded her of Wemyss. God, I'm becoming a dog lover, she thought in alarm. Thinking of the dog made her think of McCleod. She hoped she would not have any difficulties in getting hold of the recorder that they needed for the bothy. She frowned. She couldn't really blame McCleod for not wanting to go directly to her superiors with the suspicions over Campbell – nobody liked a whistle-blower. But she would have done, and she couldn't help but feel that the DS would sacrifice a lot if it stood in the way of her career. It wasn't a major stumbling-block in what she hoped might turn into a long-term relationship. Hanlon wasn't looking for a fling, a casual holiday relationship, but it was a warning sign nevertheless.

She lay back on the old cracked leather chaise longue that had found its way into Morag's comfortable, chaotic kitchen. The room was warm from the old cream enamelled Aga. A weathered wooden table, stained by age and decades of spills, with half a dozen chairs, filled most of the space and there was a leather armchair with horsehair stuffing visible through a gash in the covering in the corner. The kitchen smelt pleasantly of soot from the stove, cooking and dog, courtesy of Bridie's basket. She stared idly at the antiquated wooden clothes-drying rack that hung from the ceiling on a pulley.

She thought back to a couple of hours previously. There was nothing she could touch Big Jim with. Her word against his and Harriet's. No witnesses.

She thought about her near drowning and Eva, who hadn't been so lucky. She could imagine Eva tied up on Big Jim's boat, or more likely lured there on some pretext, probably the worse for wear on a combination of drink and drugs, driven into the middle of the sea between Jura and Scarba, near the Corryvreckan, and thrown in the sea. If you were drunk and drugged, you wouldn't stand a chance. Let the Atlantic do the dirty work. She felt impotent anger start to well up inside her. It was the old feeling, that she had to do things with one hand tied behind her back. Without her relentlessly pursuing him, Big Jim would never be held to account for his crime. It was that simple.

The euphoria at simply being alive had faded. It was replaced with the familiar restlessness. The usual endless, gnawing ache that was her life. She stood up and went to the window. She would have to get him on the drug-dealing charge; that would be something. That should be provable at least.

There was an outhouse across the yard, like a small barn, with the bonnet of a 4 x 4 poking out. Something about it looked familiar. On the inside of the back door of the kitchen was a pair of wellington boots. Overcome with curiosity, Hanlon pulled them on and walked outside.

It was a Mitsubishi Barbarian, a deep dark blue. Hanlon's heart sank. She moved along its body; sure enough there on the rear window was the sticker with the double entendre that she remembered from the hotel car park the other night, the night of the orgy.

*SWOA Give Good Wood.*

## 21

McCleod drove the old Volvo up the rutted track that led to her house, an old croft that the last owners, city dwellers, had lovingly restored before their dreams of an idyllic life in the west coast of Scotland had turned sour, wrecked by endless rain, midges making their lives hell in the summer, and a lack of things to do. She parked outside, stretching and yawning as she got out of the car and opened the hatch for Wemyss to jump out. The dog leapt gracefully onto the track outside her cottage and then stopped and sniffed. He looked around, as if puzzled.

'What is it, boy?' asked McCleod, immediately suspicious. Wemyss had never done this before. She glanced around her, frowning. In the course of her life in the police she had, over the years, had a fair number of people threaten her: 'I'll kill you, you bitch...', 'I'll track you down and...' That type of thing. Nothing had ever happened but one day it could; she wondered if this was the day.

Someone was there, either inside the house or close by. She knew it. For a brief moment she thought about getting back in the car and fetching help. Then she dismissed the thought. She was not a faint-hearted person. If someone was there, she would deal with them.

She went over to the small shed by the wood-store where logs were neatly stacked ready for the winter. She walked round the bulk of her old quad bike that she sometimes used if she had to access some of the rougher tracks into the hills. She opened the door and took down a crowbar that was hanging on a hook just inside on the wall. She hefted it in her hand; it felt good and heavy. If there was someone there...

'Come on, boy...'

Wemyss walked to heel, looking happy and excited. She frowned at the dog. She wished he would look a bit more menacing. He was certainly capable of it. She'd seen her dog protective of her, hackles raised, body low to the ground ready to spring, jowls drawn back revealing long, sharp white teeth, an ominous low growl in his throat. He could be very scary; now would be a good time. By the front door she noticed a pair of boots that didn't belong to her.

What the hell? Whose were they?

McCleod frowned. She put her key in the lock, then the door opened.

'Hello, Catriona!'

Wemyss gave a bark of joy and leapt forward to greet Hanlon.

'What the fuck?' McCleod said, in astonishment, then she stared at Hanlon's clothes. Morag was much taller and bigger than Hanlon; the old jumper she had lent her hung like a sack on the smaller woman and the patched cord jeans were low in the crotch and the bottoms were rolled up. Hanlon looked like a scarecrow.

'And what the fuck are you wearing?'

* * *

Ten minutes later the two women were drinking whisky in McCleod's front room.

'I think I should get back-up and go and arrest him,' McCleod said. Hanlon shook her head.

'That's the last thing you should do.' She drank some whisky.

'He nearly killed you,' protested McCleod.

'He'd just deny it.'

'We could bring him in anyway, and Harriet. She might back you up.'

Hanlon shook her head. 'The main thing is that we don't disturb whatever is happening next week. That way, we should be able to see Big Jim sent away for a considerable amount of time.'

'Yes, you're right, of course.' McCleod sighed and had another drink of Scotch. 'How the hell did you get here, by the way? All the way from the end of the island?'

Hanlon had told her all of what had happened up until Morag had left. Now she finished her account.

'When I saw that Barbarian and knew she was one of Big Jim's clients, participants, groupies, whatever you would call them, I was worried that she'd call him, and he'd be back for a second attempt. Maybe even helping him. God knows, if anyone would know where to stash a body it'd be her.' She drank some more whisky. Morag's forestry work would take her all over the island; she would, quite literally, know all the back roads, all the little-known or scarcely used trails. She would make an ideal accomplice. She continued, 'So I walked back to Donald's place, cross-country so no one would meet me.' She looked at the clock on the wall: 6 p.m. 'It took me a couple of hours. When I got there, I took his bike. I left a note.'

McCleod nodded. 'You must be shattered.'

'I am,' Hanlon said. 'It's been like some nightmare triathlon, swimming from a sunken boat, running away from a potential ally of an attempted murderer and then a ten-mile cycle, wearing bloody steel-toed wellington boots.'

'Well,' McCleod said, smiling, 'you did tell me you were in training for an Iron Man event. Maybe it'll do you good in the long run.'

'Perhaps,' said Hanlon drily. 'It's not how I usually train, I can assure you.'

'Come here,' McCleod said, standing up. 'I want to hold you.'

The two women put their arms around each other and McCleod hugged Hanlon fiercely. Hanlon felt McCleod's body jerk as she repressed a sob and when they looked into each other's eyes, she saw that the other woman's eyes were wet.

'I'm sorry,' she said, 'but you nearly died out there. I don't want to be attending your funeral...' She took another drink of whisky. 'I can't help but think of those two girls being sent home, back to Germany, back to Latvia or wherever she came from... They should be travelling economy, getting pissed on the flight and looking out of the window, not freight in a cheap coffin in the hold. That could have been you, so I don't want you worrying me like that again. I guess I'm being a bit over-emotional...' Her voice choking slightly, she smiled, rubbed her eyes, tried a smile. 'You're supposed to be here on holiday.'

'That's exactly what my psychiatrist says,' Hanlon replied.

'Well,' McCleod said, her hands exploring Hanlon's body, 'since you're still breathing, perhaps we ought to try some kind of therapy.'

'Let's,' said Hanlon.

\* \* \*

Later, as they lay in bed, McCleod said, 'What do you want doing about the hotel, then?'

'Nothing, for now. They won't know what's happened to me, if I'm dead or alive, unless Morag called them. Let them stew for a bit.'

'OK. By the way, I got this.' McCleod unzipped her handbag and handed Hanlon what looked like a USB stick. Hanlon looked at her enquiringly.

'It's a voice-activated recorder, starts when you speak, stops when there's no conversation. Neat, eh? Just press on, here.' She showed Hanlon the button. 'It's good for fifteen hours' running time.'

Hanlon marvelled at its tiny size. 'This will be perfect. I'll drop it off and hide it somewhere at the bothy tomorrow.' She looked at McCleod.

'I obviously can't go back to the hotel – can I stay here with you for a couple of days?'

McCleod shook her head. 'I'm sorry...'

Hanlon looked at her questioningly, surprised and hurt.

She had been expecting something along the lines of, 'I was hoping you'd ask me that,' or, 'Of course, after all you've been through...' Certainly not a 'no'.

McCleod said, apologetically, 'Look, this is the west coast of Scotland and I'm ambitious. I'm making no bones about it. It's hard enough for a woman to get promotion at the best of times. I just can't afford to be associated with you, I'm afraid. You've got quite a reputation... Please, no hard feelings, OK?'

'No,' Hanlon said, laughing a little, to show how impervious she was to the feelings of others. The truth was, it hurt. God, she thought, I really have no friends. *I just can't afford to be associated with you...* That really hurt. Wemyss nudged her hard and rolled on his back so she could scratch his stomach. At least someone cared, she thought bitterly.

'No, it's fine, I quite understand,' she said, trying to keep the hurt tone out of her voice.

'And,' McCleod said, 'to be honest, I don't want it coming out that I'm having a same-sex relationship.'

Hanlon nodded. She could understand that. McCleod's job would be hard enough without a barrage of lesbian jokes or homophobia. She was probably correct that association with her would do her career harm, but it was still upsetting. The truth is, she thought, nobody really likes me. She felt a tongue lick her hand and saw two brown eyes staring devotedly at her. Not McCleod, Wemyss. Apart from one person, she thought, scratching the top of the dog's head between his ears.

'How did you get in, by the way?' asked McCleod. 'Here, I mean?'

'The door was unlocked.'

'What? I always lock it!' McCleod suddenly looked very worried.

'Shit,' Hanlon said, throwing back the duvet.

The two of them frantically pulled some clothes on and searched the cottage, just to make sure. It didn't take long. Downstairs there was just the living/dining room, the small kitchen (Hanlon's heart sank at the sink piled with unwashed dishes), the upstairs spare room (more chaos), the bathroom, every surface covered with bottles of shampoo, quite a few of them empty (why not throw them away?) make-up and perfume. Hanlon had seen McCleod, hair and make-up immaculate, her two-piece skirt-and-jacket suit sharply tailored, her blouse crisply laundered, creases you could cut your finger on, heeled shoes polished to military gloss – the contrast between her appearance and the absolute mess bordering on squalor of her surroundings was amazing. It was as if she had some kind of split personality. It was such a bizarre contrast.

But the house was obviously empty. McCleod shrugged, defeated.

'I'm sure I locked the door.'

The last room that they checked was the bedroom. Hanlon opened a wardrobe door, shelves groaning and buckling under yet more junk.

'Jesus Christ, Catriona... How can you live like this?'

'Fuck off, Marie Kondo,' McCleod said.

Leaning at the back of the wardrobe was a serviceable-looking shotgun. Hanlon pointed at it. 'Shouldn't you have a safe for that?'

'I know, I keep meaning to get round to it. One of these days.'

'Well, promise me you'll do it soon. You might live to regret it if someone does break in and finds that,' Hanlon warned.

'OK, OK,' McCleod said. 'I'll do it next week.'

'Promise?'

'Promise.'

They relaxed for a while, chatting, then they went into the disorganised kitchen to get something to eat. Hanlon cooked some pasta, following the instructions on the packet; McCleod, who was equally clueless in the kitchen, the blind leading the blind, made some kind of tomato sauce. As they ate they talked.

'I've had an idea,' McCleod said, looking dubiously at her food. 'You can stay at Donald's place.'

'What, the chef?' Hanlon looked at her, surprised.

'Yeah, I know him fairly well, through his brother.'

'Do you?'

McCleod frowned as her teeth crunched on some penne.

'Is this cooked?' she asked.

'Yes,' lied Hanlon, 'it's al dente, it's supposed to be like that. Anyway, we were talking about Donald.'

'Everyone knows everyone on Jura – how could it be otherwise?' McCleod said. 'You could stay there tonight, go to the bothy tomorrow, plant that recorder and pick it up later in the week after the meeting.'

Hanlon considered. 'OK. If he'll put me up.'

'You're a woman,' said McCleod, 'of course he'll put you up. Donald's ever hopeful.'

She reached for her phone. Hanlon, warm, drowsy, half asleep, watched as her thumbs darted over the phone with impressive speed.

She turned to Hanlon.

'He says that'd be fine, meet him at the cottage tonight at half ten.'

\* \* \*

At ten thirty Hanlon, wearing clothes, jeans and a hoodie, borrowed from McCleod, Morag's clothes folded in a plastic bag, waited in the shadows by Donald's cottage. It was still just about light. A short while later she heard the heavy footsteps of the chef scrunching up the stone-chip path.

She stepped out into view.

'Evening, Hanlon,' said Donald cheerily. 'Could nae keep away, eh?'

He opened the door and ushered her in.

In contrast to McCleod's pigsty of a house, Donald's was a model of cleanliness and neatness. He opened the fridge; as far as she could tell from a glance across the room, it seemed to be just full of lager.

He took out a can.

'Like one?'

'No, thanks.' Her head still felt slightly muzzy from McCleod's whisky. 'Did Catriona tell you what happened?'

'Aye, I called her after the last of the mains went out to ask what all of this was about. So Big Jim tried to drown you in the Gulf of Corryvreckan? Unbelievable...' He shook his head, opened the can and tipped the contents down in two goes. He belched. 'That's better. You should go to the police.'

'I am the police,' said Hanlon, 'in a manner of speaking.'

He reached for another can and closed the fridge door. He looked questioningly at Hanlon.

'He'd deny it, as I said to Catriona. Besides, I'm not sure he would even remember doing it.'

'Well, his boat's back,' Donald said. 'I have nae seen Harriet though.'

'What sort of condition is he in?' wondered Hanlon.

'He's absolutely fucked, steaming,' Donald said. 'I saw him passed out in his office earlier. He was slumped across the desk, snoring his head off.'

Good, thought Hanlon. I'm glad you're suffering some kind of meltdown, you murderous bastard.

'I'll go and collect my stuff tomorrow,' Hanlon said, 'then I'll be off.'

'You're welcome to stay as long as you want,' Donald said seriously. He looked at her for once without his habitual come-hither/bedroom-eyes expression. He looked concerned. 'Catriona's a friend.'

Hanlon found his care touching. Delayed shock, she guessed. First Wemyss, now Donald.

'You know her through your brother,' she said.

Donald nodded. 'Yeah, that's right. He met her at an exercise class. He's a wee bit slimmer than me.'

'Oh, God...' She suddenly remembered – how could she have forgotten? 'It was his bloody kayak... I'll get him a new one. I can hardly speak to Big Jim about it.'

'I'd forget it, if I were you,' Donald said. 'As for Big Jim, he's not going to have a pot to piss in soon. Don't worry about it. John never used that kayak anyway.'

'I can't do that,' Hanlon said. 'I always pay my debts.'

And I will to you, Big Jim. I can promise you that. I'll give you what's due to you, from me and Eva and maybe Franca.

Donald shrugged. 'Have it your own way.' He shook his head, looking at Hanlon. 'I can't believe he tried to drown you. Did Harriet not try to stop him?'

'In fairness she did.' Well, she had stopped him shooting her, but was that because it would have been too obvious? 'But I'm not sure how hard she actually tried.'

'Well, if Big Jim got carted off to prison or died, she'd be better off, I guess,' Donald said.

'How come?' asked Hanlon.

Donald stretched out luxuriously in an armchair; he downed half his lager. 'Harriet is a good hotel manager – she does all the work and Big Jim ruins it. If he was removed from the helm, the ship would be sailing towards safer waters, not towards the rocks. But, as it is, I can confidently expect to pick the business up cheap in a fire sale from the receivers when he goes bankrupt.'

'But she's still around?' asked Hanlon.

'How do you mean?' Donald looked puzzled.

'Big Jim didn't shoot her or throw her overboard?' explained Hanlon.

Donald laughed. 'Not unless she's come back as a ghost. I saw her earlier, I didn't speak to her.'

'Well,' Hanlon said, 'thanks for putting me up. I'm off to bed.'

'Remember,' Donald said, reverting to type, 'if you get lonely...'

'I won't, Donald,' Hanlon said firmly. 'I really won't.'

* * *

The next morning, Hanlon got up and walked over to the Mackinnon Arms. The sun was high in the sky and there were only a few clouds floating high above the Paps. The hotel seemed eerily deserted and she met nobody as she retrieved her case and her clothes from her room. There was no sign of Big Jim, but she did meet Harriet.

Hanlon encountered her in the lobby as she walked down the stairs holding her bags. The two women stared at each other, both stony faced. If Harriet was discomforted by meeting Hanlon, there was no sign of it on her face. Hanlon felt a surge of anger towards Big Jim's accomplice. Most of all, she remembered Harriet at the wheel, accelerating the boat away from her, leaving her to the cold mercy of the sea.

'I didn't drown,' Hanlon said coldly. Unlike the others, she thought.

'Please come into the office,' asked Harriet.

She did so.

'Take a seat.'

'I'd rather stand,' said Hanlon.

'What can I say?' Harriet opened her arms expressively, pulling a sympathetic face. 'I did my best, but I'm afraid he's so far gone these days – that's why I was on the water with him in the first place. He was in no fit state to be steering a boat... At least I got that gun away from him.'

'I know,' Hanlon said, 'but I very nearly died out there. You left me out there. In the sea. With a sunken boat, by a whirlpool. I'm here, but it's no thanks to you.'

*'Well, if Big Jim got carted off to prison or died, she'd be better off, I guess.'*

Donald's words resurfaced in her memory. If she had

drowned, Big Jim might well be taking his first unsteady steps towards a murder trial, star witness Harriet, star exhibit, one very dead Hanlon. And if Big Jim was involved in drug smuggling his profits would be in cash, easily available to be appropriated by Harriet. They wouldn't be invested in ISAs or national savings bonds, that was for sure.

'All I can do is say sorry. What more do you want from me?' Harriet looked at her appealingly. Hanlon felt a surge of incredulity. It was as if she were saying to Hanlon, *'Look, I'm the victim in all of this.'*

'I'd like you to get that shotgun off him, for a start,' Hanlon said, 'so he can't do any damage to anyone with a firearm.'

'He's got three,' the manageress said, 'and a .22 rifle. They're in a gun cabinet in his bedroom.'

'Well, that's just great, isn't it?' Hanlon's voice was heavily sarcastic. 'He's heavily armed.'

'Don't snap at me,' said Harriet irritably. 'What should I do about it?'

'OK, Harriet,' Hanlon said angrily, 'here's what you can do. First, get in touch with the chief police officer of the area and let him know how dangerous he is and try to get him to revoke his licence, and right now maybe you could get the key to the cabinet and his car keys and chuck them both in the loch so he can't get at either.'

'I'm leaving next week,' Harriet said, changing the subject. 'I've had enough.'

That did surprise Hanlon. It certainly made her rethink her theory that Harriet was Big Jim's accomplice. 'Have you told him?'

'Not yet...' She shook her head. 'I think he might kill himself, to be honest. He's very depressed.'

Very depressed? He's certainly very homicidal, thought

Hanlon. She thought of Big Jim killing himself – well, she certainly wouldn't mourn his passing if he did so.

'He's talked about shooting himself,' she said.

'Well, suggest counselling to him,' she said sarcastically. 'Alternatively you could get the guns away from him, like I suggested a minute ago. Anyway, Harriet, I'm leaving, as you can doubtless see. Here's your key back.'

Harriet took it from her.

'You paid for your room in advance, of course.'

Hanlon waited for Harriet to say that the money would be refunded in full. Instead, 'There is some money outstanding on the room for food and drink.'

Hanlon stared at her in astonishment.

'You're seriously suggesting...' Outrage struggled with disbelief. 'You must be out of your mind, Harriet. I am not paying a penny. You can chase me through a civil court, and if you do I will leave an honest appraisal of my stay on Trip Advisor. I think it'll go viral.'

She stormed upstairs and packed her bags; when she returned the office was empty. She left the key on the reception desk and walked out into the bright sunlight of the morning.

Hanlon returned to Donald's cottage. She was still furious with Harriet for suggesting she pay after what she'd endured, and toyed with the idea of going back down to the hotel and screaming at her some more. The nerve of the woman!

Wondering if anyone was booked in to lunch that day, she turned around and glared at the run-down hotel. A cracked pane of glass in one of the upstairs windows had been replaced with a piece of cardboard. The place looked even shabbier in the sunshine. The Mackinnon Arms was becoming like the *Mary Celeste*, although a ghost hotel rather than a ghost ship. The boar on the sign leered at her.

Staff were dead (Eva), about to leave (Harriet), on notice (Donald), presumably looking for another job (Johanna) or engaged in criminal activities (Kai). The guests were walking out (the home counties scuba divers, her), or dead (Nose-stud). The owner was also either absent mentally, or prowling around half-cut and crazy. Talk about the ship of fools.

She walked along the road back to the cottage, went upstairs to the guest room and dropped her cases off. Downstairs, she pulled on a pair of walking boots and headed off into the hills. Buzzards wheeled over the summit of Ben Garrisdale in a cloudless sky. Still angry, she strode off along the road and then up the forestry track into the hills. Although it wasn't all that warm, the exercise had her perspiring freely and her shirt stuck to her back as she climbed up the twisting steep track.

An hour or so later she was at the bothy where Kai was due to meet DI Murdo Campbell on Thursday.

She pulled on a pair of latex gloves – if they were using the place for drug storage it might well become a crime scene – found the key to the door, as he had said, by the water butt. She opened it and went in. She closed the door behind her and looked around. The bothy was just one large room with a table and four chairs, a single bed in the corner and, screened by a partition, an ancient, very deep porcelain sink. Despite the heat outside, the place was very cold and Hanlon felt her skin breaking out in goosebumps. On the wall was the mounted skull of a deer with small, twisted antlers. The tap above the sink dripped continually. The sound was magnified by the old marble by the plughole and it echoed eerily in the gloomy room. The dull brown stain from the peaty water looked like old blood on the cracked, off-white of the glazed surface of the basin.

The walls of the bothy were of course stones that had been mortared together. The mortar was rough and flaking. Hanlon went to the wall by the door, dug a chunk of the cement out with her fingers and, checking that the device was switched on, placed the voice-activated recorder in the gap between the stones. She stepped back and checked her handiwork.

The room was dark and the gaps between the rough stones were deep. Unless you walked right up close and stared intently at the gap between the stones, it was invisible.

Satisfied, she left the cottage, locked the door and replaced the key. In a few days' time, that tiny machine would be holding the information that would hopefully send Big Jim to the prison cell he richly deserved. Him and Murdo Campbell. She had a particular visceral dislike of corrupt cops. Incontrovertible evidence, which, although inadmissible in court, would prod McCleod into action.

She walked home the slow way, down the path. As she neared the road she saw Big Jim's Land Rover parked by the side of it near where the path rejoined the strip of worn tarmac.

What on earth was he doing? she wondered.

She approached the stationary car cautiously; an observer would have thought she was stalking it, as if it were an animal likely to rear and pounce. There was no sign of Big Jim on the road. She was very wary of Big Jim now, particularly if he was armed.

She looked over the drop down to the rocks of the shore and then she saw him. Or rather she saw his legs, poking out from behind a large, smooth boulder looking out to sea. The rest of him was screened by the stone. He was absolutely motionless. Hanlon wondered if he was dead. Harriet's words about him taking his own life returned to her. Well, she, for one, would not grieve if he had.

She thought she'd better check. If he had blown his head off, better she found him rather than someone unused to sudden death or a bloody crime scene.

She dropped lightly down to the rocks and walked along the beach towards him. Big Jim had built a sort of three-sided shelter for himself out of fishing boxes, driftwood and a tarpaulin, the large boulder making up the third side. He was far from dead. His eyes were closed but his chest rose and fell and occasionally she heard him give a faint snore. She studied the blotched red skin of his face, his cheekbones criss-crossed with threads of blue veins, his nose a fiery red.

Next to him, his left elbow resting on it, was a crate containing a dozen vodka bottles. She nodded to herself. This place was Big Jim's fine-weather bolthole, his secret drinking place. At the hotel there were too many distractions, Harriet pestering him for decisions, phones ringing, people wanting to talk to him. Here, there was just the sea, tranquillity and alcohol.

It was obviously where he had been coming when she had taken his Land Rover. No wonder he had been furious, his quality time with his best friend Smirnoff had been compromised.

She prodded him experimentally with the toe-cap of her boot. Part of her wanted him to wake up so she could plausibly 'defend' herself and hospitalise the bastard. He muttered something but didn't open his eyes. She was tempted to take his car keys and steal the Land Rover. Abandon it halfway up the forestry track.

But she didn't. She left him where he was and walked back to Donald's.

## 22

The following afternoon, Hanlon borrowed Donald's bicycle and cycled into Craighouse. It was about half five and she stopped at a tea rooms in the centre of the picturesque village.

It was at around six that she heard the sirens. Three police cars and two ambulances, blue lights flashing, roared down the main road heading in the direction that Hanlon had come from. Then the *whump-whump* of a helicopter's rotor blades from overhead. It was incredibly loud.

The waitresses and customers alike went outside to see what had happened. People united by alarm shed their accustomed reserve. Only the one question: what's happened? What's going on?

Phones were produced, either frantic calls or frantic searches. Then another helicopter joining the first one.

'There's been a shooting!' shouted one of the people in the café, a man who looked to be in his early sixties with white hair, looking up from his phone.

'Two people dead.'

She raised her head in alarm. Immediately she thought of Big Jim – had he gone crazy with his shotgun?

A shocked murmur ran through the café. Terrorism? Domestic? An accident?

'Where?' asked a woman with a baby in a buggy.

'Kinuachdrachd.'

'Kinuachdrachd,' repeated several voices in tones of almost relief. Wherever it was, it wasn't just round the corner.

'Where's Kinuachdrachd?' Hanlon asked one of the waitresses, a girl in her late teens.

'It's right on the end of the island, near the Mackinnon Arms hotel.'

Oh shit! Hanlon didn't wait for her bill, she thrust a twenty-pound note at the waitress and ran outside to her bike.

As she pedalled down the road towards the hotel various scenarios ran through her mind. Big Jim shooting Harriet and Donald; Big Jim shooting – she knew it was far-fetched but it was a terrifying possibility – McCleod. It had to be Big Jim; there couldn't be two maniacs with a shotgun, surely.

She seemed to be travelling incredibly slowly, like in a nightmare. Then she heard engines before she saw the vehicles and she pulled over to allow the ambulances past. They were obviously returning to the ferry. There were no flashing lights now.

The time for urgency had passed.

# 23

'What the hell happened?' Hanlon demanded of McCleod. It was 9 p.m. and the DS had called in to Donald's to update Hanlon. She'd sent her a terse text soon after the ambulance incident, reassuring her.

I'm fine. Busy. See you later.

McCleod looked tired, upset and irritable. It had obviously been a stressful day.

'A member of the public phoned the emergency services to say that there had been a shooting at the old bothy on the forestry road near Kinuachdrachd, just down from Loch Ciaran. He declined to leave his name, but obviously he had to be local, if only to know the names of these places.'

'Anyway, I was working from home, so the call came to me to investigate, and sure enough...'

She described the crime scene to Hanlon. The door had been open; she'd gone in there first to find Kai dead on the floor. He'd been shot. 'A horrible sight,' said McCleod. She'd then walked up to Big Jim's Land Rover, which had been parked some distance away.

'He'd blown his head off,' she said simply, shuddering. If Kai had been bad, this was worse.

'I knew it was him immediately. I recognised the tattoos.'

Hanlon put her arms around her and they stood for a moment, locked together. She could well imagine what McCleod had witnessed; she'd seen herself first-hand the damage a shotgun could do. It must have been a horrific sight.

'There was nothing left...' whispered McCleod. 'It was horrible...' She shook her head as if to clear it and pushed Hanlon gently away.

'I'll be all right,' she said.

'So what happens now?' Hanlon asked.

'DI Campbell will head the investigation. I imagine that he will find that Big Jim shot Kai and then killed himself. There's plenty of evidence that the balance of his mind was well disturbed before this incident.'

Hanlon nodded. That was certainly true. She could easily imagine a drunk Big Jim emerging from one of his beach drinking sessions, seeing Kai walk up the forestry road, deciding to follow him, a drunken argument followed by a murder, then turning the gun against himself.

After all, she'd warned Harriet herself about Big Jim's behaviour, told her to get the guns away from him.

But although it was easy to picture, it all seemed somehow too convenient. Too many loose ends tidied up. And there were other things that aroused Hanlon's suspicions. For example, she only had Harriet's word that Big Jim was suicidal. Was he? Homicidal, certainly. She'd seen that, but self-harming?

And once more, Donald's words came back to her. Harriet would now be free to run the hotel as she pleased without Big Jim screwing things up, being rude to guests, misplacing bookings, sexually harassing staff.

'And where was DI Campbell when all of this kicked off?'

'At home with his granny. It was his day off.' At home with his granny, thought Hanlon. Not in the office or on the mainland.

'Why wasn't he sent to investigate?'

'Because I was rostered as Duty Officer, not him. I told you, I was working, he wasn't.'

'But, Catriona, he could have killed Kai, then Big Jim. Made it look like a suicide.'

McCleod shook her head. 'Why would he have wanted to? There's no motive, is there? Not that I can see. He was supposed to meet Kai there on Thursday, for a start. I can't go to my bosses and say, "I think DI Campbell killed Kai McPherson on the say-so of a woman suspended from duty pending investigation by the IOPC." There's no proof.'

'Oh, but there might be,' Hanlon pointed out, slightly needled by McCleod's attitude. 'The voice-recorder, that should throw some light on the proceedings. When we play that memory stick, we'll know who Kai's last visitor was.'

McCleod smiled. 'That's why I took this with me. It was hanging up on a nail in the bothy. It's the spare key for the back door.'

She handed Hanlon the key.

'You can go and retrieve it from wherever you hid it. I'm going to be on the mainland at Area for the next few days. DI Campbell will be interviewing the hotel staff, co-ordinating the investigation.'

Co-ordinating or making sure it goes nowhere, thought Hanlon. A falling-out amongst thieves was foremost in her mind.

'I wonder if Harriet has an alibi,' Hanlon said.

McCleod nodded. 'Do you know, I was kind of wondering that

too. If there was a drug-smuggling operation organised from the Mackinnon Arms, it'd be her I would put money on to be running it. Big Jim might just have been an ignorant patsy. He certainly fucked up running a hotel. Well, I guess we'll see...'

She looked sharply at Hanlon, her small, fierce face frowning. 'Don't go anywhere near the bothy for the next couple of days. There's a mobile forensics unit coming tomorrow. Give it another day or maybe two to calm down, then go and get it. Then we'll know.'

'What will you do with the information on the recorder once we get it?' Hanlon asked.

'Well, it depends what it is,' replied McCleod, frowning. 'I'm not a believer in crossing bridges until I come to them. We'll talk about that when we know what's on it – for all we know the thing may have malfunctioned.'

'What if the crime scene guys find it?' Hanlon wondered.

'Good,' said McCleod emphatically. 'I don't mind if they do. They'll think it belonged to Kai, then whatever's on it will be out there, and Campbell, if you're right...' she still doesn't trust me, thought Hanlon incredulously '...will be screwed.'

'OK,' Hanlon agreed. 'I'll go on Friday.'

'What are you going to do for the next couple of days while I'm in Oban?'

'I thought I'd stay here tomorrow and go to Glasgow on Thursday.'

'Why?' She'd originally intended to visit Tremayne on Islay to say hello and make sure that everything was OK for her impending stay. But her ex-boss would have wanted to know everything that was happening and she simply wasn't feeling up to delivering any kind of in-depth report.

'I think I've had enough of Jura for the time being. I want to go and do some sightseeing, go to the Burrell collection and whatever else there is to do in Glasgow.' She looked at McCleod, who seemed disappointed. 'Why do you ask? I'm not a suspect, surely?'

'No, no, I was being selfish. I was hoping you would babysit Wemyss – he loves you. He's a dog of great taste... Never mind, I'll ask Donald.'

'Poor Donald,' Hanlon said. 'He never gets the girl, just a dog.'

'I wouldn't worry about Donald,' said McCleod dismissively. 'He does OK with waitresses.'

She sighed. 'Well, I'd better go, I've got a lot to write up by tomorrow...' She held out her arms and Hanlon stepped forward and they kissed.

'I do have half an hour...' McCleod said.

'And I've got a bed upstairs,' Hanlon said.

## 24

Wednesday morning dawned clear and bright. At 8 a.m., Hanlon was sitting on a ridge, screened by a rhododendron bush, next to a Scots pine, looking down on a modern bungalow through a pair of old Zeiss binoculars that she had borrowed from McCleod.

She had found out the address from McCleod the night before. The DS had got a text from Campbell to ask her to co-ordinate with the forensic people the following day; he was going to be working from home and could be contacted on his grand-mother's landline. Hanlon had felt a sudden urge to find out a little more about the life of the policeman she knew was engaged in criminality. Deep down she knew that she was hoping for a glimpse of some more conclusive evidence of corruption, in her dreams something incontrovertible, a hidden Lamborghini, for example, something utterly unattainable on a policeman's pay scale. Failing that, she would at least be taking some form of action.

Big Jim was dead, Kai was dead, the Mackinnon Arms was closed. She had cycled past it early this morning, the boar on the sign looking self-satisfied, well pleased with the way things were going. Well, Donald will be happy, she thought. It's made his plans to buy the place easier.

Now she was sitting on a hill watching Campbell's island home. Unlike McCleod's untidy house and weed-choked, muddy driveway or Donald's ramshackle cottage, the policeman's grandmother's house, an eighties-build bungalow with the pebble-dashing so popular in Scotland, looked immaculate. The garden, with its plants that did well on the west coast, fuchsias, hydrangeas and nasturtiums, was laid out with military precision.

Murdo Campbell's grandmother lived about two miles from McCleod on the road to the ferry to Islay. The house stood on the spur of a small hill and overlooked Islay and the distant shores of the Argyll peninsula. The view from the living room must be superb, thought Hanlon. She thought of Dr Morgan's repro Giacometti sculptures. Who needs art, Doctor, when you've got nature to look at? she thought with more than a touch of contempt.

For once, the critical voice of Dr Morgan that had been nagging her in a highly annoying fashion for the past week, the voice of her conscience, was silent. Ha! thought Hanlon. And then her complacency vanished. She was uncomfortably aware that she was managing to find someone to quarrel with who wasn't actually present, but was a good five hundred miles away.

At least the mystery of why Campbell seemed to spend so much time at his granny's was partially explained in his favour. Who wouldn't want to stay there?

There were two cars parked outside on a block-paving drive. Campbell's BMW and a small Honda that she guessed belonged to the old lady.

Just then the front door opened and Campbell appeared. He was wearing clothes not dissimilar to her own: walking boots, a green cagoule, army trousers. He had a small rucksack slung over one shoulder. She saw him stretch as if he were going running, and then he started walking up the hill towards her. Working from home, are you?

She felt a momentary twinge of alarm; she did not want to confront him hiding in his garden. Then she saw that he was on a well-beaten path that ran from the back of the house into the hinterland of the island, towards the first of the Paps that towered above them. The path ran within about twenty metres of where she was crouching. She lay down flat, screened from his view by bracken that grew waist high on the hillside.

From her hiding place, she heard him passing by, the squelch of the mud beneath his heavy boots clearly audible, and then, a few moments later, she silently slipped down onto the path behind him.

The well-worn track led through the low slopes, twisting this way and that, sometimes dipping down, but ever upwards towards a high peak, not one of the Paps themselves, but a substantially high hill. She walked along in utter silence. There were few birds around, the only sound was that of running water from the myriad of small streams invisible under the thick, tangled roots of the heather and small bushes and trees that grew up through it. To have walked off the path would have been practically impossible; it was a beautiful environment but a harsh one for the walker.

Following Campbell, unlike following Kai, was exhausting. He moved very fast along the track into the high, rocky Jura hills. The path they were on was used by sheep – she occasionally saw their excrement – and here and there were the remains of dry stone walls, some surmounted with rusty wire, that had obviously fallen into disuse over the years. The walls were grey and patched red, green and white with lichen and emerald with moss. To her right was a very tall, more modern fence, about two metres high, made of tough-looking wire mesh. It had to be a deer fence, she guessed. The track paralleled it for a while and then turned away.

She hadn't expected to be following Campbell, it wasn't part of any grand plan, but the last time that she had encountered him in the hills alone, it had been to meet with Kai. She was now hoping that something similar was going to occur today. As she walked, she thought it was funny that modern communications should be so prone to interception that it made security sense to have a face-to-face meeting rather than discuss things over hackable mobile phones. Then again, reception, or the lack of it, was a huge issue out here.

Hanlon guessed that Campbell was about a quarter of a mile ahead of her. Occasionally from the crest of a ridge she would catch a glimpse of him, far in the distance.

As they walked, she wondered who he was going to meet. Maybe the deaths of Kai and Big Jim had forced a rethink of the three-kilo drug delivery. A small plane or a drone could drop a package off in the middle of the hills, that was one possibility; another that he was meeting someone the way he had Kai. Either way, she'd be there to witness it.

Annoyingly, he never seemed to be hurrying, but he remained consistently ahead of her even though she was practically running. It felt like being in a nightmare. She could see the marks of his boots on the black, peaty mud of the path as it snaked between the wiry, tough stalks of the heather that grew waist high and the light green columns of the stalks of bracken. She saw no people, only birds. Several times she nearly fell over a pheasant, the birds giving their weird metallic cry as they flew almost vertically upwards, startled at meeting a human.

She rounded a bend in the path and then dropped down flat below the skyline, disturbing several small black-headed birds that had been lurking in the heather. She didn't want him to see her silhouetted against the blue Hebridean skies. She saw the buzzard again, high up in the heavens, wheeling lazily over the tallest of the hills.

Below her was an awe-inspiring sight. It was a truly wonderful view. There was a flat patch of green grass surrounded by stunted birch trees, their trunks a ghostly silver in the morning sun. Just beyond it was a large loch. Its surface was like a mirror on which were reflected the few clouds that were passing overhead. On the grass was a circle of standing stones with a cairn of rocks in the centre. It was a miraculously beautiful place.

She took out her field glasses and focussed in on Campbell. He unslung his backpack and put it down near to the cairn. Hanlon's heart raced; what did it contain? Drug money? She looked at the terrain near to the loch.

The actual loch was more or less hammer-shaped and it lay in the lee of the peaks of three sizeable hills. She could see trickles of water, what looked like trickles from here but would, she suspected, be sizeable streams, running down their flanks into the waters of the loch below.

The ground near the standing stones, one piece of it anyway, was as flat as a table; there were no tall trees or power lines. It would be easy to land a helicopter there, she thought.

She swung the binoculars back to Campbell. He was unbuttoning his shirt – it was blue, standing out against the green background – and took it off. He stood there a moment and then sat down on a boulder. He was wearing a blue T-shirt and his pale freckled arms stood out against the fabric. She increased the magnification as he leaned forward to undo the laces on his walking boots. He slipped those off; all of his movements were smooth and rhythmical. His socks followed. Then he pulled his T-shirt up over his head. He had his back turned to Hanlon; she could see the V of the muscles running down his back. She wondered what he was going to do with it; she found herself nodding in approval as he neatly folded it rather than balling it up and dropping it on the rock. It was what she would have done.

He turned round and she could see his short red hair ruffled by the breeze. Her gaze travelled down. There was no fat on Campbell's belly. She could see the ridges of muscle on his stomach. His fingers undid the belt and then unbuttoned his army trousers. They dropped to the floor.

He stepped gracefully out of them. He stood a moment and contemplated the loch, maybe about fifty metres from the stone circle that he was standing in. Then he rested one hand on the boulder and pulled off his pants.

Campbell unhurriedly folded the rest of his clothes neatly, then reached into the side of his backpack and pulled out a bag with a zippered top. He put his boots and clothes in then zipped it shut. He walked slowly down to the water in his bare feet, Hanlon admiring through her binoculars.

The water must have been freezing but Campbell didn't flinch. He had to be used to wild-water swimming, thought Hanlon.

When he got waist deep, holding the bag shoulder high, he turned around and lay on his back in the water, balanced the bag on his chest and kicked out strongly with his legs. Within a couple of minutes, he was lost to sight behind a promontory that stuck out from the shore.

Hanlon guessed that he would swim round where the deer fence ended in the loch – it looked fairly unclimbable – and then return the way he came, or maybe walk down to Craighouse, which she reckoned was not too far away. From his gran's house to the village was two sides of a triangle, one up here, the other down the way.

And then someone else would come to reclaim the backpack.

Either on foot, the way they had – there was no way you could get a vehicle up here, although she suddenly thought of the deer fence. Maybe on the other side there would be a track. There had to be, she guessed, to have hauled the materials up here to build it. The track, she thought. Had Campbell made his way to the bothy yesterday afternoon along the forestry trails that criss-crossed the island, avoiding the road? Had it been Campbell who had stolen out of the hills like a wolf falling on the sheep-fold?

She gave him ten minutes more just to be sure that he hadn't just gone for a swim, although why anyone would take their clothes with them as he had done would be a hard question to answer.

She stood up, disturbing the black-headed birds again, and walked down the slope of the hill, through the heather, skirting the impenetrable bog myrtle and gorse, down to the standing stones.

As she walked into the space between the birch trees she felt a sense almost of being in a holy place, like walking into a church or a cathedral. The jagged, weathered stones, covered in moss and lichen, were like pillars flanking a nave.

She walked up to the cairn and up to the backpack. It was green canvas, heavy duty so it wouldn't get ripped or torn by vegetation or tree branches.

She knelt down and put her hand on the backpack zipper.

'What the fuck do you think you're doing?'

She looked round.

Campbell was standing over her, a heavy tree branch like a club in one hand. His eyes furious.

## 25

Hanlon slowly stood up. Campbell's face was pale with anger. She had been caught red-handed. Several explanations sprang into her mind, none of them remotely plausible.

'I think you're on the take,' was a non-starter.

'So, it's your bag, DI Campbell,' she said. She emphasised the 'your' as if there were some doubt about it, as if they were in, say, a railway station or a café rather than in the middle of nowhere. It sounded horribly lame. The moment that she said it, she wished she hadn't.

He was now fully clothed and almost literally shaking with rage. She watched his face redden; it happened from the base of his neck upwards like mercury rising in a thermometer. His normally pale face was flushed and she didn't think it was from exertion.

'Of course, it's my bag, as well you know, since you followed me up here.'

She started to speak and he silenced her with a chopping motion of his hand.

'And don't try and lie. I've known that someone was behind me for the past couple of miles. I didn't imagine it would be you, of all people.' He threw the tree branch angrily aside. Hanlon mentally breathed a sigh of relief.

'How did you know someone was following you?' she couldn't help but ask. She was genuinely curious.

'What?'

'I really am curious,' she said. Hanlon's natural self-confidence was beginning to reassert itself. Campbell shook his head in disbelief.

'If you must know, since you startled those pheasants... and then the stone chats,' he said. Hanlon raised her eyebrows, impressed by Campbell's impressive country tracking skills. 'But we're not here to discuss the birds of the west coast, DCI Hanlon. It's your behaviour that concerns me. Oh, and I spoke to my sister, you've been stalking her too! What the fuck are you up to? Why have you got this hard-on for me and my family? Presumably you've been camped out on the hill staking out my granny's house.'

She looked into his green eyes, which seemed to have changed their colour to a kind of hostile emerald.

'Are you insane?' he demanded. 'I'd heard about you. I made enquiries, people said you were a bit nuts. I can see now that was very much an understatement.'

'It was a training exercise,' she said.

'WHAT?' he practically shouted the word.

'I'll be frank with you, DI Campbell,' she said. 'Mind if I sit down?'

She indicated the boulder set in the mossy ground. She was playing for time, her mind whirling to come up with a halfway credible explanation for her behaviour.

'By all means...' he said.

'I promise I'll tell you the whole truth,' she lied, looking into his green eyes with great sincerity.

She sat down and looked up at him. 'As you probably know, I am suspended pending the completion of an investigation by the IOPC. I think in a fortnight's time I am going to be asked to leave the police. Now, DI Campbell, just how many openings are there for a forty-year-old woman detective with, I freely admit, limited people skills?'

Campbell didn't reply, but she felt that he was falling for her explanation, which had the merit of being based in truth. So far, she was just giving voice to what was in her head. It felt good to admit it. He looked at her, his face impassive; it was impossible to know what he was thinking.

'Very few,' she said, answering her own question. 'The security business being one. So I have plans to set up privately.'

'A private detective,' he said sceptically.

'Exactly.' She nodded. 'It'll be virtually all spying on spouses, I imagine. That and insurance-fraud claims involving injury. I think I am going to be spending the next few years lurking in hotel lobbies following people around, photographing errant husbands with other women or vice versa, and people with whiplash playing five-a-side or dragging their bins out on collection day. So, like I said, you're a training exercise.'

'And my sister? She was a training exercise too, was she?'

'I followed her chef to a pub,' she lied.

He shook his head contemptuously. 'I don't believe a word of it, and I don't want to see you again, Hanlon,' said Campbell. He pulled out the zippered waterproof bag he'd used earlier from a back pocket, stuffed it in his rucksack and swung it over his back.

He turned away and walked up the track, then he turned to face her, pointing a finger at her.

'If I hear you've been hassling Ishbel, in fact, if I hear your name mentioned again, I'm issuing an official complaint. Have you got that in your thick skull?'

He turned again and disappeared from view.

She gave him ten minutes and then followed.

## 26

Hanlon got off the bus by the abbey in the centre of Paisley. It was the second time she had been here and she was growing to like this part of the city.

She had travelled from Jura at first light, not that it had ever really got dark. Donald, yawning and swearing gently at having to get up so early, had driven her to the ferry. She had left her luggage there in a locker and now, tired but determined, she set off to the Rob Roy. Hopefully things would go a lot better than they had the day before. She was still smarting from her encounter with Campbell. She couldn't believe how badly she had screwed everything up. Now he would realise that she suspected him and would take corrective measures. For all he knew, she was on the island specifically to target him. Anyone involved in large-scale drug smuggling would by nature be more than just a little paranoid.

It was two o'clock now and the pub was probably as quiet as it ever would get during the week. Although maybe time didn't matter for the habitués of the Rob Roy. It wasn't as if they had anything better to do. And so it proved.

She took a taxi to the pub, the driver looking a little bemused as he dropped her off, his expression saying, *'Are you sure you want to come here?'* The same three old men were at their usual places; they regarded her with silent contempt. Tam was there with his two mates, in their usual places. He turned round as the door opened, saw who it was and turned his back on her with a kind of petulant ostentation. Groundhog day at the pub. Stasis. Leo was propping up the bar, talking to the barman, Frank, the same guy with his pencil moustache and bouffant-style hairdo who had been there last time. The only difference were two tables of tough-looking men with football scarves, black and white, and replica shirts. St Mirren colours seemingly. Perhaps there was a match, perhaps they'd just dressed up for the visit to the pub.

Hanlon's arrival attracted universally hostile looks from the football supporters but not from Leo and the barman. The latter smiled to himself as if at some private joke. Leo looked delighted to see her.

He looked even more pumped than the last time Hanlon had seen him, the veins on his large biceps swollen up under the skin like writhing blue cables. He was fearsomely strong. Tam said something to his mates. They laughed, but nobody moved to actually threaten her. Hanlon put this down to the Leo effect. He did look absolutely crazy, his light blue eyes dancing around, full of what looked like good nature, but you had the feeling that there was some kind of disconnect between what lay on the surface with Leo and what was going on underneath.

'Hi, how are you?' Lunatic, meaningless grin; his eyes seemed to stare through her at some far horizon, as if she were transparent, made of glass. 'Francis, get ma friend here a wee drink.'

'Diet Coke, please.'

Frank opened a bottle and poured her drink.

Leo watched intently; Frank gave her the Coke. 'Your good health,' he said, toasting her with his pint of lager. She smiled her thanks.

'Can I have a word with Manny, please, Leo?' she asked.

'Surely... come through.'

With relief, Hanlon left the bar and its hostile male audience, annoyed at her for polluting the atmosphere, and Leo escorted her into the back room. Manny was sitting behind his desk, smoke from a cigarette drifting up to the ceiling through his nicotine-stained fingers. It was as if he hadn't moved since she had last been here. Christ, she thought, what a life.

What is it with this place? she thought. Nothing ever changes.

'Hello again, and what brings you tae see me this time?' Manny said. He gave a gurgling cough and spat yellow phlegm into a stained, crumpled handkerchief. He inspected the sputum closely and wadded up the handkerchief and thrust it into his pocket. He coughed again.

'Have you heard that Kai McPherson's dead?' Hanlon asked.

Manny coughed, an alarmingly prolonged wheezy sound, his face turned slightly purple and he started fighting for breath. He grabbed an inhaler, put it in his mouth and pressed the plunger.

'Naw, I hadnae heard that, who did it?' He put the inhaler back in his mouth and gave himself another blast, then he grinned.

'Probably a lassie. Or maybe a small child – Kai couldnae really handle himsel'. Fucking bampot.'

'I don't know,' she said. 'Should you really be smoking, Manny? You sound terrible.'

'Och, I'm OK.' He waved a hand, batting away her concern. 'I've got my wee puffer... I'm fucked without it, mind.'

Hanlon shrugged and carried on.

'I was hoping you could give me the number of the girl that Kai attacked. I'd like to speak to her.'

Manny gave her a suspicious stare; he took another drag on his cigarette.

'Why would ye want tae do that?'

'McPherson was a suspect in a suspicious death, not just his own,' Hanlon said. 'I suppose he still is actually. I need to know a little more about him.'

Manny thought a while. 'I don't have a number for her, but we could take you to the place where she lives.'

'Just give me the address,' Hanlon said. 'I don't want to put you to any trouble.'

She was slightly incredulous at the thought of Manny leaving the pub. Can he even walk? she wondered. She had seen no evidence of it.

'It's nae bother, Leo will take you. Besides, they would nae let you across the threshold without someone tae vouch for you.'

'Aye,' agreed Leo, 'the Gillespie family are none too trusting of strangers, y'ken.' Particularly the police, she thought.

'OK,' Hanlon said, 'thanks.'

'Nae bother,' Manny said. 'You can go oot the back way. The car is a white Mercedes.'

Leo turned to lead the way. Manny looked at his phone and frowned.

'Oh, I need a quick wee word with you, Leo. Hanlon, you go on aheid...'

Leo closed the door behind Hanlon and looked at Manny.

'Yes, boss?'

'Our friend on the Isles just got in touch, Leo. Hanlon's nae here officially, they're going tae sack her.' Manny's voice was quiet, serious.

'What's she up tae?' Leo wasn't smiling any more.

'Fuck knows, Leo, but she's snooping around, that's for sure. Get rid of her... There'll be nae consequences, she will nae be missed.'

Leo smiled at Manny beatifically. 'It'll be a pleasure.'

Manny reached in a desk drawer and produced a flick knife. He clicked it and a ten-centimetre blade sprang out; he retracted it and held it out to Leo in his open palm.

'Want this?'

Leo shook his head. 'I dinnae need that, she's just a lassie.'

Manny shrugged. 'Just silence her, Leo, silence her for good.'

Leo nodded and left the room.

* * *

Hanlon let herself out of the back door and crossed the yard of the pub with its empty beer barrels and stacked boxes of empty mixers and beer bottles awaiting collection. A black metal fire escape ran to the first floor upstairs.

She drew the bolt back on the gate, went into the street and leaned against the white Mercedes saloon that was parked nearby.

She wanted to see the girl that Kai had beaten up so badly, to let her know that she could have closure, that Kai would never be able to hurt another woman again, and partly because she wanted to know if Lee Anne had any background information on Murdo Campbell. She was thinking, I'm this close to catching him. McCleod would get the glory, she'd get the girl. Campbell would get his just deserts.

Hanlon saw Leo appear from around the corner, the sun glinting on his short blond hair, his vestigial mohican. He had pulled a blue denim Levi's jacket on over his T-shirt. There was a lot of blue ink on Leo. The blue tattoos that he had over his body, the spider-web on his neck, the letters spelling out love and hate on his knuckles. His name inked indelibly on the centre of his collarbone.

He pulled a remote from his jeans pocket and the car doors clicked unlocked. Leo put it back in his jeans jacket pocket. Hanlon got in the passenger seat and Leo slid behind the wheel.

'OK?' he said to Hanlon, giving her one of his high-wattage smiles. His eyes looked even crazier than normal, their colour a faded light blue.

'Sure.' Hanlon felt a twinge of unease at being alone again with Leo. He didn't inspire confidence.

Leo drove through Paisley's back streets – at least he drove normally, thought Hanlon, even if his behaviour was weird – and then onto a dual carriageway. Hanlon had absolutely no idea where they were going. The road ran through the industrial-looking suburbs of Glasgow. As he pulled off the road she saw a sign marked Govan. He drove slowly along a potholed broad street that led past abandoned warehouses, an old industrial area; she could see the occasional crane and guessed they must be near the Clyde. Where they were driving to had certainly seen better days. He drove past soot-streaked and blackened tenement blocks. They couldn't have been cleaned in decades. Very few people were around. Shops were shuttered; they passed two burned-out cars, one on some waste ground, one parked by the side of the road. Poverty and abandon lay all about them. Weed-choked waste grounds, sagging wire fences topped with rusting barbed wire. They hardly passed a soul, the occasional pedestrian, people with Staffy terriers on leashes, a liquor store with barred windows. Hanlon felt a prickle of unease. There was a silence in the car that was hardly companionable. She was suddenly very aware that nobody knew where she was or who she was meeting.

Leo turned off the main road into a side street. He stopped outside a block of flats, about three storeys high. One of the flats was abandoned and had boarded-up windows. Leo drove around the side and there was a garage underneath the building with a barred gate accessed by a sloping drive. He put his hand in his jacket pocket, took out the keys, pressed a button on a remote attached to the Merc fob and the door slowly slid open. He drove in and stopped the car.

This isn't Lee Anne's address, thought Hanlon. How could he have a remote for her basement garage?

She got out of the car, her face expressionless, a sinking feeling in her stomach. The iron barred door slid closed with a hollow, reverberating clang. No escape that way.

Leo got out of the car.

He smiled meaninglessly at her.

'What's going on, Leo?' she asked, her voice level.

Leo walked around to her side of the car.

'What's going on, Leo?' he said in a high falsetto, parodying her voice. 'What's going on, Leo?'

He stared menacingly at her, no fake good humour any more. Just hate, violence and lust.

'Bitch!' he said flatly. 'Fucking police bitch.'

He opened his mouth wide and waggled his tongue at her; the stud embedded in the pink leathery flesh glinted dully in the dim light that filtered through the bars of the door. Oh shit, thought Hanlon.

'I'll tell you what's going on, bitch,' he said, no smile now. 'I'm going to hurt you.'

'... *things are escalating. You deliberately put yourself in positions of extreme danger...*'

Dr Morgan's voice in her head.

Leo drew his fist back, the one with 'hate' tattooed on his knuckles.

'Here ye go, Hanlon. Here's tae you!'

## 27

If Leo had thought Hanlon was going to just stand there like a lamb to the slaughter, he was in for a rude awakening. He had almost certainly had other people fall on their knees pleading for mercy, or back away trembling with fear. 'Please no' were words he'd heard many times. He had almost certainly never had anyone he'd regarded as a helpless victim fight back as professionally as Hanlon. Leo was a violent, capable thug, but he was a big fish in a small pond and Hanlon had met and beaten worse.

After days of being the victim, of being drugged, attacked and semi-drowned, she was keyed up to dishing some punishment out. She was in tremendous physical shape as well as more than mentally prepared. She sprang towards Leo off her back foot and drove her own fist towards the centre of his face.

Leo was taken by surprise. He was not expecting this. He stumbled backwards to avoid the punch, jerking his head to one side, but not quick enough to stop Hanlon's knuckles grazing his cheekbone. The blow jarred her hand; it left a red weal on Leo's face.

They squared up to each other, Leo looking at her with astonishment.

'Och, I'm so feart!' he said contemptuously. Hanlon didn't reply; she waited, fists raised, her body side on, minimising the target.

'I'm police, Leo, you shouldn't be doing this,' she said.

'You're finished, Hanlon,' he jeered. 'Manny tells me you're an auld has-been.'

Hanlon threw her head back and laughed scornfully. Has-been. I couldn't attack the person at work who called me that, but you'll do, Leo, you'll do nicely.

Her narrowed eyes scanned him contemptuously. Come on, then, Leo, you prick.

He feinted at Hanlon, who stood there, waiting. The punch would be short, she knew that. *An old has-been*, well, let's see, Leo. She didn't flinch or move, then he took a step towards her.

He was in range. Hanlon threw a fast jab at his face. Leo snapped his head away, but as he did so another jab, same hand, he wasn't expecting that, lightning fast connected with his nose. It didn't break, but it was a solid blow and it must have hurt. He took a step back in surprise as much as anything; blood started trickling from his nostrils, very red on his pale face. He rubbed it with the back of his hand, then stared at the red stain with something like bewilderment. Hanlon threw a straight right at his head. He blocked it with his palm, wincing in pain from the force of the punch and as he did so, Hanlon whipped a hard left into his ribs.

It was a powerful body shot, a left hook, the weight of her body behind it and Leo was not expecting it. He was completely taken by surprise. Off balance, he staggered under the force of the blow and Hanlon slammed a right hook into his temple. Leo fell back, shaking his head to clear it. Hanlon was amazed he was still standing; he must have a head like a rock, she thought.

Angrily, Leo advanced towards her. Things were not going to plan. He started throwing a volley of what seemed like endless punches. He was breathing hard through his mouth, his lower face smeared with his blood. Hanlon blocked most of his punches with her upper arms and hands, ducking, slipping the head shots. The body shots were hard and painful, they slammed into her like hammer blows, but she was used to being hit, she was used to pain and she knew she could take these. One or two got through to her head and she saw stars. Leo wasn't smiling now, his face was grim; he had realised the unthinkable. He was a lot heavier but he wasn't as fit and he simply couldn't match her for speed, accuracy or skill. This wasn't a kind of cat-and-mouse game; Hanlon was fully capable of beating him.

Hanlon for her part knew that if Leo won, she could well end up dead or seriously injured. Leo was stronger than Hanlon, but she was fitter, she was faster and she was better. She was a survivor. And she was angry. A roll call of tougher, meaner men than Leo that she'd fought and beaten flashed through her head, not to mention that fucking whirlpool. She grinned at the tattooed Glaswegian. Is that all you've got, Leo?

Leo dropped his right hand low and swung his shoulder back. He was obviously winding up for an enormous right that would smash down Hanlon's defence and knock her down, if not actually knock her out.

To Hanlon it was so obvious what he was intending to do and it was the break that she had been looking for. She stepped close to him; the right side of his body was completely unprotected and she slammed a looping, vicious left hook into the exposed side again. It nearly dropped him and she finished up with the same punch again, this time with her right, this time to his head.

Leo went down to the floor, practically unconscious, and Hanlon kicked him as hard as she could in his groin with her Doc Martened foot. His body jack-knifed and she kicked him again in the stomach. She rolled him on his back, straddled his body, pinning his arms down with her knees. Leo was barely conscious and she hit him again at short range in the face, four times. His nose exploded in blood, his face was covered with it, and his eyes closed.

She stood up, panting for breath, her knuckles crimson with Leo's blood – it was everywhere, over his clothes and hers – and feverishly went through his pockets. Leo was unconscious, still breathing, still alive, but currently no threat to Hanlon.

She found his wallet, the fob for the Merc and his keys. There was a plastic bag with several grams of white powder in his pocket, coke, she guessed. She took that too. She pulled his phone from his jacket pocket; it was cracked but otherwise intact.

Hanlon dragged him by his feet to the back of the Merc, opened the boot with the remote and heaved Leo up. First his head and shoulders and chest so he was half inside, then, grabbing his feet, she pulled the rest of him upwards and inwards. The boot was sizeable and he fitted in comfortably. He moaned and his eyelids fluttered. His face looked terrible. His nose was swelling, as was the flesh around his eyes, his lips were a bloody mess and one of his teeth was missing, either on the garage floor or somewhere inside his mouth.

Hanlon took him by the right hand and pressed his thumb on the circle at the base of his iPhone. To her relief, the screen lit up. She went to Leo's contacts; there was a Lee Anne Gillespie listed. She brought up the details. There was an address as well as a landline and mobile number. She photographed them with her own phone and then, for good measure, took a couple of photos of Leo. Then she slammed the boot shut.

Now she could relax. The fight had taken more out of her than she had realised. That could have been her in the Mercedes. Her legs suddenly felt very weak and she sat down heavily on the cold, rough concrete floor of the garage. For a horrible moment she thought she was going to faint or throw up.

Get up and get out, she told herself angrily. This is probably where Leo lives – his mates could come at any minute. It would be unbelievably stupid to win the battle and lose the war.

She stood up. She heard muffled shouts from the boot and dull thuds as Leo, who had now come round, struggled in the confines of the Merc's boot. She walked over to it, leaned her mouth close to the metal. Have a word with the guy who was going to beat the shit out of you, she thought. Let him know who won.

'*Das beste oder nichts,*' she said. 'It's the Mercedes slogan, Leo, you fucking loser. I saw it a lot in Germany. It means *the best or nothing*, like me and you Leo. I'm the best, and you, Leo, you're a nothing.'

She listened to Leo shouting something inaudible through the metal of the boot; she thought of the ink on his skin. 'You're a fucking nothing, Leo, you fucking bell-end. *Das beste oder nichts,* you can remember that, it'd make a nice tattoo.'

She walked away from the car, pressed the button to open the electric gate of the garage, slipped out into the street. She listened carefully to the sounds coming from the garage. You could hear a very faint noise, which was Leo trying in vain to get out. Could you force your way out of the boot of a Mercedes? Probably, if you knew what you were doing; she doubted Leo did.

Leo was as thick as two short planks. What had Manny said to him before they had left in the car? This was all almost certainly Manny's idea. Leo would be able to get dressed in the morning by himself, but that would be about his limit.

She pressed the button again and closed the barred door behind her, putting the keys in her pocket.

It shut with a satisfactory clang.

Hanlon walked off into the streets of Govan without a backward glance.

## 28

Hanlon checked her location on the maps on her phone and walked off in the direction of the Clyde. As she had thought when she'd been in the car, the great river was very close. Until today, she had only seen it from the air. Now here it was, in all its grotty glory.

She made her way down the wide, quiet, shabby streets to the waterfront and walked along by the river. It was an industrial wasteland down here. Warehouses and abandoned office blocks. A few hundred metres later, she came across a rubbish-removal barge, which was moored to a couple of bollards on the quayside. It had two holds, which were open to the air, and a kind of large mechanical grab like a scaled-up child's toy with which it could remove junk that had found its way into the water. The twin holds were filled with detritus – shopping trolleys, bicycles, tree branches, all the flotsam and jetsam from across the spectrum, both natural and man-made, that had found its way into the waters of the Clyde that the boat had scooped out of the river. She reflected that it could well have been her body, floating face down in the water, that the barge might have found.

An old has-been.

Someone had tipped Manny off about her past, someone who knew her career history. And who might that be? Campbell, you bastard.

And you, Manny, I'm looking forward to renewing our acquaintance. As she walked past the *St Mungo*, as the boat was called, she casually tossed Leo's iPhone into one of the holding areas with all the other rubbish.

She hadn't gone very far when she heard the engines onboard start up with a loud throbbing roar. A figure in high-viz overalls appeared out of the cabin, jumped onto the quay with effortless agility and cast off, leaping back on board as the *St Mungo* pulled into the mid-stream of the river.

It disappeared westwards carrying Leo's phone. She wondered where it would end up. She liked the thought of Leo, once he had eventually managed to free himself or, more likely, after someone found him, using the Find My app and tracking it down to some landfill site somewhere hopefully gratifyingly far away.

Good luck, Leo, she thought. I hope you spend a long time rummaging around in the shit on a vast municipal rubbish tip surrounded by flies and squawking seagulls shitting on you. And good luck explaining your facial injuries – a girl did that, Leo. Don't forget that detail when people ask.

And as for you, Manny, you fat, smoke-ridden gut-bucket, I'm coming for you.

She walked off in search of a taxi.

* * *

The black cab pulled up in front of a tenement building near the centre of Paisley. She thought of Leo's coke in her pocket. I bet

Leo's the dealer, she thought, not Tam. And Manny's the guy pulling the strings. And Campbell is ensuring supplies keep on coming. She got out of the taxi, pulling out her purse, now bulging with notes taken from Leo's wallet, and got ready to pay the driver. He looked at her critically,

'Are you OK, hen?'

'I'm fine,' Hanlon said, surprised. 'Why do you ask?'

'Umm, well, will ye look at the state of yoursel.'

Hanlon looked down at what she was wearing: jeans, pink Doc Martens and a cream blouse over a white T-shirt. The blouse was spotted and stained with Leo's blood, including a big smear over one sleeve, which must have come from when she pushed him into the boot. Fleetingly she wondered how he was getting on in there. She hoped he was claustrophobic.

She bent down and looked at her face in the taxi's wing mirror. There was an ugly bruise under one eye; by the following day her eye would be black.

'My yoga class got out of hand,' she said, adding a large tip from Leo's wad. 'Have a nice day.'

The taxi drove off, the driver waving at her cheerily – it had been an enormous tip. Hanlon went to the front door. She looked up at the building. A depressed, blackened tenement. The windows smeared and dirty. The pavement outside was cracked and marked with the ghost of chewing-gum traces and cigarette butts. There was a panel with a dozen buttons on the wall next to the tall, shabby, forbidding door. It looked a thoroughly depressing place to live.

She pressed the bell.

'Who is it?' asked a female voice.

'Police,' said Hanlon. 'Which floor?'

'Second floor right,' the voice said. At least she didn't sound aggressive. Just tired.

There was a buzz and Hanlon pushed the door open and walked up the grey, worn granite steps to the second floor. She knocked on the door and a girl opened it.

'Come in,' she said.

Lee Anne Gillespie looked about sixteen. She was small and slim with short hair, dyed orange, parted on one side, and a pierced nose, lip and ears. Colourful tattoos decorated her forearms. Hanlon could see the striations of faint scars, the results of self-harm, that bisected some of the tattoos with faint white lines. She was very pretty.

There was more than a hint of weed in the air.

The flat was sparsely furnished with cheap furniture. As well as the smell of the cannabis, there was a strong smell of poverty. The carpet was threadbare, the sofa had been fixed with duct tape. The armchairs were of the sort that old people were sometimes discovered dead in.

'So how can I help you?'

Hanlon could see her looking puzzled at the state of Hanlon's clothes. It wasn't hard to read her mind: what kind of police turn up covered in bloodstains? She opened her bag and showed her warrant card. Lee Anne looked at her questioningly.

'Kai McPherson,' said Hanlon.

A faint smile played around Lee Anne's face.

'Whit's he done the now?'

'I'm afraid he's dead,' Hanlon said.

'Deid?' Lee Anne looked shocked. She sat down on the edge of the sofa.

Hanlon said gently, 'He can't hurt you any more.'

Lee Anne frowned. 'What do you mean, hurt me?'

Hanlon was puzzled. 'I thought he used to beat you up?'

'Beat me up? Who have you been talking to? That's nae true.' She shook her head emphatically.

'Manny Johnson.'

'Manny!' Lee Anne spat the word out. 'Manny! That auld cunt. Him and that arsehole Leo. And you believed him! Are you fucking stupit? If ever there were two congenital liars it's those two!' She now looked absolutely furious. Lee Anne obviously had a temper.

Hanlon made placating motions with her hands.

'So it's not true? It's not true that Kai used to knock you about?' Hanlon was puzzled. Manny had ordered her either dead or injured, she certainly had no reason at all to trust him, but she had believed his story about Kai. It had made so much sense. It matched so well with what she knew of him.

Lee Anne shook her head angrily. 'Kai is a nice guy. You would nae want tae mess with him, but he's nice. I was gang oot with him and then I stupidly fucked it up.'

'So Kai didn't put you in the Royal Alex?'

'No, no one put me in the Royal Alex. Well, obviously I've been in the Royal Alex.' She said it as though it were self-evident that this would be the case. 'This is Paisley, who has nae? But never because of Kai, or any man, come to that.'

'What about Tam?'

'Whit aboot Tam?' She frowned. 'I, like a numpty, pissed as fuck, had sex with Tam and Kai found out and left me. But he never hurt me.'

'So what is the story at that pub?' Hanlon asked.

Lee Anne sighed. 'Look, the way it is, is this. Manny is a coke dealer and Leo is his minder. Manny pays him in drugs. I say coke, but he'll do you anything, ket, smack, spice, whatever...'

'That much I'd worked out,' Hanlon said.

Lee Anne nodded. 'Guid. Tam is one of Manny's best customers. He's also one of Paisley's biggest burglars – you should know, he's got a record as long as your arm – and he's also a fence.

Tam might be able to get you some drugs, if you're a mate, but he buys from Manny. Anyway, Kai *did* get busted but the copper cut him some slack and Kai went straight. He told me that the police man got him a legit job. Kai had had enough of the game, he told me.'

'And what about you?' asked Hanlon.

Lee Anne shrugged. 'You ken, I've tried tae get clean, loads of times, SMART, NA, CA...' she reeled off a list of organisations specialising in addiction, a whole list of acronyms '... even the church... no good. Maybe one day, ye ken. But not right now... I do OK. I'm a sex worker, I'm self-employed, I don't have a pimp.'

That's reassuring, thought Hanlon.

Lee Anne continued, 'I work out of the hotels in the West End, a good class of customer, some regular clients, it's nae too bad.'

Hanlon thought of Nose-stud, another sex worker, dead, her hair drifting like seaweed in the cold Atlantic swell. Kai dead. She wondered fleetingly if Lee Anne worked for the guy who ran the company who had supplied the girls to the Hart brothers. How long would Lee Anne survive?

'Poor Kai,' Lee Anne said. 'I really thought he'd make it. I was happy for him. He'd escaped.'

But he hadn't, had he? thought Hanlon.

She took the bag of coke out of her pocket, Lee Anne's eyes widened.

'What are you trying to do? Fit me up?'

Hanlon shook her head and stood up. 'Nobody's trying to plant drugs. You can have this. It belonged to Leo.'

Lee Anne looked at her as if she were crazy. 'Are you really in the police?'

Hanlon thought of what she had done, what she was doing now and what she was going to do. She thought of McCleod, who was so career conscious she didn't want her staying the night in case that raised question marks about her judgement or her sexual orientation. McCleod, too frightened to go to her superiors to tell them about Campbell. Hanlon felt a twinge of contempt for her Goody Two Shoes behaviour. Then she thought, Well, she's the sensible one, she may be a bit boring but she's not the one in trouble like me. Or indeed the one doling out class A's like a box of chocolates.

'Only just,' she said truthfully. 'Probably not for much longer, to tell you the truth.'

Lee Anne digested this, then looked at the baggy in her hand.

'You stole that from Leo, he'll go mental.'

Hanlon shook her head. 'I didn't steal it, I took it from him.' She pointed at the blood on her sleeve. 'That belongs to Leo too.'

Lee Anne looked at her open-mouthed.

'You beat Leo up?'

'Yes,' said Hanlon simply, without elaborating.

'Wow, I'm impressed.' The girl shook her head in wonder. 'Well, how can I help you? What do you want me to do?' asked Lee Anne.

'Take the night off,' Hanlon said. She opened Leo's wallet and counted out ten twenties, handed them to the dumbfounded girl. 'It's on Leo.'

## 29

Hanlon caught another taxi back to the Rob Roy. She had cleaned herself up as best she could at Lee Anne's but when the taxi driver caught a glimpse of her in his mirror he decided not to try to engage in small talk. It wasn't the bloodstains this time, it was the expression on her face.

It was set and hard, sinister. Hanlon was after revenge. Manny had sent her off with Leo to be given a beating that would have landed her in hospital. Or worse. Manny had lied to her. He had a great deal coming to him. That was what was written on Hanlon's face; that was what the man behind the wheel could see. A gathering storm.

And what the hell to make of what Lee Anne had told her about Murdo Campbell and Kai? Had he simply fooled her, or had Hanlon managed to make a monumental error of judgement? Had Murdo Campbell simply cut him some slack and steered him onto the straight and narrow? Surely not, not after what she'd heard in the bothy – they'd definitely been discussing drug deliveries. Had McCleod been right all along to doubt Campbell's involvement in drug smuggling? Or had Campbell recruited Kai for some hidden reason to embed him into the Mackinnon Arms?

But these questions could wait until later. Manny was her priority right now.

She paid the taxi off and walked to the back door of the pub. The street door was still unlocked. She slipped through it, then across the yard to the back door of the pub. She crept up to the office window and looked through.

Manny was still sitting behind his desk, a cigarette smouldering in his fingers. Where else would he be? He was talking on his mobile. Probably trying to track down Leo, thought Hanlon. He had to be worried by Leo's silence. He'd be expecting a call to say that Hanlon had been dumped somewhere either dead or beaten to a pulp.

There was a small window by the back door. She peered through it, no one around. One of Leo's keys opened the back door. An alarm mounted on the wall had started blinking ominously, but a swipe across it with a black plastic disc also on the key fob disabled it. She stood in the back hall and looked about her. The bottle store was in front of her, then the door that led to the bar, then a door that led upstairs and, to her left, Manny's office. She toyed with the idea of just bursting in, but she suspected that Manny might have some kind of panic button. He did after all run the kind of business in which there was a reasonable chance that a rival might come calling and Manny was in no state to fend off an aggressive small child, let alone a violent criminal.

She stood to one side, opened the office door and slowly pushed it open. Now she could hear Manny talking on the phone.

'He's on a boat, gang doon the Clyde towards Dumbarton. Whit do ye mean, am I sure? I'm looking at fucking Apple Maps... Yes, I'm looking at *Find my iPhone* or whatever it's called... It says he's on the river... He's nae answering... Go after him... How the fuck should I ken whit he's up tae? Look, go tae Erskine, call me from there... It's not fucking far, you lazy cunt... now the fucking door's open, Jesus. It never rains but it fucking pours... I'll call you back.'

She heard him groan as he hauled his ageing body up. She could hear him wheezing and coughing and complaining to himself as he shuffled to the door to close it.

'Fucking inefficient bastards, cannae even close a door properly.'

As it started to shut, Hanlon charged it with her shoulder; she slammed into the wood and the door burst open, taking Manny with it. It sent him sprawling, his weakened legs gave way and he collapsed down onto the floor. Hanlon booted the door shut behind her. The key was in the keyhole and she locked it.

Manny lay on the ground staring up at her. *Oh, fuck,* his expression said.

'Hello, Manny,' said Hanlon brightly, 'remember me?'

'Oh, Jesus...' he mumbled. 'What brings you here?'

'Me and Leo had a bit of an altercation,' said Hanlon. She prodded him with the toe of her boot. 'Do you comprehend the meaning of the word "underestimate", Manny?'

'I know well what it fucking means. Where's Leo?'

'Good question. Let's just say he's in a safe space,' Hanlon said. 'Let's just hope he's not claustrophobic. But let's not talk about Leo. You can tell me about Kai McPherson. And it had better be true this time.'

'Fuck you...' Manny started coughing. His face went puce, he rolled on his side and pulled himself onto all fours.

Hanlon brutally kicked his right arm hard on the elbow and Manny collapsed face down back on the floor.

'That was Leo's attitude too,' she said conversationally. 'Leo's not feeling very well as a result.' She squatted down by Manny, who looked at her with hate-filled eyes. She pulled her phone out.

'Here's Leo after I'd finished with him.'

Manny stared at Leo's bloodied, unconscious face. 'Jesus,' he whispered, 'you did that?'

'Impressive, eh?' said Hanlon. She took hold of Manny's left ear – it felt unpleasantly flabby and fleshy – and rotated it brutally until she saw tears of pain come to Manny's rheumy eyes. 'Now, are you going to tell me what I want to know or shall I start on you?'

'OK...' Manny groaned. 'You win.' She relinquished his ear. 'Kai, well, he *was* lifted, done for possession with intent tae supply and he *did* cut a deal... One of my boys was busted, that's why Kai had tae leave Paisley – he grassed me up.'

'I heard he'd gone straight,' Hanlon said.

Manny shook his head. 'I dinnae think so. I heard that there was a cop in Strathclyde connected with bringing coke in from the islands. Kai was involved in that, that's why he got that job out there. He bragged aboot it tae Tam, said it was huge, far bigger than piss-ant deals down the Rob Roy... That's all I know.'

Hanlon straightened up.

'So, you're telling me that Kai had a deal going with a cop in the islands. Do you know who this cop is? I want a name.'

'I can't...'

Hanlon placed her right heel on Manny's outstretched fingers and leant her weight on it. Manny gasped. 'Jesus, you're breaking my fingers...'

'I know.' She smiled pleasantly down at Manny's anguished, elderly face. His yellowy eyes stared up at her, his mottled cheeks with a crimson network of spidery veins turning a purple-red. 'Please give me a name.'

'Campbell, Murdo Campbell,' he said.

She removed her heel, satisfied. 'OK, then, you'd better pray that I don't come back,' she said. 'Oh, and if I hear that anything has happened to Lee Anne, I will be back. That's a promise. I'll burn your fucking establishment to the ground and you with it.'

'Where's Leo?' Manny asked. 'Please tell me...'

Hanlon pointed at her face. 'Leo hit my head,' she said. 'It must have given me amnesia, oh... hang on, I remember...' She paused as if struck by a thought. 'No, sorry, thought I had it... It's gone again. Hopefully he'll be OK. I'd be very upset if anything happened to Leo. He's got so much to give to the world.'

She took the key from the door.

'Are you going tae help me up?' asked Manny plaintively. He started coughing, then fighting for breath; his pasty white face turned a kind of deep red.

'No,' she said.

'I cannae get up by mysel',' he pleaded.

'Tough, you shouldn't smoke so much.'

Hanlon heard a voice outside. She opened the window. Manny burst into a paroxysm of truly alarming coughing, alternating with breathless wheezing as he fought for breath. Hanlon stepped out of the window into the yard, then pulled it down almost all the way behind her.

There was a knocking on the door.

'Are you OK, Manny?'

'No, I'm not fucking OK.' There was another alarming outbreak of terrible wheezing coughing. 'I'm doon on the flair!'

'Whit the fuck are you doing doon there, Manny?' she heard Frank say from behind the door.

'I need a hand up, Frank... my fucking legs gave way...' Explosive coughing. Hanlon smiled to herself. Manny was not going to admit he'd been beaten by a woman.

'You sound awfi ill, Manny. Are you awreet?'

'Of course I'm nae fuckin' awreet, I'm on the fuckin' flair... Get me up.' More coughing.

'I cannae dae that, Manny, the door's locked.' Frank's voice was one of gentle reason, as if he were talking to a child. More coughing from Manny, lengthy pauses and then anguished wheezes as he breathed in.

'I cannae breathe, I need mah puffer... Break it doon!'

'It's reinforced, Manny, you should know that, it was your idea. I'll get a locksmith.'

'The windae! Come through the windae...' wheezey breaths '... I cannae breathe...'

'I cannae hear whit you're saying, Manny... I'd better get back tae the bar, those cunts'll rob it otherwise... Manny, I'll call the locksmith, hang on in there. He may be a while.'

Hanlon crept to the small window by the back door. She risked a look through. She could see Frank in the dim hallway, crying with laughter. He lit a cigarette and sat down on the stairs. Frank was in no hurry whatsoever to help Manny.

She slipped away across the yard and out into the street. She wondered whether to call for help; she doubted Frank would. Then she thought of Manny calmly ordering Leo to beat her up; she thought of Lee Anne.

She decided to leave Manny's fate up to the universe. She nearly had enough on Campbell for McCleod to go to her superiors. A bit more patient digging would turn something concrete up, she felt sure of it.

But right now she wanted to go home to McCleod.

# 30

The following day – after a night in the Holiday Inn in Port Glasgow, bankrolled by Leo – travelling by coach and ferry, Hanlon returned to Islay and then Jura. It was the last lap in what felt like a very long race.

Standing on the ferry, staring up at the enormous swell of the three Paps, she had an odd feeling of coming home. She breathed in the heavy, salt air, listened to the throb of the engines beneath her feet, the metal and rivets of the white-painted side of the ship cold to the touch under her hand, and wondered why.

Was it McCleod? The warmth of her willing body, her responsiveness to Hanlon's touch – could it be that simple? She somehow doubted it. She'd been alone in her life for too long to want to share too much with another person. But she was aware of a fierce affection towards the other woman, despite her criminal untidiness, her desire to do things by the book, her inability to wash her car or keep it clean inside, and her bloody dog, and she had an uncomfortable feeling that affection was very close to love.

Don't be stupid, she thought, pushing the thought aside.

Hopefully in a couple of hours she would know who had shot Kai and hopefully this would lead to leverage over how the drowned girls had died. Her money was very much on Campbell. He had been on the island when it had happened. He had made one appointment with Kai. Maybe the time had changed. Who else could have lured him there?

Harriet – she was still high on the list of suspects. Maybe she was connected with the drugs, maybe she just didn't like Kai, maybe she had already shot Jim and then Kai rather than shot Kai and made it look as if Jim had done it.

If Harriet knew, maybe Donald? Where had he been at the critical moment? She would have to ask McCleod. But the time of the murder would have coincided with a split shift. Time enough to get on that bike, pedal up there... and kill Big Jim? And make it look like suicide? It was very hard to imagine Donald doing it, and even if he had, what would have been the motive? She dismissed the idea. Besides, Donald would be too lazy, in all probability.

Maybe, of course, it was an unhinged Big Jim all along, it was what it looked like – he was certainly erratic, and he had tried to kill her, after all. So, murder, suicide. Occam's razor – the simplest explanation is likely to be the correct one.

The ferry clanked its ramp down and the vehicles drove off up the slipway. Hanlon walked up to where she had left her (Donald's) bike and unlocked it. She slung her rucksack over her shoulders and pedalled off.

She cycled down the picturesque road, through the village of Craighouse, the hills and mountains on one side, the sea, now the sun was shining, a very deep blue, the hills of the Kintyre peninsula an impressionist green haze over the water.

She passed the Mackinnon Arms hotel, its car park empty. She stopped and looked at the mournful building, now, she guessed, totally deserted. She wondered if anyone had told the psychic holidaymakers that the place was closed. Maybe it would enhance the ghost hunters' hotel experience if they arrived and the place was as inexplicably deserted as the *Mary Celeste*. They could have a seance and in answer to the question, 'Is anybody there?' they'd get the hotel owner from the thirties, the suicide, Eva, Franca, Jim and now Kai. You wouldn't need a Ouija board, you'd need the equivalent of a ghosts' group chat.

She paused briefly at the cottages and dropped the bag off outside. Donald's car wasn't there. She wondered if he was over in Islay looking for work. He certainly wouldn't be busy at the Mackinnon Arms for a while, although maybe he would be soon, occupied with fighting Harriet for its ownership. That was if she wanted it. It can't have had happy memories.

Back on the mountain bike, she passed the place – shack would have been dignifying it – where Big Jim had kept his bottles. She slowed as she went past. She thought of that fateful afternoon.

Here his Land Rover would have been parked. She could visualise Big Jim, very pissed, putting the vehicle in gear and heading off up the track to exact bloody revenge on Kai for some inexplicable reason. He had tried to kill her for no very good motive. What was it with the barman?

Revenge, dislike – had Kai's sexual encounter with Harriet excited his jealousy? Had he seen Kai heading up the forestry trail and decided to confront him? Maybe Kai had let slip he was going to work for Donald when he took the hotel over. Easy to imagine Big Jim out of his mind, incredibly drunk (it'd be interesting when they found out how much alcohol was in his blood; her bet was it would be off the scale), jealous, homicidal anger fuelled by a couple of litres of Smirnoff.

Or, an alternative scenario, Kai's murderer coming across an unconscious Big Jim, luring him into the Land Rover and driving him slowly up the jolting road to his death. He would have had to be lured – nobody would be strong enough to drag the dead weight of an eighteen- or nineteen-stone Big Jim up from the beach, over those rocks, into a Land Rover.

Was that how it had gone? Easy enough to get a befuddled Big Jim into a vehicle, just promise him more booze.

Hanlon was here now at the bothy. She got off the bike, went round the back and opened the door with the key that McCleod had given her, ducking under the police tape.

Inside it was cool and dark. There was a faint smell of blood, maybe just her imagination, and some dark stains on the floor. Otherwise it was much as before. Hanlon walked over to the wall, just above head height, where she had secreted the machine. She looked hard, leaned up, feeling with the tips of her fingers, and there it was. She retrieved the tiny recording device, USB sized, and put it in her pocket, then she retraced her steps.

\* \* \*

Back in Donald's cottage she switched on her old laptop, drumming her fingers impatiently as it warmed up.

She inserted the device into the port on the side, opened it and clicked on 'Play'.

Excitedly, she leaned forward as she waited to discover Kai's last words. The identity of his killer. Please, God, let it be Campbell, she prayed.

## 31

The next day, Hanlon opened the door to the ring on the bell. It was McCleod.

'Oh my God, what the hell has happened to your face?' She stared at Hanlon in horror. Hanlon's left eye was swollen practically shut and was a purple-blue colour. There were several other bruises on her face, on her chin and cheekbone. McCleod's eyes dropped to Hanlon's upper right arm. This was even more badly bruised, as if she'd had an abstract tattoo inked onto the skin. It was there she had taken the bulk of Leo's punches.

'Jesus, your arm... You look like you've been hit by a truck.'

'Come in, I'll tell you about it.' It was then that she noticed that McCleod was using a walking stick and hobbling. She looked at her questioningly.

'What have you done?' Hanlon asked.

'I twisted my ankle at circuits,' McCleod said. 'It's swollen up like a bastard. I can hardly move. I cannae walk the dog. Poor Wemyss is going spare, he's got cabin fever.'

They sat down next to each other on the sofa and kissed.

'Be careful touching my arm and face,' Hanlon said. 'They're pretty sore...'

McCleod said softly, smiling, 'Please don't do anything like this again. Promise me you'll stick to official channels...'

Later, as they lay in bed upstairs, she told McCleod what had happened in Glasgow and Paisley.

'And Manny confirmed that Murdo Campbell is behind the smuggling?' said McCleod. Hanlon nodded.

'Oh, he's guilty all right, it's just corroborative proof we need.'

McCleod asked, 'Well, what about the recording from the cottage? You've retrieved that, I take it?'

'I did, and it was absolutely useless,' fumed Hanlon. McCleod raised her eyebrows in surprise.

The machine had worked faultlessly. It had recorded Kai saying, in a surprised tone of voice, 'Hello, what the fuck?' Then the sound of a shotgun. Then, after a brief pause – the machine was noise activated and had switched itself off – the arrival of the forensics team.

'We are absolutely none the wiser,' agreed McCleod. They both stared dolefully at the useless recording device.

'How about your investigation?' asked Hanlon, pessimistically. 'How are official channels working out?'

'It's really not getting anywhere.' McCleod shook her head. 'The first thing I wanted to do was trace the person who called the murder in. We tried tracing the 999 call, but they must have dialled 141 or had caller block switched on in settings. There's no tracing the mobile used to make the call. The voice is a man's voice, an English accent, we've no idea who it is. There are lots of tourists around at this time of year. Hill-walkers, bird-watchers, people fishing the lochs... The current thinking is that the person who found the bodies doesn't want it known he was here on Jura, maybe someone having an affair, maybe someone with a record who thinks they might get implicated.' She shrugged. 'Who knows? Then there's no obvious evidence from the scene of crime people. But if you're right and the killer was Campbell, he'd know what to do to avoid leaving any trace. I guess we're waiting for a break.'

Hanlon sighed.

'How did the alibis check out?'

'Donald's one is rock solid. He was working all day long, there was a coach party staying to lunch and he was the only one in the kitchen, helped by Johanna and a couple of part-timers.'

'Harriet?'

McCleod shook her head. 'She doesn't have an alibi. She wasn't working. She says that she had been out for a walk and had returned to her room, but nobody saw her.'

'So, it could be her, then?'

'It could be.'

'And Campbell?' McCleod just looked at her. The look said, Do you really think I'm going to ask my superior officer for an alibi...?

'We could still get a break,' McCleod said, 'or maybe, just maybe, things are what they seem, and Big Jim really did kill Kai.' She stroked Hanlon's hair. 'Cheer up, I'll think of a way to bring Manny in. He might talk.'

'If he's still alive,' said Hanlon gloomily. She had a feeling Frank might have finished him off.

They were silent, then McCleod asked, 'Could you do me a favour? Could you look after Wemyss for me for the afternoon? I have to go over to Islay for a meeting.'

'Sure, when do you want to pick him up?'

'I'll be round about 6 p.m. If you could walk him, I'd be very grateful. He hasn't been out today.'

'I'll see you then. Oh, can I run with Wemyss?'

'How do you mean?'

'If I go running will he run along with me? I was going to do fifteen k.'

McCleod laughed. 'You most certainly can, but I'd do it on the road. He is a sheepdog, he can get over-excited if you're hill-running and he sees animals, but he's fine on the road. He'll run to heel too, but carry a lead, just in case. There's one in my car.'

They went out to the Volvo and the DS let Wemyss out of the hatch. He jumped around excitedly and sat obediently as McCleod handed Hanlon his lead and water-bowl. He looked suitably puzzled and slightly mournful as McCleod drove off, but then shook himself briskly and followed Hanlon back inside.

Hanlon looked at the dog; the dog looked expectantly at Hanlon.

'Walk?' she said.

Wemyss looked excited and went to the door, wagging his tail enthusiastically. Hanlon opened the door, kicked off her training shoes and reached under the shelf in the porch for her walking boots. As she did so she noticed the boots that Morag had lent her.

She swore. She had walked away from Morag's house without a word in her borrowed clothes because she had suspected the woman might be some stooge of Big Jim's. Perhaps she had been, but she had undoubtedly helped her. And he was dead now – the least she could do was return the clothes and boots. Hanlon prided herself on paying her debts. Besides, Morag was probably at work in the hills, maybe not even here on Jura. She could always leave them in the porch with a note; it might not even be necessary to speak to her.

'Come on, Wemyss,' she said.

\* \* \*

They walked down the road to Morag's house near the tip of the island. Hanlon guessed that it would take them an hour. She tried to think of some other way that they could get some leverage on Campbell. Nothing came to mind. Well, something would turn up. The main thing was, she was still alive, that and for once she had someone in her life, Catriona McCleod. She recalled the horrified look on her face when she'd opened the door. It was unusual for someone to care so much about her.

There was a part of her that was slightly irritated by McCleod's concern. Well, it was her own fault for not calling her to warn her, she supposed. She would have to learn to keep others informed of her actions; she would lose the freedom to simply do what she wanted when she wanted if she was going to seriously be in a relationship. She hadn't texted McCleod since the previous morning. In Glasgow there had been too much going on, and then over here on Islay and Jura there was the technical problem, the lack of a signal.

The dog trotted obediently beside her. The road was a dead end, of course, and they met no traffic whatsoever. The only sign of life was a couple of boats out in the loch and once a low-flying jet, travelling faster than sound so she had the peculiar experience of seeing it before she heard it. Up in the sky she saw the buzzard circling and, down on the shore, fast-darting small brown birds that skimmed the grey rocks. They walked past Big Jim's drinking retreat in the boulders on the beach, then the path that led up to the loch, then the forestry road that she'd run up earlier that day.

As they strolled along, she lost herself in pleasurable fantasies about life with McCleod. She could transfer to Glasgow, Hanlon would leave the force, maybe make a living doing personal training or security. They could live together somewhere in the city, away from the prying eyes on Jura. McCleod made her laugh, wasn't intimidated by her, and she loved the way that the other woman lay by her side with one arm thrown over her, fiercely clinging onto her, as if terrified of losing her. It was nice to be needed.

The tarmac road petered out and became a rough track made of impacted stone. Hanlon rounded a bend and now she could see the stretch of water between the tip of Jura and the island of Scarba, the Gulf of Corryvreckan, where Big Jim had tried to drown her the other day.

She stopped and patted the dog. She looked across to where she knew the whirlpool was. She had survived that; she had survived Leo. She felt a sudden surge of invincibility.

Now she could see the roof of Morag's house.

She walked along the track up to the gate in the dry stone wall and then she saw the Mitsubishi Barbarian.

She sighed; she'd have to make conversation after all. She opened the gate and went in. She walked round the house. She had noticed that Morag didn't use the front room; it was kept for best. She knocked on the back door and she saw the forestry woman get up from the chair in the kitchen by the stove and open it. She noticed Morag start slightly at the sight of Hanlon's swollen eye, but she was too tactful to say anything.

'I was wondering if I'd see you again,' said Morag pleasantly. 'Would you like a cup of tea?'

'Can the dog come in?'

'Of course he can, Bridie won't mind. Don't worry about your boots.'

Hanlon handed her the clothes and wellingtons. 'Here's your stuff, thank you.'

'Thank you for bringing them back,' said Morag. She looked tired and unhappy as she ushered Hanlon into the untidy kitchen. Morag indicated a chair and she sat down.

'Look, Morag,' Hanlon said, 'I'm sorry I left so suddenly.' She decided to come out with what had happened. 'My kayak did sink, but not by itself. Big Jim tried to kill me out on the loch.' Morag simply nodded; she didn't look remotely surprised. 'I swam to shore and when I saw your pick-up truck, well, I'd seen it before. I panicked.'

Morag handed her a cup of tea; she took it.

'At one of Big Jim's parties, I take it,' Morag said bitterly. 'You were right to be worried if you thought I was a pal of Big Jim's – that man was scum.'

'You're telling me!' said Hanlon. She described what had happened out by the Corryvreckan. Morag nodded.

'Thank God he's gone.' She sighed. 'Well, here's my Big Jim story.' She picked up her mug of tea and clutched it tightly, her eyes unfocussed, looking into the past. 'Two years ago I was at a party at the Mackinnon Arms. Oh, don't get me wrong, I knew it was a kind of swingers' party, but, well... I don't know, things had been happening, I was in a bad space, I thought it might be exciting. I got drunk, more than drunk – I think Big Jim spiked my drink. I woke up the next morning in his bed.'

'Bastard,' said Hanlon.

'Oh, but it gets worse,' Morag said, 'much worse.' She stood up, put down her tea, walked over to a cabinet and got out a bottle of the Famous Grouse. 'I need a drink, want one?'

'No, thanks.'

Morag poured three fingers of neat Scotch. She looked at it and then shook her head.

'Dammit, I've got to drive into Craighouse soon...' She put the glass back in the cupboard with the bottle and turned to Hanlon.

'It wasn't just him, there was another man too. I... they... well, it was disgusting and someone, probably Harriet, had filmed it.

Basically, Big Jim threatened to upload it to the net unless I came along to his parties every now and again.'

'I'm not sure he could have done that. Upload it. Legally, I mean, as well as content-wise...'

Morag shrugged.

'Exactly, you're not sure. Who knows how these things work? Not me, that's for sure. Besides, illegality wouldn't have stopped him. He could certainly have texted explicit images of me to everyone he knew, that much is certain. I've got two kids at uni – do they want to see their mother doing God alone knows what? Especially with him...' There were tears now.

'Well, now it's over. I'm glad he's dead. I just wish he'd suffered a bit more.'

'Morag, where were you when Big Jim died?' asked Hanlon, suddenly suspicious.

Morag laughed and shook her head. 'Up in the hills, working. I didn't have anything to do with it. But I will tell you, I was very pleased to hear his head had been blown off.' She nodded fiercely. 'I was bloody delighted. Shame Harriet didn't join him.'

'And Kai?'

'He was at the party the other night.' Morag smiled. 'But no, I don't know anything about him. To be honest, I avoided that hotel unless Big Jim insisted.'

'Someone drugged me,' Hanlon said. 'I thought it was because they didn't want me snooping around their sex party.'

'Maybe, I wouldn't put anything past that old bastard – nothing about him would shock me any more,' said Morag vehemently. 'But you're much better-looking than me and I was drugged for sex. I think you just got lucky somehow.'

So, Hanlon thought, if I hadn't taken that coke off Franca, Big Jim could well have been in my room. Was that why he tried to kill me? He turned up in my room expecting to find me unconscious, unable to resist, found I wasn't there, guessed I was down-stairs, knew I'd seen what was going on?

Well, I guess we'll never know.

'Whose is the dog?' asked Morag suddenly. 'I think I've seen him around.'

'Oh, it's a friend's,' Hanlon said. No need to bring McCleod into it.

Morag didn't pursue it. 'Anyway, I quite understand why you ran off when you thought I'd grass you up to Big Jim. Thank God he's gone.'

'Thank you for telling me. Was there a man called Murdo Campbell there? At the sex party the other night.'

She frowned. 'I don't recall the name?'

'Very red hair, green eyes, handsome.'

'A good-looking guy with red hair?' She smiled. 'Yes, there was, but he got very drunk and passed out. Unless Big Jim Rohyp-noled him too. I think Big Jim would've screwed anything that moved. Anyway, they had to carry him upstairs.'

For some reason Hanlon felt inexplicably relieved that Camp-bell hadn't been shagging Big Jim's clients. Morag stood up. 'Do you want a lift? I'm going to Craighouse.'

Hanlon nodded. 'I'm staying at the cottages near the hotel.' She hesitated, 'Let me give you my number. Just in case.'

'Thanks.'

Morag took the number and the two of them, accompanied by their dogs, left the house.

## 32

Back at Donald's, Hanlon made a cup of tea and lay curled up on the sofa with Wemyss lying in the crook of her legs. Soon she would be out of Donald's house and moving from Jura to Islay and Tremayne's B & B. She felt a pang of regret. The island had got under her skin in a way she could never have foreseen.

But right now, she felt flat, deflated by what she had heard from Morag. Big Jim, even more of a bastard than she'd imagined. Rapist, blackmailer, homicidal maniac, probable drug dealer. Arsehole.

Well, he was gone. Finished. What wasn't finished was Murdo Campbell, the drug smuggling, and, she suspected, bringing the guilty to account for the actual murders, the drowned girls. And the really frustrating thing was, there was nothing she could personally do about it.

She had no proof. Only what she had overheard in the bothy, seen with her own eyes. Her earlier optimism vanished. Manny was hardly going to testify, and that was assuming Frank hadn't killed him. McCleod believed her, well, maybe, but she wasn't going to do anything that might jeopardise her career, certainly. At best, she would keep a suspicious eye on Campbell.

And Campbell was untouchable. Using Kai as his middleman to help move drugs, positioning him in the heart of the community in a job where he could come and go easily, going out to sea to meet an incoming boat to pick up the drugs. No questions asked. If Kai had just moved onto Jura people would have wondered what a Paisley hard man was doing relocating to an obscure hotel on a remote island. He would have been the subject of a great deal of speculation and observation. But not based in the Mackinnon Arms, in a job he had been tailored to courtesy of Murdo's compliant sister, Ishbel.

And what a great way to launder money, through The Sleeket Mouse. Doubtless there would be other restaurants; other 'backers' would appear to explain the quantities of money that Ishbel Campbell would have access to.

Well, lying around staring at the ceiling wasn't helping.

She stood up and went over to the small bookcase and picked up the book of collected Robert Burns that Donald had pointed to when he had told her the origin of the restaurant's name. The only book Donald owned that wasn't a cookery book.

She saw to her surprise that Burns had written 'Auld Lang Syne' amongst other things. Well, if that was the case he had a lot to answer for, in her opinion. She hated New Year. She read 'To a Mouse'. It was quite touching really, a farmer apologising to a mouse for destroying its cosy home with his plough blade, just as cruel winter was approaching.

Well, she knew the feeling. Five hundred miles away the IOPC was steadily compiling a doubtless damning report. She was the mouse, the IOPC was the destructive, remorseless, implacable blade inexorably moving in on her. Hanlon had received an e-mail from her rep suggesting that there was an offer of resignation on health grounds available. This would mean she would keep her pension rights, she would just lose her job. But at least she wouldn't be sacked.

He heartily recommended she take it.

*'Thy wee bit housie, too, in ruin...'*

Like the mouse house, her career now lay in ruins. She could fight on, but she wasn't sure she had the heart for it. She thought of McCleod. It was two now. She'd walk Wemyss over, it'd take quite a while. She wanted sympathy and advice. McCleod, the resolute career woman, wedded to the police force, she'd know what to do.

She got up and went to the door. Wemyss, eager at the prospect of another walk, leapt from the sofa. Hanlon sat on the front step and pulled on her boots, looking out at the blue sea, the sun beating down and a cold, salt breeze ruffling her hair.

They could talk about their relationship too. Anything was better than morose inaction. That was just a recipe for disaster.

She stood up and whistled the dog and they set off down the road.

## 33

Hanlon and Wemyss walked up the track to McCleod's house. As they rounded the corner she froze: Donald's red Nissan Micra was parked next to McCleod's Volvo.

There was something in the cosy proximity of the cars that suggested a similar relationship of the owners. It's my imagination. It can't be, thought Hanlon.

*'I'm working on Islay, I'll be round about six.'*

It was five now. Your imagination is going crazy, she told herself sternly. It's two cars, that's all. It's meaningless.

She felt sick.

Perhaps she got back early, perhaps Donald had come round to offer cooking tips or something. God knew McCleod needed it.

She thought of the mouse, secure in its nest, oblivious of the iron plough headed towards it, until it burst through the walls.

Perhaps it's nothing.

She walked to the front door and knocked.

Perhaps it's nothing.

The door opened.

McCleod. Short belted dressing gown. Naked underneath.

Tousled hair. Smelling unmistakeably of sex. Shock on her face at the sight of Hanlon, then replaced by an imperturbable mask.

'Who is it?' called a male voice.

And Hanlon's dreams lay in ruins.

Donald appeared, barefoot too, jeans and a T-shirt.

Betrayal. Anger. Disbelief. Jealousy. Rage. Nausea

'Hello, Hanlon.' He grinned. 'Come to join in?'

## 34

McCleod took charge with exemplary efficiency.

'Go and wait in there, Donald,' she said sharply, pointing at her bedroom door. He shrugged and obeyed.

Our bed, thought Hanlon stupidly. Our bed. She felt like throwing up. I feel betrayed. Duplicity. Hanlon hated being lied to and people lied to her all the time. Usually at work: lies, half-lies and omissions. She didn't need it in her private life. McCleod sat down on the sofa and Hanlon took the chair opposite.

Was this the meeting on Islay? What other lies? She felt a burst of anger, blazing, sharp, towards herself. How could she have been so stupid, so gullible?

'Well, this is unexpected,' McCleod said brightly. Then, 'Let's be adult about things.'

For a mad second Hanlon felt like back-handing her. She fought down the urge to wipe the irritating smile off McCleod's face. I don't want to be adult. I want to break your fucking nose.

Dr Morgan's voice in her head. *'Yes, that worked brilliantly last time, didn't it?'*

Hanlon's phone rang, no caller ID. It would have been polite to have ignored it. Hanlon was in no mood to be polite. She wanted to make a point. A man's voice, an English accent.

'It's Morag...'

'Really?' She actually looked at the phone in surprise. What?

Morag noted the surprise in her voice. 'Aye, really. I've got an app does it,' she explained. Of course, thought Hanlon, she knew another single woman who had the same thing on her phone, for the same reason. Morag carried on in her digitally altered man's voice, McCleod staring at Hanlon with annoyance.

'I remember who the dog belongs to, that policewoman...' Hanlon felt a faint stir of alarm, like the rumble that signals the start of an avalanche. 'I did see a car in the hills that day, driving away from the bothy, the one where they say it happened...' Oh my God, the killer's car. Hanlon kept her face expressionless.

'Go on...' her voice level.

Hanlon's eyes went to McCleod, who was leaning forward rubbing her foot, the swollen ankle.

'Her Volvo.' McCleod, the killer. Not Campbell at all, not Big Jim. Her friend and lover, the woman sitting so calmly in front of her at this precise moment.

Hanlon ended the call. McCleod met her eyes.

'Who was that?' she said pleasantly, but with a hint of steel. Their eyes were locked together. She knows I know, thought Hanlon.

'Nobody,' Hanlon said. She stood up.

'I'm going now. I need to think about things. I'll leave you and Donald in peace.'

'I don't think you should,' said McCleod, also standing up, her voice hard. 'I really don't think you should. Who was that on the phone, Hanlon? Donald,' she shouted. There was real urgency in her voice now, panic too.

The chef ran out of the bedroom towards Hanlon and

McCleod grabbed her arm. Good, thought Hanlon. You started it. Time for some justified violence. She drove a hard right hook into her body, real venom in the punch. God, that felt good, and McCleod staggered back, tripping over a shopping bag on the floor. She landed on her back. Donald threw a punch at Hanlon. She jerked her head out of the way and hit him hard on the nose with a straight right. He reflexively stepped back, clutching his face, then she pushed past him and ran for the door.

'Get the shotgun!' she heard McCleod shout as she ran outside. Shit, she thought, it'll be to hand as well, in the wardrobe, ten feet away, not locked away in a safe. It'll only take him a couple of seconds.

She looked around. The drive, too long to reach the road before Donald, armed with a shotgun, caught up with her in a car. She ran to the left and started scrambling up the steep slope of the small hill behind the house to put as much distance between her and the place as possible before Donald ran out.

She pushed her way upwards through the greenery, relishing the steep slope. You try it, Donald, you fat bastard, she thought, through the ferns and stumpy, lichened bushes and past bog myrtle, alder and birch trees. Clouds of midges arose around her and within a couple of minutes she was covered with sweat. She thought grimly of Donald trying to follow her. You haven't got a chance, you fat prick. McCleod could have bounded up it like a gazelle, but thank God for that busted ankle, about the only thing she hadn't lied to her about. No way, she thought. No way could Donald get through this.

I'm home and free.

After about five hundred metres of climbing, the foliage thinned and she could look down on the house and the sea beyond. She sat down and caught her breath. She could see the drive to McCleod's cottage, a dark line from up here, running down to the road that ran parallel to the water and then, far below now, she caught sight of the two cars parked outside the house.

She watched, grim-faced, as Donald came out of the house with McCleod, who was leaning on her walking stick. Donald was carrying a shotgun. He'd obviously decided he didn't care about trying to disguise Hanlon's death in the way he and McCleod had done when they'd decided to kill Kai. Killing Hanlon now was the main thing.

Hanlon looked around her. There was certainly plenty of Jura to hide a body in. Not like at sea where it could wash up anywhere.

She did a quick mental calculation. It would take Donald about twenty minutes to get to where she was now, by which time she'd be about twenty minutes ahead of him, half an hour realistically. The chef certainly was in no shape to follow her.

Above her, and in the distance, rising up majestically, the sun glinting on the silvery grey scree, were the peaks of the Paps of Jura that ran along the spine of the island. All she had to do was head towards them, using them as a marker, until she reached where the ferry came in.

He could hardly shoot her there.

She narrowed her eyes and started to move, the muscles in her legs like iron rippling under the skin. Home and dry, she thought, home and dry.

\* \* \*

Ten minutes later, Hanlon was cursing under her breath. Until now she had thought nothing of the burns that criss-crossed Jura except as picturesque. Now she was more than just aware of them. This one she was looking at was a major headache. It wasn't the burn itself so much, it was what it had done to the hill-side. The stream, as it flowed down from the hills towards the house, had, over time, cut a deep gorge into the ground and there was no way she could realistically cross it.

She had come across it totally by surprise. It was hidden by a fold of the hill and screened by a line of trees and then suddenly, unexpectedly, there was a cleft in the earth maybe thirty metres deep and twenty wide with the brown powerful waters of the stream and giant boulders worn smooth over the aeons, far below.

Uncrossable. Except of course down at the road where there was a bridge that she must have crossed a dozen times on car and bike without noticing. It hadn't been important. It was now.

Uncrossable, unless you had a rope and plenty of time, neither of which she had. And while she stood here, wasting precious time, an armed killer would be coming for her.

The side of the bank was treacherous, mud and stone and practically vertical; you'd need a rope to get down. She looked around her in desperation. She had to get across the gorge to get to the higher ground. Only up there would she be safe. Here she was horribly exposed.

To her left, below, maybe half a mile away, she could see the sea. Bordering that was the road that led north to the Mackinnon Arms and now she could see, slowly making its way along the road, a quad bike. She knew who would be driving it. Hanlon's heart sank. Between her and the road the land was open, boulder-strewn fields of grass and rushes, dark patches of emerald green decorated with yellow, gorse bushes, and yellow-green splodges of bog. Nothing at all that would stop or hold up the quad.

Hanlon cursed. The idea that she would be untrackable disappeared. It was obvious what her choices were now she had hit the hidden obstacle of the impassable gorge. She would be forced along parallel to it. Donald and McCleod would have known that she couldn't cross it and would be forced inland, towards the mountains, until there was a ford or crossing place.

She took her phone out of her pocket. No coverage. No calling for help. She put it back.

Well, she couldn't outrun a quad bike but, screened as she was at the top of the huge field by bushes and the trees, there was still a slim chance that Donald wouldn't see her. At least she wasn't being pursued by Murdo Campbell, whose tracking skills had so impressed her the other day. How could she have been so blind? No, she thought, that was unfair on herself. McCleod had been remorselessly cunning. And if it hadn't been for Morag's phone call, she'd probably be dead.

She crouched down by a gorse bush, momentarily wondering at its vivid yellow flowers and the deep emerald green of its spiky foliage. The snarling noise of the powerful quad bike engine grew louder and louder and then she saw its olive-green shape on its squat tyres come into view. It was about a hundred metres away.

Donald, she found it easy to imagine a look of calm concentration on his face, stamped on the brake and clambered laboriously off. You wouldn't know by his expression that he was hunting down a woman with a view to killing her. It was probably the same look of quiet absorption that had made him such a good chef in top London restaurants.

The shotgun was slung over his shoulder and as Hanlon watched he broke it open and loaded two shells. He clicked it shut, and looked down, checking the safety catch. A good chef, in no hurry, making sure of his equipment, making certain everything was in place. That wasn't good, but what she next saw made her heart sink.

Bounding effortlessly up the slope of the hill was Wemyss. Hanlon could see McCleod's Volvo parked at the bottom of the field. The dog stopped by Donald, who ruffled his fur and gave him a biscuit from his pocket. Wemyss wolfed it down gratefully. He then pulled out a T-shirt from under his jacket and gave it to the dog to smell. Hanlon recognised it as the one she had been wearing when she and McCleod had been at the exercise class together. She'd left it with McCleod, taking one of hers.

The dog looked questioningly at Donald. She heard him, the breeze carrying the words, 'Good dog, FIND!' The dog took off at speed; Donald remounted the quad bike and followed.

Wemyss ran in a zigzag fashion, pausing and sniffing the air, his keen nose sometimes down on the ground, sometimes pointing skywards. The breeze was blowing from the sea, fortunately for her, and the dog couldn't get wind of her scent. He was puzzled, she could see that.

The two of them were now headed in the direction she had come from. All she could do was start jogging along the side of the ravine, up into the hills, hoping for some way of getting down the sheer side of the gorge and accessing the stream so she could wade upstream and lose the scent. Then, to her horror, the wind direction changed. It was now blowing down from the hill, carrying her scent towards the collie.

Any hope Hanlon had of escape quickly disappeared. She was aware of a movement by her side and looked down to see Wemyss at her heels, the muscular dog grinning at her as he effortlessly kept pace with her, enjoying the unexpected game. He barked happily, in sure expectation of another treat. Hanlon slowed to a walk, she couldn't outrun the dog, and then, sure enough, she heard the quad bike and turned to face her pursuer.

He awkwardly and stiffly clambered from the machine, unslinging his shotgun as he approached her. Donald walked carefully and slowly towards her. His feet, supporting his seventeen or eighteen stone, sank up to their ankles in the soft ground. The expression on his face was one of quiet amusement, as if they'd been playing a game of tag and now he'd managed to catch her.

Hanlon stood facing him. She, by contrast, was light, muscular, elegant and poised on her feet. The time for running was over. The shotgun in Donald's hands was large, ugly and menacing.

Hanlon breathed deeply. With the adrenaline coursing through her body, she was hyper-aware of her surroundings. Mindfulness, she thought ruefully, so prized these days, but look at the price I'm paying. Right now, she was conscious of the sloping rough pasture falling down to the track and the sea. She was conscious of Donald inexorably marching towards her. She was conscious of the gorge just a couple of paces backwards behind her, a violent, jagged slit like an irregular scar in the flesh of the rush-strewn field. On the opposite bank, the green pines rose impenetrably up. Hanlon could hear the noise of the water from far below, its powerful brown current with flecks of foam tumbling over both smooth and jagged boulders. She cast a quick glance over her shoulder. The sides of the gorge, virtually sheer, shaded by the trees, were covered in vivid green lichen, moss and other plants, and the emerald flash of the occasional fern.

'Shame it had to end like this, Hanlon,' said Donald. She noticed he was careful to stop a few feet away from her. 'I never did get my threesome.'

'You're not my type, Donald, you fat arsehole,' she replied.

Her keen grey eyes scanned the ground to either side of her. From where she was standing, she could see where the soil had eroded the edge of the land, creating treacherous overhangs at the edge of the ravine, the last couple of metres of the edge of the gorge lacking any underpinning. If an unwary person walked to the edge it could collapse in a heartbeat.

The ground behind her, like the brim of a hat or the peak of a cap, jutted out. She was standing practically on the edge of the cliff. A step backwards and she would be in freefall. Very little supported the ground that she was on. A kind of turf diving board. She knew that, Donald didn't. As far as he was concerned, the ground beneath his feet, although boggy, was rock solid. Hope flared within her. The slightest heavy pressure and the ground could give way. The burn was about thirty metres down; a fall would be fatal.

Her heart beat like crazy. There was a chance! If she could lure Donald to the edge, the ground could fall away beneath them, collapsing and sending them hurtling down into the burn below. And Donald was heavy, very heavy.

Donald gestured with the shotgun and took a step closer to Hanlon. She moved back fractionally nearer the edge; she felt the ground give slightly beneath her feet. Good! she thought. Any moment now it would collapse. The low leaves of a tree growing by the edge brushed her wiry, unruly dark hair. She looked upwards at its branches. She could see the blue sky and sunlight through its leaves. The bough whose leaves were touching her hair was about twenty centimetres directly above her. It was a thick branch. It would take her weight. She guessed that the fine roots of the tree were all that was holding up the ground on which they were standing.

'It is drugs, I take it?' she asked.

Donald nodded; while he weighed his options he was only too happy to talk. He would much rather her death looked natural – the closer she was to the edge, the better. 'My brother's fishing boat meets a yacht, over from the Azores, the transfer is made at sea, we pick them up, bring them back here, then to the mainland. It's sweet.' He looked at the gun in his hands and at Hanlon and then at the ravine. His thinking was obvious: better that she fell or was pushed rather than be shot.

He came closer. Her body would be found, eventually. An accident, a slip. Easily done. Especially to someone with a track record of cross-country runs, no local knowledge and known to be impetuous.

'And Eva?' she said. Donald smiled unpleasantly.

'I was shagging her, she found out what was happening. She was a terrible swimmer. We threw her into the Corryvreckan.' He shrugged.

So, not Big Jim, she thought. Hanlon's lip curled in disgust. He took another step closer and Hanlon shuffled back a step. She was nearly over the edge now. Donald could see that; he smiled. Nothing could go wrong; he held all the aces. Keep the idiot woman talking while she walked backwards until her foot met air...

'And Franca, why kill her? I know Kai didn't give her all that coke that was in her system.'

'She'd turned up at Kai's to beg for coke, but got the wrong cottage. I was bagging up half a kilo when she burst in. We partied hard, she was a good fuck, and I called Catriona. She was waiting for her when she returned back to the *Lorelei*.' Hanlon nodded, remembering the expensive yacht from Portsmouth. 'Couldnae risk her blabbing, loose lips sink ships, ye ken the saying.'

'And Kai?' She felt the ground sink again. She pretended to slip, easily done on the wet, treacherous, boggy ground. One knee thudded down heavily on the black peat. A nice hard blow to further weaken the overhanging turf. Any second now it had to give. They were practically standing on thin air. All that there was between them and space was about three or four centimetres of soil. It had to give.

Must keep him talking, just a little longer... The hammer blow of her knee had done it!

Seen by Hanlon, unseen by Donald, a fault-line crack had appeared on the soil just in front of his feet. He gestured at her, oblivious of the fragile nature of the ground, with the shotgun and jerked his head at the gorge.

'Stand up, Hanlon,' he ordered. 'You look undignified grovelling down there.'

With pleasure, she thought. She stood up, pushing down hard with her bent knee as she did so; the crack widened and spread beneath his feet. Yes! she thought. We're so close...

'Jump,' he said, his voice hardening. She looked over her shoulder at the huge drop, the stream and its rocks far below. She tried to look terrified; it wasn't hard. 'Or I'll pull the trigger – you know what that'll do, don't you?'

She did indeed. From the waist up she'd be mince.

'Tell me about Kai first...' he frowned '... please,' she begged, playing for time, praying that the insecure ground would hurry up and give way. 'Then I'll jump, I promise...'

Donald sighed, humouring her. 'I don't know how he found out about the shipments, I didn't even know he knew, not till you told Catriona. I just thought until then that he was a barman with a shady past who sold a bit of coke on the side. You tipped us off. She went to kill him, found Big Jim passed out by the side of the road... made it look the way it looked.'

'Now—' he waved the gun '—jump.'

'Make me,' she said defiantly. She was banking on him not wanting to shoot. On his desire to make her death look accidental. Hanlon dead from a fall, natural causes; Hanlon blown to pieces by a shotgun, murder. He shook his head irritably, the shotgun held in one hand, not wavering, and picked up a tree branch from the ground. Bits of old timber were strewn about everywhere under the tree canopy. He hefted it in his muscular right arm, the gun in his left now pointed to the ground. He was obviously intending to push her into the gorge.

'Move!' he ordered.

Hanlon stood there pushing down as hard as she could with her feet. Surely the overhang couldn't take much more. He took a step towards her. He was now well over the fault line. The critical point. She could see the crack zigzag wider as his weight pressed on the fracture. NOW! she thought.

Hanlon stamped her right foot down as hard as she could.

Donald for a nanosecond didn't understand what was happening. Maybe he thought it was a show of pointless defiance on her part. He raised the heavy branch ready to push her backwards into the gorge to be smashed on the rocks below.

The ground shifted downwards, tilting alarmingly. Donald had no idea he was standing on a kind of platform made of soil held by tree roots and about to give way. He looked puzzled, thinking it was his balance that was at fault, not the ground itself. He slipped slightly and jabbed the stick hard down to keep his balance, shotgun in one hand, branch in the other, causing the overhang to accelerate its movement downwards. Now, too late, he realised what was happening, that the ground was giving way beneath his feet. His body swayed and his arms flailed as he tried to regain his footing and move back to safety.

Eighteen stone of pressure pushing down hard. The crack yawned wide and Hanlon leapt upwards, the force of her leap adding to the pressure on the ground, her hands grasping the bough of the tree that had scraped her hair earlier as the over-hang gave way silently.

About four metres of the overhang disappeared into the depths below and Donald fell with it down into the gorge, his arms windmilling once, his voice bellowing wordlessly before he crashed onto the boulders beneath.

Then silence.

## 35

Hanlon hung for a very long moment from the tree, staring down at what had been ground beneath her feet and was now a drop of thirty metres down to the burn. Her grip was strong, she felt exultant, she was alive! She could see the pieces of black turf far below her. She swung herself hand on hand back along the branch until she reached the body of the tree and clambered down the trunk.

She stood by the side of the ravine, one arm hugging the tree, and looked down at Donald's body sprawled on the rocks far below. He was lying face down on a large boulder, motionless. She thought of the dead girls, Eva killed by Donald, Franca killed by McCleod, who had also murdered Kai and Big Jim. She thought of Big Jim and his attempts to kill her. She thought of his sexual and emotional blackmail of Morag.

She looked around her. I'm alive, she thought, relief flooding through her. It's over.

The blue sea, the majestic mountains, the Paps in the distance. It all looked so idyllic, but of course there were serpents in this Eden.

Her grey eyes narrowed and the wind tugged at her corkscrew hair as she gazed pitilessly at his shattered corpse.

She felt a nudge at her side and looked down; two adoring eyes stared up at her.

'Good boy, Wemyss,' she said, patting the dog's head.

They turned and walked down towards where the quad bike was parked. Donald had left the key in the ignition. Hanlon stared down the hill towards the sea.

Down below on the road, the Volvo was gone.

## 36

Murdo Campbell handed her a pen to sign her statement. He turned off the audio recording.

'So,' he said, 'there we are.'

Hanlon had been giving her statement at the police station on Islay. It was hardly a full account, but it would suffice, and Campbell was in no mood to make life hard for her. Hanlon's face still looked dreadful from the beating that she had taken from Leo. Paradoxically, to Campbell, it made Hanlon look even more attractive.

'What was happening down at the Mackinnon Arms exactly?' Hanlon asked.

Campbell pushed a hand through his red hair.

'HMRC and the drugs squad had a mutual interest in the place. They knew that cocaine of an unusual high purity was coming onto the mainland via the Western Isles, well, no surprise there, but they had narrowed it down to Jura, specifically the Mackinnon Arms.'

He drank some water.

'My drug squad colleague knew I had an informant who worked in the catering trade...'

'Kai McPherson,' said Hanlon.

'Exactly. Kai, poor bastard, had given me quite a bit on crimes in Glasgow and Paisley. I used to turn a blind eye to his wee deals on the side. Anyway, he was keen to get out of Paisley, get out of crime in general. So I leaned on my sister to give him a job at her restaurant, which is up for a Michelin star.'

'The Sleeket Mouse.'

'Well, you've eaten there.'

'I've eaten there,' she said coldly, 'as well you know.'

'Well, then.' Campbell was wearing a dark suit and tie, which he now adjusted; he looked elegant and careworn. 'When the bar-manager vacancy at the Mackinnon Arms came up, I suggested him. He was ideal for the job. They bit his hand off.'

'So now you had a man in there.'

Campbell nodded. 'I did. Firstly, Kai tipped us off about the sex parties. I went, I said I was an Oban businessman. I didn't take part. I pretended to be too pissed.'

'Did you learn anything?'

'No, other than it cost three hundred and fifty pounds, drinks and drugs included, to attend if you were an unattached man, a hundred if you were a couple, that there was no obvious coercion and that although drugs were available it was no big deal. Kai was doing well out of that. Of interest if we'd wanted to object to Big Jim renewing his licence, but otherwise no.'

'Did Kai know who was behind the alleged drug smuggling at the hotel?'

Campbell shook his head. 'No. Well, we both assumed it was Big Jim and Harriet. He had the boat as well. But we needed proof. The problem really was our informant, who knew that the drugs connection centred on the hotel, but we thought that meant the hotel as a business, making Big Jim the main suspect, rather than someone who worked *in* the hotel. It never crossed our minds that Donald Crawford was involved.'

'So Kai knew that something was going down rather than who was behind it.'

'Exactly. To be honest, we thought that the drugs were probably going to be attached to Big Jim's lobster pots.' Just as I did, thought Hanlon.

'To be more specific, I mean the buoys that marked the pots. Donald's job involved collecting the lobsters. When coke was delivered, he'd collect that too. Waterproof packaging. Then he could just sail out at his leisure, collect the lobsters, collect the drugs.'

'So when Big Jim attacked me there...'

'Exactly. When McCleod told me that you had been attacked by Big Jim by the lobster pots, it just confirmed my impressions, so I was right about the pots but completely wrong about the man. Big Jim had nothing whatsoever to do with drugs and neither did Harriet.'

Hanlon pushed her hair out of her face. Campbell glanced down at her hands, slim and muscular, a couple of blue plasters on the knuckles of her right hand from where she'd had the run-in with Leo.

'So how much did McCleod know about your investigation?'

Campbell pulled a face. 'In an ideal world, nothing, I obviously wanted as few people to know as necessary, but in reality...'

'You told her, didn't you?' Hanlon's voice was accusing.

'Bits and pieces. I trusted her.' He smiled. 'As did you. Catriona was very plausible. So when she found out, from you...' he nodded intently at Hanlon, the payback for her blaming him for trusting McCleod '...that Kai was meeting me with definitive details at the bothy, Kai had to die.'

'Well, I suppose that explains that. Why did Kai turn up at the bothy two days before?'

'I can only imagine that McCleod had contacted him and told him that I had said to meet me earlier. He knew who she was, he would have no reason to disbelieve her. She drove her car over the back way, via the forestry tracks, avoiding the main road.'

'What if Kai had checked?'

'McCleod knows there's no signal where my granny lives.'

'And Big Jim?' asked Hanlon.

'To take the rap for Kai's death.'

'What's the story with McCleod?' asked Hanlon. She hadn't told Campbell about their relationship; he didn't need to know and she wasn't going to have the police sniggering over them like a group of schoolboys.

'We found a lot of coke hidden at her place. SOCO and forensics are all over it at the moment.'

'And McCleod herself?'

'No trace of her. Crawford had a boat with quite a powerful motor – that's missing. I think when Donald failed to reappear, she ran.' He smiled. 'I think she guessed the outcome. We can assume that she made her way to the mainland. I'm guessing she'll be either out of the country or somewhere like London. I think, too, that you are lucky to be alive.'

'Well, obviously.'

'No.' Campbell shook his head. 'After you told her that you thought I was on the take, that you had seen me and Kai together, et cetera, she would have known that you wouldn't have let it go. The last thing that McCleod needed was an intelligent, suspicious police officer obsessed with the Mackinnon Arms. Even if Morag hadn't intervened, your days would have been numbered.

I think she'd have removed the problem – you would have had a tragic accident while hill-running...'

He sighed. 'She was a very efficient police officer, a very efficient criminal. I have no doubt she'll be a very efficient fugitive.'

Hanlon nodded. Campbell looked at her. 'And you, what are you up to? Are you really going to be a private detective, chase cheating wives and husbands? Like you told me, remember?'

'I've resigned from the police,' Hanlon said.

Campbell looked at her keenly. 'That's a big step...' She smiled; she noticed he didn't say, please don't, please reconsider.

'I don't want to talk about it,' she said to forestall any queries.

'Immediate plans?' he asked.

'I'm staying here a while. I do have a holiday booked.' Hanlon gave a sardonic laugh.

'Well...' Campbell slid a card over the table that separated them '... I have friends in a legal team in Glasgow. They do corporate stuff – they often need a good investigator. It would be a hell of a sight more interesting than divorces. And they pay well.'

'Thanks.' She genuinely meant it.

He leaned forward. 'You're too good to be wasting your time on cheating husbands, even if you do need to brush up on your stalking skills...'She smiled at him and their eyes met, green looking into grey.

'How did you get over that fence?'

'There's a ladder for walkers to cross, that simple...' He sat back in his chair. 'Think about my offer. If you're interested, there's my card, it's got my mobile number on, call me.'

'Possibly.' She hesitated. 'Thank you.' She leaned forward and took his card. 'I owe you an apology. I was convinced you were dirty.'

Campbell smiled. 'It's the red hair. Judas had red hair.'

'Did he really?'

'So they say. Mind you...' he smiled again '... they also say that Jesus came to Dumbarton. You can't always believe what you hear.'

They shook hands.

Hanlon stood up and walked out of the interview room. Campbell watched her go, her back straight, utterly imperious. He found her disturbingly attractive.He stared at her firm, emphatic signature at the end of the witness statement. He hoped they'd meet again.

\* \* \*

Hanlon walked out of the Port Ellen police station and down to the harbour front. She stared out across the darkening sea. It was fascinating how it changed colour so much. Black clouds were moving in from the west and there were occasional white horses outside the tranquillity of the harbour.

She thought of Donald's broken body lying on the rocks of the burn far below, the icy water running over him. So much for his plans of running a Michelin-starred restaurant on Jura. So much for his plans of killing her.

Hanlon had a retentive memory; the lines of Burns she had read in Donald's book, on Donald's sofa, in Donald's cottage, came into her mind.

> The best laid schemes of mice and men
> Gang aft agley,
> And leave us nought but grief an' pain
> For promised joy.

She pushed her hand through her hair, her grey eyes as

expressionless and unfathomable as the Atlantic she was looking at.

'Come on, boy,' she said to Wemyss.

The two of them walked off, away from the sea, towards the centre of town.

## MORE FROM ALEX COOMBS

We hope you enjoyed reading *Silenced For Good*. If you did, please leave a review.

If you'd like to gift a copy, this book is also available as an ebook, digital audio download and audiobook CD.

Sign up to Alex Coombs' mailing list below for news, competitions and updates on future books.

http://bit.ly/AlexCoombsNewsletter

# ABOUT THE AUTHOR

**Alex Coombs** studied Arabic at Oxford and Edinburgh Universities and went on to work in adult education and then retrained to be a chef. He has written four well reviewed crime novels as Alex Howard.

Visit Alex's website: www.alexcoombs.co.uk

Follow Alex on social media:

facebook.com/AlexCoombsCrime

twitter.com/AlexHowardCrime

bookbub.com/authors/alex-coombs

# ABOUT BOLDWOOD BOOKS

Boldwood Books is a fiction publishing company seeking out the best stories from around the world.

Find out more at www.boldwoodbooks.com

Sign up to the Book and Tonic newsletter for news, offers and competitions from Boldwood Books!

http://www.bit.ly/bookandtonic

We'd love to hear from you, follow us on social media:

facebook.com/BookandTonic

twitter.com/BoldwoodBooks

instagram.com/BookandTonic

Printed in Great Britain
by Amazon